Cabin Crew
Julie Hoag

Table of Contents

Proofread in partnership with Bumblebooks in The Amana Colonies, Iowa

Cover by Katherine Magpie Design

Tropes: YA Contemporary Romance, Romantic Comedy, Empowerment of Women, Drama, Forced Proximity, Friendships, Enemies to Friends, LGTBQ supporting character, Minnesota setting.

Triggers: Past recalling of attempted sexual assault and physical abuse. Talk of anorexia. PTSD. Mental Health.

Dedication:

To those whom I love, those who love me and have supported me, all the readers and my fellow tough Minnesotans. For all who read this, may growth, love, and peace settle upon your life.

Chapter One

I almost raise my hand and admit, *my name is Ashley and this all my fault. I'm the screwup again.* I glare at my phone, I could hate it, but it's been my savior on too many dreadful nights for that.

The truth is, my leaving it made us come back. Now my friend is suffering from more parental anguish, a whole torrential mess of it. I shrink further into the seat as Melissa's face grows more tense as she stares at her phone, just waiting for the call to hit.

She grimaces, then answers, timidly saying, "Hi." She's been nervously running her freshly manicured pink-tipped fingernails through her blond hair since she got her mom's text. Her brilliant blue eyes flick to me with fear in them, and I give her my best apologetic look.

She sighs, gives me a tiny smile clearly to soothe me, and looks out the window at the heavy snow falling. "Mom, I know, I know, but we had to come back. Ashley forgot her phone." She shoves her perfect thumbnail in between her teeth and nibbles, threatening the smooth integrity of the finish. She yanks her finger from her mouth and stares at it, her lovely pouty lips stretched into a frown. She always bites her nails when nervous, which is a damn shame with that perfect nail job I gave her last night.

Mandy is over to our right, lounging, scrolling on her phone taking up the whole love seat with her feet up, smirking as she flicks. Her phone tinkles a tune for a text and she responds with a smile and a shake of her silky dark hair. As usual, she seems unperturbed by our predicament. But perhaps, that's another reason I love her, because she manages to be unphased by most problems.

I'm all jumbled inside, as usual. I really need to strive to be low-key, like Mandy. I give her a small smile. She returns it. That helps.

Melissa shakes her free hand rapidly in front of her chest. "Mom, I know, but now the snow has started here. It's really looking bad. I'll try some neighbors and see if anyone has gas." She pauses and puts her hand on her forehead while squeezing her eyes tight. "I know, I screwed up big. I should have gotten gas last time I was in town. I had planned to get it right away when we started for home, but I forgot, then with Ashley's phone..."

Poor girl, not getting gas was probably her only screwup for the entire year, and her mom won't let her forget it. Just...crap. Total crap.

Her eyes widen and lighten up. "Oh? School's canceled again for tomorrow?" She fist pumps the air and meets our gazes with her eyes still flared, a large grin splays across her perfect little face. She's like a doll, she's so pristine and petite. White blond hair, perfect porcelain white skin against striking brilliant blue eyes; her Swedish descent is completely clear. She jumps, her tiny size two frame jolts in the air. "So, we can just stay the night? For real?" Her eyes are popping as she bites her lower lip. She's won the lottery.

My jaw drops. Her parents are okay with us staying here alone for the night? This freaking rocks. It will be a minute before they clear the roads, too. But will my mom go for it? What choice does she have? Because...the storm. I smile. I've won the lottery, too.

"We won't drive anywhere in the storm, I promise." She pauses. "Yes, we will right away when the roads are plowed tomorrow, Mom. I promise we'll try to find a ride to Joe's for gas in the morning. Yep, I'll call him if I need to." She pauses and nods quickly. "Yes. Get home safe now, it's looking pretty nasty out there already." She nods again as her face blossoms into further elation. She jumps in the air, shaking her fist as she makes eyes contact with me. Her body then slumps; she she's still smiling as she rolls her eyes. She stays on the phone for another full minute; her mom is obviously dictating the rules to her, again. "Yes, Mom, I know. Yes. Okay. We'll stay safe. I promise. Bye. Love you, too."

Melissa ends her call with her mom and squeals with a full leap into the air. "Sweet motherload of freedom!"

"Wow, what the...?" Mandy sits straight up and looks out the window as a car drives past. Through the large front window, we watch as the car turns into the driveway next door.

"Dang," Melissa says. Her face falls. "They probably can help us get gas and we'll have to go home, but my mom said not to drive home in the storm, so..."

I creep over and watch as a car door pops open and a tall boy with dark floppy hair gets out. He looks sort of familiar. "Wait, Melissa. Who has the cabin next door again? That boy looks familiar." I peer out and squint my eyes, trying to figure out who the boy is. I gasp. "And...oh my God! Melissa! It's Liam."

"What?" Melissa shrieks as she runs to the window and watches.

Sure enough, Liam Holstrom, resident heartthrob with a voice that melts every teen girl in the tri-state area, shields his eyes from chunky flakes of falling snow. It's falling so heavy he bats it away from his gorgeous face, his lips set in a lazy sly grin. His dark hair becomes quickly speckled with large snowflakes in mere seconds. He runs his hand through his hair, causing Melissa to sigh.

"Wow. Incredible. He's so amazing." Melissa's hands fly to her cover mouth as she watches in apparent ecstasy as he stretches his arms up into the swirling snow. He isn't wearing a jacket so when he stretches, a tiny line of his abs becomes visible, and she gasps. "His abs! Ashley! Did you see that? I saw his abs and they look delicious even from here."

I smirk expecting she might actually drool with that look on her face. "Who owns the cabin?" I ask again. Next to exit the car is Lucas Hamilton who moves to the back of the car to open the trunk. His dark brown skin looks stunning against the white snow. That guy could make millions as a model and his girlfriend, Lily, could make more. Together they'd make billions. Lily appears from the other side of the car, and wraps herself around his waist when he bends over to dig in the trunk. He glances back at her with a pearly white smile and tries to wiggle her off, but she doesn't budge. Instead, she lays her cheek on him and her blond hair gyrates across her back as he wiggles them together. He grabs a pile of winter jackets from the trunk. I smile. Right. No one actually wears their jackets in Minnesota. They're extra. We're tough.

"Lucas Hamilton's family owns it. I don't see his parents yet though," Melissa says, her eyes still transfixed on Liam.

We watch as the last guy stumbles out of the car into the snow. My cheeks flush as my heart plummets to my toes, then flutters like a ping pong ball on a hard surface.

It's Kian. I can't help it, I sigh. If there's one person in the world I'd want as a boyfriend, forget any perfect book boyfriend, it's Kian, he trumps them all. But he'd never even give me the time of day let alone have a conversation with me. I dream nightly of his sexy, goofy smile, his lush floppy hair, and how incredible it would be to be wanted by him. I'd die happy if he ever asked me out; that act alone would make my life and I could perish right on the spot. He's a straight-A student, a star athlete, class comedian, and the most popular guy at school by a long shot. I fantasize about him curling me to his broad chest with his strong muscular arms, and staring down at me with desire in his eyes. But, my hopes bottom out because that will never happen. I watch him; can't take my eyes off him.

Kian shakes himself all over like a wet dog as he peers up into the heavy falling snow, a smile on his gorgeous face as he's talking. I'm sure spilling a joke because Liam laughs and smacks him on the butt. Kian doesn't even flinch from the slap, rubs his thick muscular arms and I almost drool. What I wouldn't give to be the one doing that rubbing. I close my mouth before saliva falls out. Be still, my saliva glands. Simmer down, now.

Mandy scoffs and I glance back at her. She rolls her eyes. "What? We're lucky enough to get stuck in a cabin without parents around, and the two guys you are both hot for magically appear next door. You two get all the dang luck." She sighs and heads back towards the kitchen. "I'm hungry. I hope your parents left food here."

"Yes, they always do," Melissa says without taking her eyes off Liam.

"I'll go get you two some drool rags," Mandy says as she laughs. "Your mama got any bibs left here? Damn lucky, that's what you two are." She scoffs, then snorts. "So unfair."

Kian grabs three bags of groceries from the back and trudges through the fast-piling snow on the driveway. It's like a foot deep over there. Clearly the drive hasn't been plowed recently, but he trudges on like it's nothing but air. The benefits of being a jock with thick leg muscles. I swoon, imagining him in shorts.

I suck in a breath and hold it for a second. "Wow. I can't believe they're right next door, and we have no parents," I whisper as I nudge Melissa. "You sure your mom isn't going to come back to retrieve us?" I won't have the guts to talk to Kian. But, God, do I want to with every stinking cell of me.

"No, she won't risk it with the snow. Plus, she's supposed to work tomorrow morning. So is my dad. She said it isn't even snowing in Aitkin yet and that's like an hour from here. I told her we already have, like, four inches on the ground." Melissa licks her full pale pink lips as she watches Liam with a smile. "We're gonna get to stay here tonight. Next door to him."

Kian. "Yeah, I think it's even more than that, like six inches already. I cannot believe we have another day off of school. Two in a row; that's unheard of!" I turn my gaze from Melissa back to Kian as he disappears inside.

"Bless you, Superintendent." She sighs.

"I know, right?" I clap. "The man is an angel."

"The plows will be slow, plus with this cold, it's dangerous out there. Mom would freak out if we started driving in this crap, my one and only saving grace right now, Mom is petrified to have me drive in a snowstorm." She sighs. "Those are the only reasons we get to do this, otherwise she'd hightail it back here to make sure we don't do anything wrong."

"You're always the good one. You never do anything wrong," I say, shaking my head making my blond curls dance across my shoulders. It's true. She's the best rule follower I know. That's not a title I can claim; I tend to break them. "That's Mandy and me." I smirk even though she isn't looking at me.

Remembering the troubles I had at a recent party starts to take over my brain. My heart starts to beat faster and feelings of panic rise as I struggle to not think about it. A frown overtakes me, and I wipe it off fast, physically grasping my lips hard to fully erase it. I need to keep calm and not think about that party. I sigh and count slowly to three. Whew, it's working. I'm calming down. I need to focus on the moment. That always helps me. Thank goodness, Melissa didn't see me starting to freak out since her eyes are still glued on Liam. I don't want any questions right now. It's safer that way.

"I know, and my mom acts like I do bad stuff all the time. She'd kill me if she knew what I fantasize about doing with Liam." Melissa smirks, her eyes lit.

I smile and giggle. "You're going to elaborate more on that." I take in Liam's frame. He's not hard on the eyes by any means. "I'm not surprised you love a bad boy like him. He's the opposite of you, like, in all ways. He's a rebel."

"I know, right? I'm no rebel. That's exactly why he's so hot. It makes him even hotter." She watches intently as Liam grabs sleeping bags and pillows from the car and barrels through the snow, giving a loud battle cry as he runs. "Wow." He almost falls in the snow, and she gasps. "Oh, poor baby," she says when the next charge he does lands him laid out flat, face first in the snow.

I chuckle at Liam. He's cute, but Melissa stares at him like she's brainless.

I'm not so sure I'm any different when I stare at Kian, though.

Lily stands over Liam, hands on her hips, her lovely face grimacing as she yells over him. She plucks pillows out of the snow and shakes them. Liam just laughs and throws snow at her. Lucas arrives to rescue her and heaves a whole armload full of snow on Liam's head, which he flails away wildly with his arms, cracking up. Liam grabs Lucas by the ankles and yanks him down into the snow. Lily runs with the pillows into the cabin as Lucas bear crawls after her kicking his legs as he fights off Liam.

Kian appears outside again and heads over to the boys wrestling in the snow and snatches up the sleeping bags before they can tackle and pull him down, too. Kian runs with three sleeping bags in his arms but trips over something and falls belly down on top of the sleeping bags. That's just enough time for the boys to scramble up and run at him. Liam grabs Kian's feet and Lucas grabs his underarms, and they carry him to the driveway. They swing him, heaving him into the over three feet of snow in the yard.

"Oh my gosh," I say. "They're so cute. I love watching them play like this."

All three of them have bright red, rosy cheeks. No jackets on them which makes more eye candy for Melissa and me. Their muscles ripple as they run, throw snow at each other, and then they disappear inside. I sigh. "That was hot."

"I'm surprised they lasted that long out there in this cold." Melissa hugs herself, nodding and ending with a shiver.

I nod back. It's even a bit chilly inside the cabin. "I know, right? But we're Minnesotans; we are tough." I turn away from the window now that the show is over. "Melissa, you really going to go door to door asking for gas?" My heart ramps up to quick beat as I imagine going with her to ask.

"No. I'm going to follow your lead and be a rebel this time. I can't pass up a free night with you two here. This is going to be an awesome night." Her eyes shine with glee as she shivers again. "Besides, I don't even want to drive in this, mom doesn't want me too, and if we had car trouble with these below-zero temps, we'd be in big trouble." She crumples in a shudder. "Geez. I better check the thermostat. My dad must have turned it down before he left. It's really freaking cold in here."

Melissa heads off to check the thermostat and I meander into the kitchen to find Mandy digging in the cupboards.

"You're still here? I thought you'd be knocking next door asking to borrow a cup of sugar so you could see Kian up close." Mandy sports her teasing look, smirking at me with an impish half grin.

"If I had your confidence, I'd do that in a heartbeat." I lean against the counter and cross my arms across my chest.

"I'll go with you, Ms. Ashley Larson," she offers with a smirk, wiggling her fingers in the air at me. Her pink nail polish looks so nice against her dark skin, like pink rose petals on my deep brown kitchen table. She kisses the air at me. Then shakes her head. "Denial doesn't look good on you. I know you want to go see him. Admit it."

I'm ignoring that. "I love this color nail polish on you. It really pops." I opted for red last night when we did manicures on each other, a rogue red when they both chose pinks.

"Yeah, I like it, too. I'll have to buy this one for myself, have to ask Melissa where she got it. I need it." She slips two tarts into the toaster. "Want me to leave these out?"

"Nah, I'm not hungry." My stomach is a constellation of nerves and excitement, not a rumble of it due to hunger.

"Oh, you're hungry, just not for food." She laughs at me and bats her eyelashes. "Am I right, or am I right? You want a Kian-size snack, with chocolate on top." She opens the fridge. "I saw whipped cream in here, too, unless Melissa's mom took it." She snatches it and shakes it at me with a big teasing grin.

I take a step and smack her arm, ready to tease her back. "Will you stop? You're awful! Mandy Rodriguez, you're ever the pervert, aren't you?"

"Damn straight. And you love me, and I know you think the same way I do; you just hide it." She gives me a direct look, wiggling her eyebrows.

"Ha! You don't hide it at all." I plop down in the wooden chair at the table and open my phone to text. "Better tell my mom and dad we aren't coming home. They're probably going to hate this."

"So, what? At least I'm honest." She's still stuck on the pervert comment. See...? A one-track mind. She takes a giant bite of her tart, raising her eyebrows at me several times. "Perverts get the goodies." She sits next to me and slips the hair elastic off her wrist, then whips her dark smooth hair into a ponytail bun on top of her head. Her irises match her hair color. She licks her lips. "You doing okay?" Her face twists with concern. "You seem, a little off." A look of concern floods her face. "Are you thinking about the party?"

I nod, sigh, and roll my eyes at her. She means well, but I don't want to talk about the party. "I'm good. Really, I am." I don't need to go anywhere near the real answer to that at the moment. I need a distraction from those thoughts, so I text my mom all the details of our predicament. She actually agrees we shouldn't drive in this storm and cold temps. It really is dangerous—no one's overreacting this time. I'm utterly shocked that she isn't pissed. A grin fills my face as I set my phone down. "Wow. That went way better than I expected. Probably because school is canceled, but she didn't even care. You call your dad yet?"

"Yeah, he's fine with it. He trusts me." She takes another chomp and chews aggressively through a grin. "Though we both know he shouldn't." She chuckles, her eyes ablaze with fire.

"Yeah. That's so true." I smirk back at her. We have our juicy secrets, and they're streaking through my brain. *And so is Kian.* Despite talking with her, I can't get Kian being next door out of my mind. I'm so obsessed with Kian. I fully admit it.

"But I won't tell anyone what we've done." Her face is full-on blooming with a gritty naughty girl grin. "Secrets to the grave."

We link our gazes and smirk in unison. I nod sealing our pact. Mandy and I go on wild escapades together, perusing parties that Melissa refuses to try, not that I blame her. Things sometimes do get crazy, but we have loads of wild fun together.

Most of the time.

"My lips are forever sealed, my friend." I put a finger to my lips.

"Ditto."

Melissa appears. Her delicate features are scrunched up, making her look cute as a baby bunny. "We have a problem. The heat isn't working. Dad always turns down the heat before we go and he forgot to do it this time, so it's still set at the usual mark, but it's really cold in here." She rubs both arms with her palms.

"Oh shit," Mandy says. "And with below zero temps hitting today and tonight, it's gonna get damn cold in here." She sighs, throwing her hands up. "There goes our fun night." Her smooth calm expression is now frazzled by a frown. "Should have known, it was too good to be true."

"I know. A comfortable night alone here with you two was just too perfect to happen, I guess." She picks up her phone with an exasperated sigh. "Maybe Mom will know what to do."

I slap her forearm. "Wait. Don't call your mom. Let's just wait it out. We can pile on clothes and our jackets, hats, gloves...we can make it." I don't want to give this up. It's too good, and too damn rare. "Plus, what would we do anyway? We have barely any gas to drive anywhere, the tiny amount left in the tank is probably frozen by now, and the roads are now covered in way too much snow. We might get stuck even if we do try to drive."

Melissa shrugs. She looks nervous, but a bit intrigued by my idea of staying. "I don't know. But there's a hotel in town. Problem is, we have only fumes for gas, so, you're right. We're stuck here. We could call the police for a ride?" She grins, then shakes her head as Mandy and I grimace, scowling like we're eating habanero chili peppers. She shrugs again, plops down at the table. "We're gonna freeze our asses off," she spits, sneering through her wide grin.

"No way, Miss Goody Two Shoes!" Mandy growls like a beast, making me smirk. Her sassy grin flares. "Did you really just say 'asses'? Loving it!"

We all bust up laughing. Once the laughter dies, we all stare at the wood surface of the table; there are dents all over the top where Melissa's twin brothers sit. They must have taken spoons or forks and jabbed the table over and over again when their mom wasn't looking. I trace the dips with my index finger...I can't believe her mom didn't sand it down and re-stain it to make it perfect again. She's just anal enough to do something like that to bring back perfection.

"We're screwed." Mandy puts her head in hands, runs her fingers through her silky hair, then pulls out her hair binder and slips it back on to her wrist. "Wait," she says with a massive grin. "Is there still only one car next door?" She hops up and runs to the window. We follow hot on her heels like her groupies. "Yep, still just one car." Her expression turns devilish. She nods as she rubs her hands together like she's cooking up a perfectly evil idea. "We don't need to go next door to beg for sugar or gas...we need to go beg for a cabin of warmth."

"No," Melissa says shaking her head and her hands wildly. "No way. We can't do that." She gives a fervent final head shake. "Nope."

"Come on, you chicken. Why not? The cabin looks big enough. Plus, you two could ogle the boys of your dreams live and in person." She gets this naughty rascal grin on her face, running her tongue on her lower lip like a hungry savage. "Juicy fodder."

I shudder at the thought of being so near Kian. It sends huge chills through my torso and grips me hard like a lurch in my gut. "God, could you imagine staying there with Liam, Melissa? That'd be like a dream come true, right?" My brain starts to shift, wanting Mandy's idea but being terrified by it.

She shakes her head vehemently, with a look of terror on her face. "But we can't go over there." Her eyes go wide as her head wobbles. The girl's going to shake that pretty head right off her shoulders.

Mandy turns her back to us and saunters away. We follow again; we have no shame.

"Or won't?" asks Mandy with an accusing finger jab to the air as she spins to face us. "You want to freeze your tushes off here all night?" she asks in a sassy tone.

"They are way too popular for me to go knock on their door. Lucas and I used to play together years ago, but, ya know, he's nice and all, but he doesn't talk to me, like ever. Sometimes when I see him here, he waves, says a few words if I'm lucky, but that's because our parents are friends, and he has to when we all get together. He avoids me like the plague though. I just can't do it." She sighs. "Plus, *she's* there," she says with extreme disgust, as she makes a gross face, sticking out her tongue. "Bleck."

"I'd give anything to have a cabin next to him. Watching him and Lily in swimsuits jumping off the dock? Talk about your double twist cone pleasure." Mandy smirks and exaggeratedly sways, then pretends to faint, falling to the couch. "Those two are smoking, effing, ever-loving, chill-inducing, volcanically hot together." She shudders, fanning herself as she's splayed across the couch.

I giggle and shake my head. "You're funny."

Melissa laughs. "Yeah, she's here all the time, too. She comes along just about every time. She won't talk to me at all and when Lucas does, she stays away. She's way too cool for me."

Her disdain for the girl is so obvious, but I happen to agree.

"Who needs talking when that's your view?" Mandy chuckles as a snarky snarl graces her face. "Staring at those two all summer, geez, I'd have to live in the cold shower."

I shake my head at her, rolling my eyes. "You're too much," I say with a grin.

Mandy nods as she sits up abruptly. "Yes, that I am, friend, that I am." She pauses, then rises off the couch, jerking her arms up in the air. "I'm going next door to ask if we can stay with them. They've got to say yes in this cold. Besides, we could die." She winks, then spins away, only to look back at us. "It's literally a perfect setup." She raises both her hands in a shrug. "I gotta do it," she says with confidence. "You'll both soon be thanking me."

Melissa quickly rises and blocks her. "Please, no, Mandy. No. Don't do it. Let's just try to stay here, maybe it won't get that cold. We have lots of blankets." Her voice is so full of pleading it almost hurts to listen to her.

"Are you nuts?" She sidesteps Melissa easily, her basketball skills showing as she dodges Melissa's lame grab attempt. "I'm going. I'm not freezing my ass off all night in this cold cabin when there's a warm cabin next door—that's also full of total freaking hotties." She dashes across the living room.

"What if Lucas's parents come?" I ask, not hiding my own hesitation over her plan.

She turns back to us. "So, what if they do? It's still a warm cabin full of sexy people we all like looking at. It'll be epic. Besides, parents are parents. They will help us." She does a little dance in place, wiggling her butt in celebration. "Hey, it's a once in a lifetime opportunity, and I'm not going to squander it." She approaches the front door. Melissa and I follow her like puppies.

This is getting embarrassing. How did we get to be such wimps?

"Are you really doing this, Mandy?" I'm in awe. She has balls of steel for someone who has no balls at all. "You're my hero." I smile at her, though I'm scared to death to go over there. But it would be so incredible if it happened. Being snowed in with hot guys? Yes, please.

"I know, love. I know." She slips on her boots and pats my arm. "You will love me forever for this, right?"

I nod. "Maybe?" I'm shivering, I'm so nervous, but I want it, bad. Like I want air. I gasp as she sets her face in firm determination.

She slips on her coat and a hat with a white glittery ball on top. She's out the door before we can snag her, and before I forget to breathe. She's prancing along in the falling snow as she glances back at us with the most giant grin possible.

"She's amazing. I could never to that in a million years." I watch her strut down the driveway. "She's a pro."

Melissa wrings her hands. "I don't want to go. But then there's Lily. Lily, like, hates me, and I hate her. I can't be in the same cabin with her for that long."

"I don't like her either. She's a stuck-up bitch. They might say no." I shrug.

"They won't." Her eyes are so worried, I give her a big hug. "I might have a heart attack being that close to Liam." She looks so serious I almost laugh in her face.

I rub her back; she's shivering, too. "I get it. It'll be okay. We will all be there together. We could always come back here if they're mean to us." I don't believe myself either, but hell, I'm trying to. "Right?"

She nods as her face shows she's trying to not panic.

We watch as Mandy bounds up the driveway next door, dragging her black leather boots with the bows up the backs through the snow like she shouldn't be.

"Girl is gonna wreck those beautiful boots," Melissa says, shaking her head.

Chapter Two

Mandy is inside the cabin and I'm fretting like a crazy person. My insides are swarming. Melissa and I stand with our sides touching, arms around each other and stare through the window at the whirlwind of snow slicing the air, both of us shaking from our wacked out nerves, and the cold. Outside it's like the tornado exhibit at the science museum, but on steroids. The mighty wind is sending the giant white flakes in swirls, then it lifts the loose snow off the top of the snow packed layer beneath and blows it in gusts of white sheets across the front lawn of the cabin. It really is beautiful. Absolutely frigid below zero temps and a wind chill of 40 below is dangerous, but also undeniably gorgeous.

There can be beauty in evil, if we look.

The front yard has been fully blanketed in a fresh layer of snow in the short time Mandy has been gone. Before the storm hit, it had been packed down with a bazillion small boot prints from her brothers who played in the snow almost every waking hour this weekend. The footprints have now been obliterated by the oppressive heavy snowfall. Not one is visible. The forts the boys made of snow block walls are losing their shape with the new snowfall, as are the snowmen, the snow dogs, and the tunnel. It was an oasis of fun for the boys. I glance back next door and gasp as Mandy pops out and sprints down the driveway.

I gasp. "She's coming back!" I shriek, releasing my death hold on Melissa.

Melissa stiffens as if she's bracing to be hit.

Mandy trudges through the piling snow in the street and plows up the driveway at lightning speed, the ball on her hat bouncing, a grin splattered across her lovely face. I knew she'd do this. I had zero doubts.

We fling the door open as she approaches.

She's got an even bigger grin for us as she steps inside. She shivers and shakes off the snow, then says, "Oh, God, that wind hurts. It's so damn cold." She stomps her boots on the soft green rug and pulls off her hat. "Pack up girls, we're going next door."

"Seriously?" I ask. Oh crap. This is really happening? My heart starts to thud.

Melissa groans, hangs her head, covers her eyes with her hands. "No, no, no," she whimpers.

"They insisted once I told them the story of how our heat went out and we have no gas in the car. Even Lily insisted. Ah, you guys, she looked so yummy in only a long red silky top that looked like pj's, Lucas had on a soft grey button down and it was open at the top all the way down to his mid-chest. Hm. I wonder what they were doing?" She fans herself. "I don't have to guess..."

I snort. "You gonna be able to be in the same cabin as them? Can you handle that?" I snicker at her.

She nods with googly eyes. "They have a shower, don't they?" She smirks like I'm a dunce, and removes her coat. "Or I can just step outside in the frigid polar vortex air for a moment. That'll work in no time. Let's pack up some food and drinks, too, so we can share what we have with them. They may only have enough for the four of them. Well, I guess someone else may be coming, but they weren't sure with the weather if they're still coming or not."

I rub my hands together and try to calm myself as I wonder who they are. No matter, *because Kian*. Yeah, the thought of being that close to Kian takes over, making my blood run around my body like a fire on a gas-soaked rope. I shiver with the sheer thrill of thinking I can gaze at him all day and not be caught looking at him awkwardly, like I usually feel when he catches me staring at him. "I'm nervous as hell, but this is gonna be amazing, I can't wait." Slow down heart. Breathe, baby, breathe.

"Thank me now, thank me later. It's gonna be sweet." Mandy hops then skips away.

Melissa sits on the couch. "You two go, I'm not going. I'm staying here." She nods for emphasis, shoving her arms under her breasts.

Mandy flips back towards us. "The hell you are, Melissa. Get your ass off that couch and get ready. You are going."

"We aren't even friends with them," Melissa protests as her lip comes out in a pout; her hands go up in the air. She stands, recrosses her arms over her boobs that are admittedly somewhat large in contrast to her tiny body. She's too thin but she's been doing better eating healthier, so that's a good thing. That's the important thing. Mandy and I constantly help urge her to do better for herself.

"Not going." She frowns.

"Don't be a dumbass," Mandy says as she heads to the kitchen, waves her hand back at Melissa.

Mandy rustles a paper bag, drops things into it with a *clunk* sound.

I sit down next to Melissa, who has sunk back down on the couch with a defeated look on her face.

I pet her thigh soothingly. "Melissa. We can't stay here. We'll be miserable. It won't be bad, I promise." I'm shaking like the last damn dead leaf on an oak tree in a fall storm, but helping her calm down is taking my thoughts off my own nerves.

"And if it's awful?" she asks. "Then what will we do? Leave?" Her eyes are big and round as she slowly flutters her eyelids. She looks sad and it makes my heart hurt for her.

Her eyes start to soften when I hold her cheek.

"Yes, we will leave and come back here and wear our coats, hats, mittens and a million blankets and just sleep here. I'll come back with you if you want to leave." I'm petrified too, but I can't let on much so or she'll feed into it. "Let's just try it. I know we aren't all friends and all that crap, but it could be good. Plus, you and I can actually stare at Kian and Liam and not be called out as stalkers. Good view and all; maybe we can even talk to them." That strikes instant fear in my heart and I almost let a gasp slip. Damn I hate being shy.

A tiny little half-smile appears on her lips. "Yeah, that would be awesome, wouldn't it?"

Yeah, if I don't die of a heart attack first. "That's it. You got it." I grin back at her. "So, you on board and won't tell your mom about the heat going out?" I bite my lip; that might be enough to make her mom actually brave the weather to come get us, which would ruin this amazing and perfect situation.

"No. I'm not going to. She'd probably rent a giant SUV and barrel down the highway to come rescue us. I'll tell her tomorrow when we leave for home, then it will all be over anyway. I'm not even going to mention we went to Lucas's cabin. She'd probably freak out."

"So...you're going then?" I hold my breath as my eyes brim with hope.

She nods, her own eyes mirroring mine. She places her hands on her skinny thighs, and carefully says, "I guess."

Then the lights go out.

I release a small cry.

"Hey, what the—?" Mandy yells from the kitchen. "Who turned out the lights?"

Melissa groans. "Oh, no. Now what? Not the electricity, too?"

Mandy comes into the living room. "No electricity either? Dang. Melissa, you're going over there if I have to carry your skinny little white bare ass. You ain't staying here with no heat and no electricity."

Melissa drops her face into her hands and releases a sob. "This can't be happening."

"What if theirs went out, too?" I ask in a shaky voice. "It could be from the high winds." I pause. "Wait, how did we have electricity before but no heat?"

"The heat runs on propane. It's separate." Melissa stands up and folds her arms across her chest, dropping her head down. "This blows."

"Oh, but now we have no electricity. I bet it's the storm and they don't have it next door either." I'm suddenly hoping the lights stay off, it might be easier to be in a room with Kian if it's kind of dark so he can't see me.

"True, but at least they have heat, I guess. I'm pretty sure my dad said most cabins here use propane for heat. We could just use candles for lighting or use flashlights." Melissa sounds so defeated, I want to shake her.

"And if their heat is out, we'll have to use body contact and snuggle to keep warm." Mandy giggles. "Maybe some friction." She laughs an evil laugh as she rolls her body from head to toe.

"You're so naughty, Mandy." I give her the look we give each other when we're at parties and we're drunk as skunks. When our eyes meet like that, it's Naughty Mode on.

She shimmies her shoulders and does a little jig. "You nailed me to the wall. We share the same brain, remember?" She mocks me with her brazen tone, rolls her eyes at me. "So...back at ya, baby cakes."

I grin because she's right.

"Oh, this is going to be so awkward." Melissa paces across the brown and white fluffy living room rug. The thing looks like it's from a dang magazine. The whole cabin could be in a home decorating magazine featuring cabins with the lake-themed original paintings on the walls, the beige and blue throw pillows on the scarlet red sofa, the dark grey granite countertops against the white kitchen cupboards, the lamps handmade from driftwood, some even with kerosene in them to complete the authenticity. Even the coasters are made of shells and clay with shiny pearly chunks littered about their surfaces that catch the light and gleam as if the sun itself is beaming down on them. Her mom deserves five stars for all that design.

"Bring that black box game of cards. You know, the taboo one," Mandy commands with a nod to Melissa. "I saw it in the hall game cupboard yesterday, so I know you have it here." She shoves a plastic bag at Melissa. "Go."

"I'm not playing that." Melissa shakes her head. "I'd die before I play that in front of Liam. Plus, my parents would kill me."

"Parents? I see no parents. Besides, you don't have to play, you can watch, and blush from a distance, by yourself in the damn corner if ya want. It's the perfect ice breaker game. Get it, or I will." She shoves Melissa, gentle, but forceful. "And any other games, appropriate or not, that you see." She laughs and rubs her hands together. "Especially any inappropriate ones. This is going to be so good."

I smile. I get where both of them are coming from. I want to play that with Kian but frick, I'm scared as hell. My hands are trembling as I follow Mandy into the kitchen. I take her lead and start tossing in cracker boxes, cans of soup, and pasta into a paper bag. I grab the flashlights from the junk drawer and toss those in, too. She pulls out a bottle.

I shake my head. "Melissa's parents will freak out. We can't take that. They'll notice—they make drinks up here all the time. There's no way they won't notice."

"We'll just take half and then add water back up to the level. No one will ever know." She smirks. "It will still smell that way. Stuff is pungent."

"You're in charge of it then, you have to make everyone stop drinking it in time so there is some left. Seriously, Mandy, you know her parents. They will go ape-balls ballistic all-out nuts if they think we drank it." I glare a warning at her. "I think it's a bad idea."

She shrugs. "Don't tell Melissa." She holds her finger to her full dark lips. "*Sh*!" She narrows her brown eyes at me and smirks. "Keep the secret," she whispers.

I shake my head, then nod. It's a recipe for trouble.

We pile the food bags, blankets, pillows onto the sleds from the garage, slip our backpacks on our backs and head out into the frigid cold. This weather is so harsh even Minnesotans need coats today. The wind whips us, pelting snow at our faces. It hurts my skin. It hurts really bad, so much so that I want to scream. Even breathing sears my lungs with pain. I gasp sharply.

"Damn polar vortex!" Mandy yells at the sky, shaking her fist upward.

Chapter Three

Melissa and Mandy run because it's so brutal. I have the most waterproof boots of the three of us, so I offered to trudge through the yard and make sure the back door is locked as Mandy had gone out earlier for a smoke but has no clue if she locked it after. Being eighteen has brought her bad habits with smoking, but at least she's not a full-time smoker. I smack the door, so frustrated. I can't get the dang garage door shut. I let out a fuming sigh. I stomp over then kick snow away to clear a track for the front garage door. It's a try of two stinking times before it will go down and stay because there is so much snow in the way. I run to the back door, dash through it, and lock the back door, then sprint back around front. Gosh frickin' frick, this is so painful to even just be in this wind! By the time I get down the driveway, Melissa and Mandy are already inside Lucas's cabin. My heart sinks. Damn. I have to enter alone. All eyes will fall on me.

I try to run, but I fall over a snowboard hidden in the snow. I haul myself back up, pick up the snowboard, and chuck it towards the garage so no one runs over with their car and wrecks it.

The snow is harder to walk through in their driveway for some reason, either I'm tired, or it's because they didn't shovel it this weekend like Melissa's dad did, so this snow probably froze more solid. Their car looks fully trapped already, with piles crawling up the sides. The air scathes my cheeks. It lashes me violently as a crazy wind gust flies past me sending my blond curls up in a whoosh and wild dance above my head. I get to the door and Kian opens it wide, a giant smile on his face. The sight of him freezes me to a dead stop. Oh, dear God, I can't breathe.

"Well hello, lost one! We were wondering where your pretty face went." He beams at me.

His words make my heart drop to my snow-covered boots. Did he just say that? I try to smile but it comes out too wimpy as my cheeks feel frozen solid and won't move right.

"Come in and get toasty again. It's a brutal one out there, matey! We've got the energy drinks to warm yer belly right." He winks, streams a smile my way and motions for me to come inside. The wind gusts and blows snow in with me as I walk across the threshold. He doesn't move, so I have to sneak under his arm that's holding the door for me. He's so tall, I don't even have to duck to walk under his arm, but I guess I'm short, too, so there's that.

"Wow. That sucked." My first words ever to Kian and I had to say "sucked"? How lame can I be? Did I have to say that? Geez. My cheeks flood with heat.

He smirks at me. "Yeah, it's damn brutal out there. I can't imagine not having heat in this frigid temp, so glad you guys told us." There's a sparkle in his eyes that I love. He's always joking around, a social butterfly, which is basically one hundred percent opposite of me—I'm the butterfly either trying to flutter out the door or blend into the wallpaper, whichever is closer.

I grab a brain cell and respond, "Thank you for having us. We would have been freezing like hard icicles all night long." What's with me and these suggestive phrases? Geez. My cheeks heat deeper. I stare at my toes because that feels the easiest.

I glance up at him and he's still smiling at me, like he's got a secret, so I let a little one slip across my lips.

"I still can't believe we get a second day of no school tomorrow. This is freaking awesome! When we heard school was canceled again, we all hopped in the car and hightailed it up here, barely made it before the snow got too heavy." Kian is gazing at me with an expression that confuses me, but I allow myself to return his eye contact, which feels more than amazing. I desperately hope he thinks my cheeks are red from the brutal wind.

"We were already up here with Melissa's family for the weekend. We headed out with them earlier this morning when we didn't even know about the no school thing for tomorrow yet. I realized I forgot my phone at the cabin, so we had to come back for it, but Melissa forgot she was low on gas." I roll my eyes in mock annoyance. "She had an uncommon brain fart moment...for her, at least." I scoff. "We barely made it back to the cabin once she realized it, we slid in on fumes alone." How in the world did I just say all that to him without dying? It came out of me like a rambling pile of projectile vomit I said it so fast. Speaking of, I might hurl right-freaking-now.

"Wow, that's crazy."

I take off my coat and he points, directing me to the nearby coat rack.

He smiles sweetly at me. "We can help you get gas when we all head back home tomorrow."

"Thanks," I say, slipping my coat on top of another, securing it with my fingers around the peg.

"Come on in. Do you know everyone? I mean, I know we all go to the same school, but do you know everyone?" His eyes are so bright blue this close it takes my breath away. They are like light blue Lifesavers with a light shining behind them. Just brilliant. They are tools of seduction.

I realize I'm just staring into his amazing eyes, so I shake my head. "I mean, wait, I meant, um...yes, I know everyone." I blush again and I think my blazing red cheeks must have stolen the blood from my brain because I've just gone completely stupid.

He smiles, says, "Everyone, this is Ashley."

Wait, I never told him my name. He knew it? What the...?

"Ashley, there you are! What took so long?" Mandy asks with her face set in a teasing expression. Oh, of course, he knows because

Mandy told him. I'm foolish. There's no way Kian would have known my name any other way.

"Liam, get the girl a hot cocoa? A soda pop?" Kian glances at me, then touches my lower back to guide me in because I'm not moving. His hand feels hot as fire on my back and I almost shudder from his touch. Simmer down now...breathe Ashley. My brain is working so slowly, either from the cold or being so near Kian. Maybe both.

The cabin is laid out in an open style living space where the kitchen, dining room, and living room are in one giant room. Kian's hand is still on my back, and I might faint. It's burning into my skin through my shirt and I almost groan as he applies gentle pressure to push me forward. My leggings are caked to my butt and riding up my ass something fierce, but I can't pick at it with Kian's hand just above, plus, everyone is looking at me. I try not to smile too big and just try to tolerate my leggings up my butt bugging the sanity out of me. Damn—I can't believe he's touching me. He is touching me...*oh my Gawd!* My heartbeat is rampant flopping inside my chest like a fish on a boat floor. I hope he can't feel my fierce heartbeat through my back.

Since I don't answer, Kian does it for me. "One hot cocoa, Liam."

I've gone completely dumb. I glance up at Kian and he grins down at me. Kill. Me. Now. Because now I can die happy. I manage to give him a small smile back.

Mandy clears her throat, and I glance at her. She grins at me and my smile gets way too embarrassingly big, so I try to crush it, so I don't look too goofy, but I fail. I'm sure I look like a total idiot right now. She does the silent giggle at me with a smirk as she rolls her top lip into her mouth with her tongue, her eyes tell me she's trying her ass off not to crack up. I shake my head slightly, trying to get her to stop making a big deal because I'm about to lose it. I'm consumed with Kian's hand still lingering on my back. How is he still touching me?

Liam comes near and Kian removes his hand from me to take the drink from him.

My heart sinks. I want his hand back on me so badly.

"My lady," he bows slightly as he hands the hot drink to me, a spectacular twinkle in his blue eyes. "To warm you up."

"No electricity here either, huh?" I ask as I sniff the mug. It smells yummy.

"I think it's the wind. Hopefully it will come back on soon," Kian says. He heads to the kitchen and whispers something to Liam causing him to chuckle.

Um. What the hell was that? Don't panic, don't panic.

I glance at Melissa, who is sitting on the couch with a pillow over her stomach and a diet drink in her hand, and she's watching Liam like he's a gazelle and she's the lion, completely mesmerized. Like she's freaking eye-locked on him, in unblinking full-on-zombie-mode stare. I sit next to her to jar her into moving her gaze off Liam before he notices. I glance over and both Liam and Kian are staring at us. Too late. Liam clearly noticed based on his fat grin. *Crud nuggets*. This is going so badly, I try not to look horrified.

"Melissa," I hiss. "You're staring way too hard at him. Look at me." I nudge her shoulder.

She turns towards me slowly and mouths, "Oh!"

I whisper to her, "Breathe, just breathe. 1-2-3 in, 1-2-3 out, slow, and repeat."

Mandy is in the kitchen, making herself at home finding spots for all the food and drinks we brought over. Lily is helping guide her in the kitchen. Thank goodness Mandy is doing it. I didn't want to be that close to Lily; she'd probably kick me. Mean-girl vibes are the worst from her.

Liam approaches and doesn't stop until he's three feet from Melissa. Talk about making a beeline. His thick dark hair is swept to the left in a wave, and he rakes his hand through it before dropping his arm to his side. Melissa's eyes follow his every move. His pale blue eyes are like a wispy cloud over the sky. His gaze at her is aggressive, direct, and sexy as hell, even to me. "Want a little something something with your diet?" he asks Melissa.

We all know he's a super senior, and over eighteen—not that it matters, but in Melissa's world of overachieving, he's more than a black sheep. He's likely to be seen as the devil himself, at least to her parents.

She remains silent. Her eyes now lock with his. She never drinks, but here is Liam asking her if she wants some. His presence has made my straight-A friend as dumb as me. She says, "No," but nods her head "yes."

He laughs and slips the drink from her hand. "I'll fix it for you. I'll just add some vanilla flavoring." The can no longer in her hand, I notice her fingers trembling.

"Fold your hands together," I whisper hoping this will get them to stop shaking. "Breathe. Remember, Melissa, breathe." I pause. "You don't want to faint."

She glances at me, finds her voice as she whispers, "I can't drink." Her eyes are wide, her mouth is slightly open, her breathing is very rapid.

"He's not getting you that. Close your mouth and smile, he's coming back," I hiss.

She smiles but it's a total forced smile and her eyes are googly. She takes the drink from him and nods. "Thank you," she mutters without taking her eyes off him.

I'm so proud of her for at least speaking when she's this shell-shocked.

"You're very welcome." His grin is the kind of smile that makes every female in the room take notice. He's a rocker, a total charmer, and his sexy grin is going to take him far, along with his voice. He's the singer in his own band and they play local events. We've been to three of his shows. He's amazing, utterly so.

Melissa looks like she just slipped into a hot tub. Her face is almost displaying sheer joy, like an orgasm is gripping her.

I stifle a laugh, clear my throat, but she still stares. This is not good.

Liam looks amused and smirks, which only serves to make him sexier. There's at least a million words in that smile. "Try it. Hope I didn't make it too strong for you." He takes a sip of his drink; his smile returns as he swallows.

Yeah, a quarter of a shot would be too strong for my girl here, the virgin-drinker she is. This will lead to serious badness. I refuse to let that happen.

"Okay," she says, a dazed zoned out look still on her face.

Dang. They might think she's high, which is the furthest thing from her personality.

She takes a giant gulp and forces it down, though it looks for a second like it might come back up. But she gets it down and then coughs.

Liam chuckles. "Guess I'm a bad bartender, huh?"

She shakes her head. "No, it's perfect. Totally perfect. I just took too big of a swallow." Her face flushes a deep red. She looks like she wants to swallow her own face.

He chuckles again with a giant grin. Kian comes over and slaps him hard on the back. "Being kind to our guests?" He cocks his head. His eyes are so twinkly again like blue glitter was sprinkled into his eyes.

"Yep, only the best." Liam nods at Melissa.

It's awkward as crap. I plead with the universe that this gets better.

I look for Mandy. She and Lily are still talking in the kitchen about food and drinks. I see Lily pick up the bottle and smile. She nods. Mandy is so close to her I'm sure she's just a puddle inside right now, but she looks calm, cool, collected, just so very typical Mandy. I see her waiver though when Lucas walks into the kitchen in a towel. She drops the can of soup, and it slams onto the floor with a loud clunk.

Lucas smiles that famous killer smile. I watch Mandy visibly swoon.

"Oops. We have visitors. Hey, Lily, are my pants still in the dryer?" he asks as if it's normal to wear a towel in front of everyone.

"Yeah, I bet they are dry by now. I'll get them." She starts out of the kitchen.

"No, I can do it. You stay here. I got it." He nods a hello to Mandy whose jaw is actually dropped open, rather un-Mandy-like.

I hold back a laugh. Rarely have I seen Mandy so rattled. I sort of love it. I call out, "Mandy, you need help with food in there?" Geez, the three of us are like star-stricken morons, like we landed in a cabin full of hot celebrities. We have got to get a grip and stay grounded. I almost laugh out loud, but manage to crush it.

Mandy shakes her head and gives me a thankful look for the distraction. "We're good, thanks." She recovers quickly, manages a smile, but I can imagine how her heart is just ravaging the blood through her veins right now.

Kian and Liam sit in the chairs across from Melissa and me. They're talking about basketball. Liam doesn't seem like the type to care about ball, but he's carrying the conversation with Kian like he knows what he's talking about. I can't think of a damn thing to say to Melissa right now, my brain is frozen, hers is clearly an iceberg, too, in her silent gaze at Liam. Good grief, I need to help her.

"Take more sips," I whisper. This will relax her. I need to do that too, so I take a sip also.

Mandy announces, "Lily and I are on lunch duty. We'll rotate, whoever cooks doesn't clean up and we'll take turns."

The lights flicker on, and everyone cheers but Melissa, who is still trapped in her unblinking-zombie-mode.

"Sweet! Now we have more options for lunch," Lily says excitedly as she does a little perky hop. She claps. Clearly, it's the cheerleader in her. I try to keep my hating on her contained, but the only thing that I can do is direct my eyes at the ground.

"Sounds like a good plan. I'm starving," Kian says as he picks up the black game box. "This is going to be a fun night." He smiles. "Ever play this card game, Liam? It's hilarious. And I know funny!" He nods, tapping the box with his index finger.

"I've heard of it, never played it. Sounds interesting, though." Liam nods as a grin creeps across his face.

Of course, Mandy had set it out on the table so the guys would see it.

"You girls ever play this game?" asks Kian with a raised eyebrow, which sears something wild and unmanageable across my gut.

"No," I say, blushing. I've read some of the cards before and the idea of playing that game with boys petrifies me. I'll need lots of some kind of courage to play that with Kian.

"Never," Melissa says without removing her eyes from Liam. I think the introduction of him being so near has completely fried her smart lovely brain. I cringe wishing I could just shake her out of this stunned state.

Lily screams from the kitchen. Lucas comes running out with only jeans on, totally shirtless. "You okay, Baby?" He looks like sex on a stick.

She screams. "Blood!"

Mandy grabs a napkin. "You've cut yourself. Have any bandages?" she asks Lucas with authority.

"Shit! Yes, I'll go get some." He comes over to touch Lily's arm first. Her eyes are on him, pleading with him.

"Hurry," Mandy commands. "Men." She snorts, shakes her head, holds pressure over Lily's cut.

"Need help over there?" I ask. Silent Melissa offers zero help.

"No, I've got it." She gets to be the savior for Lily. She's good; she's happy.

Lily is literally freaking out, mewling, whimpering. Her chest is heaving and she's breathing fast and repeating, "Okay, okay, okay..." in non-stop mode. A damsel in distress has never been so gorgeous. Mandy seems to be eating up being her hero, and I couldn't be more happy for her.

Lucas returns and he and Mandy patch up Lily good as new. He sits on a chair at the table pulls her onto his lap like she's a toddler. He's so gentle with her, it's rather beautiful to watch. His affection for her is so obvious, I can't help but be a bit envious. She calms immediately after he wraps his dark thick muscular arms around her.

"You okay? I can take over making lunch, baby," Lucas offers, kisses the back of her head, though if he stays shirtless to make lunch, I'm positive Mandy will slip and cut herself too out of delirium. I should go help in that case and make sure she doesn't get any knife duty.

Lily shakes her head. "I'm okay now. I can do it." She sighs. "I want to. Mandy and I are having fun." She smiles at Mandy and Mandy's face goes from happy to soft.

Lily rises from Lucas's lap.

"Let's do it," Mandy says, a triumphant smile on her face.

Chapter Four

Lily and Mandy announce they will make us a giant salad and sandwiches with a promise of cookies for dessert. Mandy walks around taking everyone's sandwich orders and typing them into her phone. I'm super grateful for food coming soon because Melissa needs to eat. Yeah, me too, I'm guzzling it a bit heavy trying to squash my rattling nerves.

Liam stands and stretches, giving us a tiny peek at his sculpted abs. They are so grab-worthy I can't take my eyes off them. I glance at Melissa and flinch. Melissa's jaw is legit dropped. I want to reach over and shut it for her but that would be too stinking obvious.

Kian clearly notices her dropped jaw because he chuckles. Both have giant grins. It's like they can literally read my thoughts. My face flushes.

Liam's smile is delicious. He remains silent, but gives a single laugh, and sits back down on the couch.

"I've seen your band play. It was so good." Melissa speaks! But her "so good" was cringey swoony, and she slurred a bit at the end.

Oh. Crap. I scramble for ideas to save her.

"Oh really?" asks Liam, clearly amused by her words. "You like my band?" He raises an eyebrow and leans forward, puts his elbows on his knees.

I'm just glad speaking helped her close her jaw so it's not hanging off her face anymore.

Liam doesn't seem offended at all. He stands back up and walks towards her, a pleased expression on his handsome face. Those eyes of his dance with delight.

I hear her gasp as he nears her.

"Um..." she says with great hesitation as he grabs her cup. "Uh, yes, the band, and you...you...you have an a-a-a-maz-ing-g singing voice." She relaxes her body. "You're so very talented."

Great. Now she's stuttering. But, alas, she recovers quite nicely. I have to hand it to her for that.

"Refill?" he asks Melissa as he brings her cup to his chest and taps it with his index finger. He tips the cup towards us. Good thing nothing was added because it's empty.

"Make it weak, like nothing added. She's not really a drinker," I say, patting her thigh.

She glares at me. "Shut up." She makes her lips a tight line, her eyes hardening.

Yikes! My jaw drops. My goodier-than-two-shoes friend has never ever said that to me before. Ever. I laugh and Kian and Liam follow in with chuckles. I don't think I've ever heard her say that before in my life.

I call across the cabin in a loud voice, "Mandy, you've got to come see this, I believe our little Melissa is transforming." I'm laughing as Melissa tears her eyes from Liam and glares at me even harder. She looks like she wants to hit me.

"Oh, my bad. I'm sorry," I say in a soothing voice, though teasing her newfound sassiness is kind of fun. "Didn't mean it."

"Am not changing one bit," she retorts in a snappy tone. "And I'm not little." Her tone is sassy, and I love it. She folds her arms over her ample chest which causes a bit of cleavage to peek out. I watch Liam's eyes go there. She smiles hugely at Liam.

Wow! Holy Hannah roly poly wild bombs! Who is this, anyway? I pull a silent gasp in my brain and my jaw goes a bit slack. There might be some sparks between these two and I don't want to mess that up. Dare I chance to believe? She is actually flirting with Liam!

She gives him a playful look and pets his thigh like three times as she speaks. "You make it however you like, Liam."

The world is shifting, and the old Melissa has been replaced with a playful one. I can't hide my smirk, but then thankfully recover myself with an innocent smile. About time, Melissa.

I hear Kian partially suppress a guffaw. There's something going on between the two and he even seems to notice it.

Liam doesn't even flinch at her continued touches, but smiles and lowers his head down towards her. He doesn't stop until his face is almost even with her. He releases a quiet chuckle.

I glance over at Mandy and unfortunately, she's busy talking with Lily so she's missing this forward display. It's so un-Melissa-like that I can't suppress it. "Wow," I say. It comes flying out of my mouth before I can stop it.

Melissa's eyes go into slits as she darts her gaze at me. "I oughta bitch-slap you!" She's gone into full sassy mode. She returns eyes to Liam.

My eyes go hugely wide. "Wha...?" Who is this and what alien stole my Melissa? Certainly, this is not my Melissa! I can't form a single word further in response. I want to cheer for her though, breaking free like this. It's ridiculously unexpected. I sit, watching dumb and mute. Must be her hormones have gone haywire being this close to Liam.

This, of course, gets Kian and Liam cracking up, I'm guessing it's Melissa's use of "bitch-slap" that has tickled their funny bones.

I let out a laugh, aghast. "Forgive her," I tell Liam as I glance at him. "She's not herself. Seriously, I'm speechless."

"What did I just say to you?" Melissa glares at me, her words are very loaded with heat. Her hands go up in the air, she shakes her head. "You want to be slapped?" A hiccup flies out of her mouth, and she covers her lips with her hand, her eyes narrowed at me.

"Are you sure that was just plain vanilla you added?" I ask Liam as a joke.

"Yup, positive," he says innocently, his arms raised, his eyes genuine.

"Shit. Mandy, you got some crackers over there or something, Melissa needs a snack or something. Like now." She's acting like my cousin Marie who is pregnant and if we don't get her food at the crack of the whip, she goes postal freak show on us. "Must be massive low blood sugar."

"Yep, help is coming," Mandy calls.

Liam heads over to the counter to play sexy bartender again making a new drink for Melissa. "Anyone else need a drink over there?" he calls.

"I'll take a cold one," Kian says. He looks at me with something in his eyes I can't quite pin down. "You want anything?"

I shake my head. It's so hard to keep eye contact with him for very long, yet it's also impossible for me to not keep staring at him. He's so hot I can't breathe right near him. "Maybe after we eat. I think I need food too before I have another."

Melissa's eyes follow Liam's every move from across the room. Kian and I both catch Liam glancing back at Melissa with a shit-eating grin on his face.

Kian and I glance at each other and chuckle. I mouth "wow" to Kian, and he runs his hand through that thick dark blond hair of his and smirks.

"Might need to be on chaperone duty, huh?" He chuckles with a raised eyebrow.

"No doubt," I say as I throw a lock of curls over my shoulder. I stifle my guffaw. No way. Never for Melisssa.

"Maybe we need an innocent game," Kian suggests. He looks over at the table in the corner that's piled high with games and cards and Gatorade. "How about Trouble?"

"Sure, sounds good to me. We need something to do," I say. Something besides stare at one another. Well, I don't need any more to do than that, but a distraction might be good for me and for Melissa, considering some force has stolen her brain.

I watch Kian walk over to the games. Whew, what an ass that boy owns. He returns and sits on the ground in front of the square wooden coffee table. I slide to the ground and tug on Melissa's pants to get her to join me. She's still in trance mode eyeing up Liam as he walks over towards us. Kian pulls the game board out of its colorful box. Being a few feet from him makes my heart bang in my chest. I'm hyper-aware of every breath I'm taking—that is, when I can actually take a breath. Half the time I feel a bit faint.

Liam hands Melissa the drink and sits on the floor at the coffee table opposite her. "What are we playing?"

"Trouble," Kian says. "I used to play this all the time as a kid." He's busy setting it up so I can stare at him casually.

"You going to join us?" Liam asks with his eyes in an intense lock on Melissa.

Yeah, he got her memo.

She nods and slides down the front of the couch after a long sip of her drink, a silly lovesick look on her face. I look back and forth between her and Liam, assessing if he thinks she's making a fool of herself. He seems like he's finding her amusing, but thankfully not annoying.

I cringe, sigh, and roll my eyes at Kian. He meets my eyes, which are glowing with amusement, too. He chuckles with me.

Kian hands me half the pegs and I fill them in on our side for Melissa and me, and he does the same for himself and Liam. Melissa is sipping her drink again.

"Mandy! That snack?" I holler, making the boys flinch. "Sorry, that was loud, wasn't it?" Very unusual for me to be loud in front of boys, must be the effects of this crazy scenario we've fallen into. At least I'm feeling more relaxed now that I'm actually connecting with Kian. I never expected Melissa to be an ice breaker for us.

Kian takes his turn. He gets a one. Nope. He can't move yet.

"Yep, I'm coming." Mandy hustles over with a plate loaded with snacks.

Liam pops the dome with the dice in it. He gets a six, so he moves his game piece out.

Melissa's eyes are still on Liam's every move. Her lips are parted slightly, her tongue wiggles her upper lip.

Mandy sets down a plate in front of Melissa with a banana and a peeled carrot on it.

I scoff. "Wow, Mandy! Really?" I throw my hands up in the air. "We're trying to cool things down here, and you bring her phallic foods? Girl, this so does not help." I shake my head as I fill too late with the mortification at saying such a thing in front of boys. Maybe I've fallen into an alternate universe with this polar vortex weather. My cheeks heat and I try to laugh it off, but there's no denying it. They all heard. Oh, the horror...

Melissa just stares at the long pieces of food. She's so out of it, she doesn't even blush.

"Shit!" Liam says, then cracks up. "Phallic?"

Kian is just dying of laughter, too. "Wow," he says through his outbursts.

I can't even. I shake my head, barely managing to stifle my own laughter. Kill. Me. Now. And. Quickly.

"What's going on over there?" Lily asks, clearly amused herself.

I glare at Mandy and she just shrugs. "Well, you know she doesn't eat crackers! She's all about the fruits and veggies. I grabbed the first ones I saw."

"I'm dying," Kian gasps as he slaps his thigh.

The boys are laughing so hard, I give in and laugh, too. I made this happen, but I still want to crawl behind the couch and stay there at the moment for a break. Heat swells in my gut as I shake my head. "Gawd, Mandy, didn't ya have an orange or grapes or something?

How about an apple?" I ask as I try so hard not to fall into extreme hysterics myself.

The boys are bellowing like donkeys and I want to shrink away. Melissa is still sipping and not eating the food but staring at it.

"Oh my god. Just take it away, Mandy." I lose it, cracking up so hard I'm now crying.

"String cheese? Lily is there a hot dog in there somewhere?" Mandy's now laughing, too. She slugs Melissa in the bicep. "I had no idea. Shit. You okay, Melissa? You're like a freaky zombie right now."

She sighs. "Just trying not to puke," she whispers.

"What?" I shriek as I scramble to rise. She might have snuck a drink of something stronger.

"Um," Mandy says, her voice softer than usual. In a louder voice, she shouts toward the Lily, "Lily, a bowl, quick!"

I reach for Melissa. "Can you make it to the bathroom? I'll help you." She will just die if she pukes in front of Liam.

She nods and tries to stand. Bad idea. She makes the sound of a hurl about to launch and I manage to turn her tiny frame towards Mandy who now has a bowl, thanks to Lily.

"Napkins, too!" I belt out in a panic.

Lily scrambles back to the kitchen.

Barely any vomit comes out other than brown liquid. No food at all. Damn, I bet she ate nothing this morning. Melissa retches. Mandy cringes then screams as Melissa's brown liquid vomit speckles her hands.

Lily rescues Mandy with a pile of napkins, dabbing frantically all along her flesh.

"Melissa!" I accuse. "You skipped breakfast, didn't you?" I shake my head. Not the time for me to berate her; bad me. "Sorry, bad timing." This most likely explains why she forgot to get gas because she had no fuel for her brain.

"I didn't see her eat anything either this morning," Mandy says with regret, shaking her head and swiping napkins on her vomit-soaked hands.

I sigh. It's too tough to stay a size-two. I rub my friend's back as she gasps.

Once she's done vomiting, her tears start.

"She's got this fainting spell thing," I say apologetically while looking Liam in the eyes, hoping he buys into the explanation. "We thought she outgrew it."

"Take her to the back room," Lily says, points to the hallway towards the back of the cabin. I stare at her in pure disbelief as she's holding a bowl with my best friend's vomit in it as if it was just full of harmless chips.

I nod and must forcefully pull my stare from her. I need to snap out of it and help Melissa. Mandy and I each take Melissa by an arm and drag her. Her tears are heavy, she's gasping and sobbing, but since she's faced away, at least the guys don't see as much. We almost carry her down the short hallway.

We lower her onto the bed in a bedroom. She's trembling through her sobs. The bed is covered in a soft lavender spread with deep purple and pink flowers. The room is clearly a little girl's room because there are also dolls on the shelves, a little doll crib, and a doll house stuffed with little fuzzy colorful animals. The sheer lilac curtains bounce as I pull the shade to dim the room. Mandy turns on the pink lamp beside the bed rather than the overhead light.

"I'm going to wash my hands, be right back," Mandy says, and I nod my answer.

"You okay?" I whisper to Melissa. She's silent for like a minute, still shaking a bit. "It's going to be okay. I'm here."

Mandy comes back into the room looking refreshed, a forlorn look on her face.

Melissa gives us a slow nod. "I guess I'm okay. I puked in front of Liam." She gasps and lets out a loud sob. "Oh, dang it. He will think I'm so gross." She's shaking her head back and forth, her hands fly to her head. "Did I dream that, or did I really pet his thigh?"

"What? You pet Liam?" Mandy scoffs, then laughs. "And I missed it? Damn. I miss all the good stuff."

I nod at Mandy, trying not to laugh, too. "Um, yeah, you pet him, sweetie. But don't worry, he clearly liked it." I nod super-fast at her, rubbing my hands together. "Seriously, he did. Didn't you see his face?"

"Oh my god! Why, oh why did this have to happen now?" Her hands go to cover her eyes.

"You've got to eat," I say while trying not to sound too bossy.

"You pet, Liam. I love it!" Mandy cannot stop laughing, so I point at the door. If she can't control herself, then she needs to go laugh out there instead. As the door shuts and she enters the hallway, she bursts into obnoxious laughter and Melissa groans.

I need to pummel Mandy.

"Oh no! I can't ever go out there again!" She rolls on her side while releasing a few sobs.

"You didn't eat, I think that's why this happened. Did you even eat a breakfast? You barely ate at dinner last night. You need to do better at nourishing your body." I rub her back. "Remember our talks. Healthy eating over numbers." I lean over to give her a hug.

She moves into my arms, and nods with her chin on my shoulder. "I know. I know. You're right." She sniffs as she leans back. "Yes, I'm trying, ya know."

"I know you are." Tears spring to my eyes remembering last year when she hit rock bottom and slipped to being too thin. Add in this fainting business and she was a mess. She barely ate and Mandy and I had to watch her like food hawks to make sure she ate at least something every day. She almost passed out walking down the hallway more times than I care to count. I seriously don't know how she could think in school on so little food, let alone get straight A's. If I don't eat, I'm like an idiot buffoon who can barely spell my own name. Luckily, we got through to her. We'd been about to intervene and notify her parents when she suddenly began to eat healthier again.

"How about you try to eat some crackers? That will make you feel better."

"And water."

"Okay, I'll go get some. I'll be right back." I place the garbage can from beside the bed and a box of tissue right next to her. "Here, in case you need to puke again." I pat the can. "It's right here."

She nods but doesn't lift her head.

Gently, I pull the bedroom door shut behind me until it clasps.

"She okay?" Liam asks as I step into the hall, like he was waiting there already or something.

I nod. "She's good. Do we have any soda crackers? And bottled water?"

Lucas is the one in the kitchen. He catches my attention with a wave. "Yep, I'll put some in a bowl." He dumps in half the sleeve then fills up a tall glass with ice water.

"Thank you," I say. "She really needs this. She's a total lightweight and she didn't eat anything today." I sigh. "This isn't new." I didn't want them to worry too much.

"Oh, geez, not a good combo," Lily says as she finishes up the final touches on a ham sandwich. "What kind of sandwich did she want again?" She looks around for her phone. "I'll make a sandwich for her." She scrolls her phone. "She didn't want one."

"Um, make her a turkey and cheese sandwich." I smile. Melissa will be so surprised that Lily went out of her way to make her a sandwich. "Please." It's hard to be mean to her when she's helping Melissa, but I still can't shake that I do not like this girl.

"Sure, no problem." Lily gives me a sweet smile which kind of irks me for some reason; she's supposed to be a bitch. "I'll make it quickly," she gushes.

Hmm...now I feel guilty. I hadn't expected her to be nice.

Liam has made his way back to the living room and Mandy is looking solemn now sitting across from him and Kian. Hopefully, she's been working on smoothing all this over for Melissa. The boys both look so serious, which sucks. Our fun has just been stolen by puke.

Back in the room I set the crackers down and nudge one at Melissa's lips. She takes it and nibbles off one tiny corner.

I rub her arm. "Keep going until you get the whole thing down. Lily is making you a sandwich."

"Lily hates me. Why would she do that?" Her face is all grumpy, her lips tight.

Lily is at the door and dammit, she heard that. Her face is aghast. "I don't hate you." She sounds sad and dismayed, her eyelids fluttering as she twitches her head. "I barely know you."

Melissa scoffs. "Yeah, maybe that's the problem. You always avoid me, even when Lucas sometimes talks to me, you stay back and ignore me." She won't look Lily in the eye, but stares at the cracker in her hand instead.

I watch Melissa study her cracker. I'm so proud of her for speaking her mind to Lily.

"Oh, I...I guess I wasn't even aware I did that." She sits on the bed, places the plate close to Melissa. She's added a small pile of chips and some orange slices. "I'm sorry, I never intentionally ignored you." She looks genuine and it twists the knife into my gut further.

"It seemed to me like you always did." Melissa's face still looks pissy, but her tone is much softer.

"Well, that ends now. We're all becoming friends here, right?" Lily's so perky, her cheerleader pep shining through. "Can we be friends?" Her face is aglow in a beautiful smile. "Sometimes I get too shy."

I lean back as I process that. Shy? She never seems shy at school. She's the life of her group of friends, giggling, talking, lively. She's the pep of the group, not to mention that of the grade. I watch her wondering how I got her so wrong.

Melissa nods, though she looks very skeptical as she stares at her cracker. "Okay. We can be friends." She finally gives Lily eye contact, and a tiny grin grows on her face. "I can get too shy, too, at times."

"Good. Now eat this sandwich and come back out so we can all play some games together. We could have, like, a tournament or something." She tilts her head with her smile, and it makes her even more beautiful. "It'll be fun."

Her mood is nothing short of infectiously contagious.

She goes out of the room, closing the door softly behind her.

"See. I told you this would be okay. Everyone is being kind. " I pat her back, rub her shoulder, move her white, blond hair away from her strikingly aqua blue eyes. I tuck the strand behind her ear. I clearly need to remind myself not to judge too harshly, too.

"Liar, you were worried too. I could tell." She sniffs then takes another nibble off the cracker. "You hate Lily as much as I do."

I sigh. "Yes, you're right. And I was super worried to come over here. I am a bit uncomfortable still. But Lily, just now. Wow, huh?" I sigh as Kian flickers to my brain. "But then there's Kian. He makes my heart race and my brain go into freeze mode." I put my hand on my heart. "He's so hot, I can't breathe right when I'm near him. I was breathing so fast and hard I felt like I was going to faint earlier." I crumple into a giggle.

"Only one of us down at a time, there, lady." There's a nice Melissa grin.

I laugh. "Yeah, no doubt, right?"

"I feel like such a fool. How could Liam ever like me now?" She drops the cracker and pinches the skin between her eyebrows.

"Oh, don't be so hard on yourself, after just one little incident? Come on. You think he's that shallow?"

"He knows I like him now." She stares gloomily at me, then reclaims the cracker taking a big bite. "Clearly." She makes a disgusted sound. "I cannot believe I pet him." She covers her eyes with her hand. "I lost total control."

I stifle my laugh so it's not too huge. "So, maybe that's a good thing, though. Right?" Yeah, that was so not like her, but damn funny.

"Ugh. This sucks." She rolls her eyes. "Hey, you want Kian to know you like him?" She glances at me with a questioning look.

"True. Hell no, I don't." I play with a curl, flip-flopping it back and forth. "But you know, Liam didn't seem turned off by it all, not even a tiny bit. In fact, he smiled a lot. He really seemed to like your attention, especially when you pet him."

She groans. "Oh, God. Why didn't you stop me? And my staring, geez. I was like a freaking stalker." Her face erupts into agony again and tears start up. She swipes at her eyes with a tissue.

"Hot as he is, I'm sure he gets girls eyeing him up all the time, especially when he's performing." Not helping here I'm sure, but true. "I bet he's used to it."

She raises both hands. "Oh, right, Ashley. That's supposed to make me feel better? He has his pick of girls, most likely when he plays. He sure does at school. He'd never like me and now I have to be trapped in this cabin all night with him knowing I'm not for him. This is just awful. I've totally ruined it."

"I think you're wrong. From where I was sitting, his face looked pretty appreciative of your attention." The guy looked downright giddy.

"I totally couldn't help myself. His thigh was right there in front of me, it was like I was like hypnotized or something." She rubs her forehead.

I laugh. "Yeah, you weren't exactly yourself just now." I suck in my lip. Probably not the best comment to make at this moment.

She drops her eyes to the bedspread and sniffles. "Do you think he hates me?"

"No. I don't at all. You'll see. Just eat more and I think you'll feel better. Feed your brain, then you'll see you're overreacting." I hop up. "I need to pee. I'll be back. Work on that sandwich, okay?"

She nods.

I flip back before leaving. "How about Lily being nice? You think that's real?"

She shrugs. "I dunno." She devours another cracker.

I face the door again, turn the knob, and step out into the hallway. Both Kian and Liam look my way. They're both laughing, not at me, but because they seem extra happy. Are they ever not laughing? I give a tiny wave, because what the hell else do I do. I'm starting to feel self-conscious as I speed across the hall to the bathroom. It's not every day your crush watches you walk into a bathroom. I suck in my breath as I scoot along quickly, taking one last glance before I reach the doorway. Yup, Kian's eyes are still on me. It makes my heart race. Once safe inside, I release my pee and sigh. This is gonna be a long night.

Chapter Five

When I come out of the bathroom, everyone is seated around the living room eating sandwiches and salads. Lily points to the counter where there is a plate with a sandwich on it and a small side salad.

"There's yours," she says with a flick of her hand. She's so friendly again and I can't get used to it.

I smile back, nod, and grab it. It's so weird to have one of the most popular girls in our class make me a salad and sandwich. She's not at all the person I thought she was, maybe I'm not the person I think I am. "Thank you, Lily," I say as I take a seat next to Mandy on the couch.

"How is she?" Lily asks as she stuffs a bite of salad with tomato into her mouth. A splash of red dressing splats on the corner of her mouth and she licks it off.

"Ah, I wanted to get that," Lucas says with a frown, which switches quickly to his toothy grin.

She smiles. "Next time, lover, I promise."

I glance at Mandy. Of course, she's watching. Lily and Lucas are hypnotic to watch, I admit it. They're both so beautiful and together they are just like a dream, like marshmallows and chocolate. Mandy closes her eyes for a second, sighs, pops them back open, a foolish grin on her face. She smirks, and then shrugs.

I know where her brain went.

"So, anybody gonna eat these?" Kian lifts the plate with the banana and the carrot on it. His eyes are lit with gargantuan smiles in them. He's on the verge of laughing again. "Cause I ain't letting good phallic food go to waste." He grabs the banana, peels it, and takes a big bite. "Um, damn good long food." He's cracking up at himself as he chews. He tries to stifle his laugh so he can chew, but it still barrels out around the mouthful of banana. He raises an eyebrow as he asks, "Any other takers? It's been so long since I ate a banana." He cracks himself up as he shoots me a look. His eyes are in mega tease mode.

Dumbfounded, I mutter, "Oh, my." I'm trying so hard not to laugh, feeling heat threatening to stain my cheeks. He's so juvenile, but I can't help but love it. Joking about such things with the guy I've been obsessing over is like a fantasy coming to life.

Liam's cracking up, too, as he says, "I'll do the carrot." He hurries over and snatches it up in a crazed stumble.

We all laugh. Poor Melissa. She'd die out here right now.

I fight my cheeks flushing, but it's no use. My brain fart mention of "phallic" is the butt of the joke that won't die.

"Got anymore phallic foods in that kitchen for us to enjoy, Lucas? Lily? Mandy? You three are the kitchen gods 'round here." Kian keeps a straight face as he stuffs the rest of the banana into his mouth. "Pretzel rods? Zucchini? Plantains?" He can't keep a straight face anymore and he loses it. Laughing, he asks, "Cucumbers?" He cracks up into uncontrolled laughter. "Anything saggy and soft like Liam, like string cheese?"

Liam blows a huge breath out, his face screwed into a silly expression. "Damn, you're so immature, bro," he says through his broken laughter. A haughty look overcomes his face. "I'm no cheese dick."

There's no one with a straight face in the living room. My cheeks are red as fire. "Damn," I say. "And to think it was my potty brain started all this."

"Ain't no limp string cheese mofo shit going on down here," Liam says with a giant snort followed by a laugh as he grabs his crotch.

Melissa would be dying to hear him talking this way, and I wish she were here to see it.

"Go stand outside and that'll change quick," Lucas says. "It's so bad out there right now. I just took the garbage out and I about died. Damn. A dude's dick could freeze right off in that. Whew! It's really bad." He shivers violently. "Not kidding. Worst of my life."

"Huh! Shush up, lover. Don't say that," Lily says with a giggle and a blush. "That would be tragic."

Lucas grins widely at her.

My thoughts go right back to Kian's phallic food jokes, and I let a laugh slip. Gawd, what is wrong with me? I giggle at myself, I've got to get a grip on my hormones, but that's damn near impossible near Kian. I fix myself a drink. I'm going to need something to occupy my mouth to get through all that crazy talk. I turn back towards the group, musing what crazy stuff will happen next. I'm having way more fun than I had expected I would, and it's incredible.

"Anyone else need something?" I ask casually, glancing around.

"Grab me a banana, will ya?" Kian says with a straight face. "Maybe another carrot and a zucchini too? I'm feeling extra hangry." He still maintains a straight face—how does he do that? He blasts into a smirk, his exuberant laugh bathes me in warmth.

He can do that all night if he's going to keep looking at me like that.

"Oh, gosh." I crack up, my face is red as my plastic cup. I shake my head and raise my eyebrows. I really don't know what to say. Floundering like a fish, I ask, "Are you being serious?" I sway slightly as all eyes are on me. I legit hate all eyes on me.

"Ah, actually, I'm full, but I can squeeze one more one sliver of length in if it's Lucas's size." Kian dodges a pillow that Lucas chucks at him.

"Aw, shut up man, I bet I have the biggest one here." He waves his hand at Kian. "You're full of piss and shit, my friend. We're in the locker room together every damn day, remember, dumbass?" He gives Kian a knowing nod.

"I can vouch," Lily says with a saucy grin.

"You'd have laughed if I had said Liam." Kian smirks confidently and rubs his jaw.

Good gracious do I want to touch that jaw and feel it on my fingertips...oh, whoa...I'm obsessing, big time. I sigh as I walk back into the living room, without a banana.

I sit back down on the couch; I want to be nowhere near that kitchen. Grabbing any long food and handing it to Kian would do me in.

"Hey? Where's my banana?" Kian accuses with a relentless teasing smile, his hands raised.

I spit the liquid in my mouth back into the cup as I guffaw. I can't get it down my throat while giggling. I roll my eyes at him. Enough with the food jokes. I feel like I'm living in that movie with the corny sex jokes I watched with my dad, which I admitted was funny at the time, unless you happened to be watching the movie with your dad in the room like I did... Geez, that sucked. I wanted to crawl away.

"So, should we play that cards game since we're all talking phallic stuff? I know there are cards that will fit right in." Kian's eyes are so alive and eager.

"Let's wait for Melissa," I say. "Though she already said she wouldn't play, but I'll get her to change her mind. In fact, I should go check on her."

When I look around, I don't see Liam. I swivel my eyes toward the bedroom Melissa is in and then to Mandy with a question in them. She nods and raises an eyebrow. I widen my eyes and drop my jaw. Mandy nods, then holds up two fingers and mouths, "two minutes".

A big gust of wind groans outside and slaps the house as it blows sheets of snow across the front window. The lights flicker but stay on.

"Just nasty out there," Mandy says as she chows down her pickle.

"Aw, pickles, I forgot to add pickles." Kian snickers.

Mandy chuckles. "Pickles are the best." She laughs harder. "Okay, we've got to stop, but I get one. It's my turn." Her naughty grin flares. "I like the big fat pickles at the state fair, the ones you have to hold with two hands and with a napkin because they are so juicy when you bite in them. The juices run down your chin and all down your hands."

Laughter bursts from everyone in the room.

"Okay, you win for the naughtiest one," Lily jokes.

"I almost always do," Mandy grins. "It's my forte."

I laugh so hard, my eyes water. I wipe them as I try to stop laughing. "She's so not wrong. She's the master."

"I like you, Mandy. You're a riot." Lily throws a balled-up napkin at her. "We should hang out more."

I smile. Everyone likes Mandy. It's impossible not to. I watch Mandy's face; she's so happy, she's beaming.

"I'm in." Mandy plays with a strand of her dark hair and flicks it to and fro. "Anytime, girlfriend. Any time."

I glance at the room where Melissa is and wonder what she and Liam are talking about in there. It's been several minutes now. I'm tempted to go knock and rescue her from further embarrassment, but if it's going well, I don't want to ruin it. Never in her lifetime would she have expected Liam to seek her out like this. She's gotta be on cloud nine. Hell, I'm on cloud nine.

"Okay, who's up for dishes, then?" Lily holds up her plate in the air. "Cause it's not Mandy or me."

"I'll do it," I say and grab it from her. I collect Lucas's and Mandy's plates, too. I reach for Kian's, but he snaps it back.

"I'll dry, if you wash. I have sensitive skin and soap makes me break out." He smirks; he's still in full joking mode.

"Liar." I don't take his plate but turn and walk towards the kitchen. My heart races at the thought of standing close to him while we do the dishes. This day is turning into a dream come true already.

He follows me and all I can think about is if he's looking at my ass or not. I'll have to ask Mandy later if he was. I almost trip over a brown stuffed bear on the floor, I'm so nervous. I've been told I have a nice bum, more than once, so I'm dying to know if his eyes are lingering there. I whip around and glance back at him, but his eyes are looking right into mine, which takes my breath away.

I dump out Lily's crusts into the garbage and the half of Lucas's salad he didn't finish.

"Ah, the bananas, finally." He grabs the yellow fruit and snaps the stem to break it, then peels one section down all in one motion.

He smirks at me as he takes a bite. I roll my eyes at him and slap him with a towel. His expression is laden with a tease.

"What? It's good?" he asks all innocent-like, but his dancing eyes are nothing but. He takes another bite while grinning.

I point at him. "You devil. You're bad," I say.

"Bad bad or good bad?" he asks as he chows the rest of the banana; what's left is gone down his throat in like four seconds flat. He smirks, his cheeks puffed out with banana; he's trying not to laugh.

"I don't want to stand near you with all that stuffed in your mouth." I pause as he keeps doing his act of showing off. "Good bad, I guess." Geez, why did I say that?

He swallows hard. "Your face was priceless. I'd pay money to see that again."

Is this boy ever not smiling?

I sigh and send him a teasing look back. Legit I'm dying to be actually flirting with my long-time crush. It's surreal. I don't want to wake if I'm dreaming. "Thanks, so glad I can entertain you," I say dryly.

"There, that's a good face, too. I'll just say a bunch of shit and watch you react. That sounds like a fun afternoon." He must be joking, but there's something else blooming in his gaze too, which I'm afraid to name.

Oh boy. Wouldn't I love that if he really meant it? I simply smile back, suddenly speechless.

"What, you think I can't make you react?" he asks, staring me down as if I've challenged him.

"Oh no, I'm pretty sure you can." The question is, can I stop myself from blushing the whole dang time?

"Okay, here goes." He clears his throat and stands up straight like a soldier, chin up.

"Crap," I say and drop my head. "I'm in big trouble now."

"Yes, yes you are. Game on, sugar, you're my captive at the sink. Dishwasher duty to my hard driving towel. Watch out, I'm a mean slapper with a wet towel," he says in a southern accent. He winds up his towel in a twist, readying it for a smackdown.

I toss another plate into the soapy water. "So, you're saying my ass is in trouble here with that towel in your hand?" I raise an eyebrow at him. My brain is stalling on that I've said "my ass" in front of boy, and not just any boy, *Kian*.

"Yowza! And you slam me in for the kill! That was a good one, sweetness. I'm proud of you." He twirls the towel tighter, and says, "And, yes, your ass is grass with this towel in my hand. Bend over." His eyes blaze with sassiness.

"Hey, quit flirting with the help over there, Kian!" Liam shouts. "Get to work."

Ah, he's back in the main room now, which means Melissa is alone again. I curb my urge to dash off to her to get the scoop.

"Stuff a long hard carrot it in, Liam!" Kian rolls with laughter. "I've got one for ya."

"It's all a fallacy," Liam blurts. "You have nothing long and hard."

I can't stop my laughter from erupting. No one else is around so it's just us three filling the room with sound, at the neverending perverted phallic jokes I had the misfortune of starting. At the same time, I'm grateful, at least it's lightened the mood.

"Goodness, dang, what did I start?" Despite my reddened face, I'm dying to know. I turn to Liam and ask, "Did you see Melissa? Is she okay? I was going to check on her but then saw you had it already covered."

Liam smiles and hooks his thumb in his jeans pocket. "She's good. She's really good." His gargantuan smile says he's really happy about this.

"Oh?" I raise my eyebrows at him. Hope flickers inside me for Mellisa.

"Yeah," he says before taking a sip of his drink and plopping down on the chair. "Really good," he repeats.

"Interesting," Kian says with a nod and a smirk at me.

"I know, right?" I ask in a whisper. I widen my eyes for further emphasis of my surprise. I plunge my hands in the hot soapy water for something to do.

Kian dips the towel into my dish water to dampen it, winds it up, and raises it. "Ya ready? I'm ready to whup ya." His eyes are naughty as heck. "It works even better wet."

"Don't most things?" Liam hollers towards us followed by an impish laugh.

I lunge away, my hands dripping soap suds and water as I move. I'm slow to think, still reeling from Liam's innuendo. "Don't you even dare!" I shriek. I raise my soapy hands and back away from him, I'm careful to point my ass away to avoid any actual towel snaps. "I will get big time revenge on you if do it. Huge." I nod aggressively, but I can't keep a straight face worth crap.

He smiles back with an evil glint in his eyes. "Oh, now I'm curious what that revenge would be." He drops the towel to his side, taps his temple with his finger. "I might just have to do it, just so I get to see what your revenge will be. I'm too curious." He twists the wet towel into a log again and raises it with a very menacing look on his face.

"You wouldn't!" I feel my cheeks heat blazing red. I take a step back and bump into the TV tray behind me. Glancing back, there's a plate of cookies on it and I fear it's about to spill as the tray teeters. Kian swoops in and saves it, his arms both wrapping around me as he stabilizes the tv tray with one hand and claims the cookie plate with the other. He's slightly bent down over me, and our eyes meet as he closes his arms tighter around my hips.

His body is fully pressed to mine. I can't help it, my heart beats so fast I'm dizzy. I gasp.

"I saved it." He grins down at me.it. His lips look so luscious.

We're legit close enough to kiss.

"You did." Heart be still, let me breathe...

Neither of us move, our faces are inches away from each other. His eyes are stunning up close, brilliant like blue sky, and as bright and clear as the sun shining off water. His eyes are anything but calm. I see a flicker of something—no, that's not it. It's fire. Something I can't quite fully grasp, but it's a definite something I'm daring to like.

He slowly stands up, snatches a cookie, takes a bite, and then brings it to my lips, all while still holding my gaze. "Cookie?" he grins, his eyes twinkling with suggestion.

Oh my gosh. My breath is stuck in my throat. What is this? It's not possible. My heart is punching my insides, my hands are shaking, and I think I might fall down. I grab the counter with a soapy hand; it's slippery and not likely to help stabilize me, but I still do it because I must do something. I open my mouth as my heart thunders inside me and prepare to take a bite of his cookie. At the same time, I instinctively reach for the cookie to take it myself.

He jerks the cookie, claiming his hold on it. "You going to eat that soap, too? Bite," he commands. He grins as I take a bite.

As I chew, he raises the towel again, but this time he unfurls it and hands it to me. "To dry your soapy hands, so you don't ruin a good cookie." He smirks at me, handing me the cookie.

"Thank you." I swipe away the suds on my hands with the towel. I'm trying to recover my composure, but I suck at it. I'm practically panting and it's embarrassing. I shove the cookie in my mouth and watch him as he watches me chew.

He watches me in amusement. "I'm the slave driver 'round here...now finish that cookie and get working on those egg dishes so we can go play silly games and drink ourselves to oblivion while the world outside freezes solid."

"Eggs? We didn't have eggs for lunch?" I give him a perplexed expression.

He points to the pile of dishes on the stove. "Oh, there are breakfast dishes, too. We ate eggs when we first got here, made by yours truly."

"And you all left the egg dishes to sit all morning?" I'm astounded he made eggs, but I love it. "You can cook?"

He shrugs. "Eh, we're lazy guys, what can we say. And yeah, I can cook. My mom insists I learn." He grabs for the towel as I jerk it away from his reach. "Give me my whip woman, in case I need to use it on you." He smirks. "Now, get to work or else." He rips the towel from my hands with a daring grin.

"You can cook eggs?" I'm still bewildered by him knowing how to cook. I raise my eyebrows. I hadn't thought he could get more perfect. "I'm skeptical. I might need proof." I grab my glass and take another chug. I need to keep sipping because this drink is helping me talk to Kian without melting into a puddle on the floor, and I need all the help I can get. But at the same time, I'm finding it easier to talk to him than I'd expected.

"Yes, mama. I'm a good cook. I can make eggs and more. And don't you doubt it. Chef Kian, at your service. No tart left unwrapped, no chip bag left unopened, no ice cream container left unlidded, I am a master chef of epic cereal proportions."

"Don't believe him, Ashley, he's really a good cook," Liam hollers from the living room. "We've been friends since first grade, I know. Trust me, he's an amazing cook."

Kian opens his hands at me in front of his chest. "See? Proof. Liam's no liar." He swings a hand towards Liam. "You can listen to him on this one."

"I'll believe it if I ever see it." I scrub hard on the egg-encrusted plates. "Darn, dried egg is like glue."

"I know, right?" He sighs. "Want the slave driver to take over? I can handle it. I'm a master dish washer, too."

"No, I can do it." I rub harder. "I'm no wimp." We work in silence for several minutes. Finally, the last dish comes clean. I stand at the counter and face the living room as Kian finishes drying and putting away the dishes. I rest my elbows on the counter and watch everyone trickle back into the living room. I watch them all as if they are a sitcom show I'm about to watch.

Mandy enters from outside and a swirl of snow flies in with her.

Liam yells as the frigid gust reaches him. "Damn, woman! What you doing opening that freaking door?" He holds his hands up as a shield.

"I needed something, had to run back over to Melissa's cabin." Mandy looks annoyed.

Melissa wanders into the living room. One glance tells me she ate the whole sandwich; there is color back in her cheeks and as a bonus, she's smiling.

She sits across from Liam and glances at his face. He locks her gaze and holy shit, there is definitely something there because they are grinning at one another. My heart does a little dance for her. I'm dying to know the details.

"You feeling better, love?" Mandy asks her as she smooths a hair strand from her eye. "You looked like the sickliest dog earlier."

I sense every move Kian makes behind me as he shuffles about the kitchen opening cupboards, putting away dishes and silverware. I'm struggling wondering why he stopped being flirty with me. Did I say the wrong thing? My heart starts to sink until I sneak a glance back at him and I'm pretty sure he's checking me out. This makes my heart jump, but I keep my body still because my heart is nothing but.

"Thanks. Felt like it." Melissa sighs. "Again, so sorry I puked on you."

"No worries. You need to be schooled on how to eat better though, sweet pea." She sits next to Melissa and wraps her arm around her, pulls her snug in a side hug.

"I'm a novice. I've got issues. I admit it." She directs her gaze at Liam again, but then quickly averts her eyes. His face is pleasant as he watches her. It's so lovely to see.

"It's damn cold next door. I had to run over for something and it's freezing in there." Mandy crosses her legs on the coffee table in front of her.

Her warning hits big as Melissa's eyes widen. "Already? Why is that happening so quickly?" She pauses, then exclaims, "Oh no! What if the pipes freeze?"

"Oh," says Liam. "If they haven't yet, they sure as hell will tonight. It's supposed to dip down to more than forty below."

"That quickly? Oh crap! My parents will be so mad! Maybe I should tell them the heat is out. I don't want to ruin our cabin. I'm sure pipes will be an awfully expensive thing to fix. They'll be livid if they find out I knew, and I didn't tell them." She starts wringing her hands and her chest is heaving up and down, worry screwing up her pretty face. She looks ready to launch into a full-on panic attack.

"Now don't panic, Melissa." Mandy takes Melissa's face in her hands. "Breathe, my little woman, breathe. Come on now. Breathe."

Melissa's face morphs into further hysterics and then she releases a little scream as she stands up. "Oh my gosh! They'll kill me!"

"Wait, wait." Liam stands up. "I can take a look. Maybe I can fix it. When my dad wasn't such a loser, he showed me some stuff so I'm good at fixing things. Take me over there and I'll see if I can fix it. I'm sure I can at least do something."

Melissa has tears in her eyes. "Really?" she asks, stepping closer to him and staring up at him like he's a superhero, which he might just be hers.

"I'd like to help, or at least try." He stretches his arms up in the air then runs his hands down his chest. "Just maybe I can do something."

"Really? That would be so awesome, Liam." She nods, and then follows him to the door like a puppy dog. She slips on her coat and without a lick of hesitation follows her long time crush out into the swirling snow like he's going to make her world right.

Chapter Six

"Fuck you!" Mandy screams at Lucas as she shakes her fist. "You don't get to buy that, that's supposed to be mine. I have two green properties already. That is mine!" She's fallen into crazy mode, her verbal explosions are big and wild; her expression is insanity.

"Eat it, bitch. I got there first, it's mine. Give it to me, Ashley, I'm buying it." Lucas reaches his arm across the board, hand open. His eyes are smug, his grin cocky. He nods. "All mine, baby." He grins at her, his triumph all over his face.

I sigh. "Mandy, you know you can't stop him." I hand Lucas the card for the property and take his payment. "He landed on it fair and square."

"I hate this game. I quit." Her usual sassafrass-tude rears its torrential head to full bloom. Her eyes flare wide, her hands both fly up to her face, palms up.

"Your only child is showing, Mandy." I shake my finger at her, narrowing my eyes, though I maintain a not-so-serious teasing expression.

"Shut it, hoebag." She stands up and trudges to the front door, slips on her coat, boots, and hat, almost knocking over the wooden coat rack next to the door in her rushing haste.

I know she's just pissy and she will get over it in a heartbeat. "Don't go out there, Mandy. It's too cold."

"I just want a smoke, but I can't find one. I saved it in my bag, but now I can't find it." She shrugs and stomps her foot. "I'm going. I'll walk to a gas station to get one then."

"You'll die," I say, fearing she might actually try it. "Stay here. Come on, don't be like that. It's way too dangerous for that." I'm scared because she'd actually do it, and die trying. She needs a fix bad, but I won't let her go.

"I have one," Lily offers. "You can have it, if you share it with me. Well, I have three, we'll save the others for later."

Mandy whips around. "You?" Her eyes are huge, her growing admiration for Lily five thousand percent apparent.

"Well, yeah, but only sometimes. It's a bad habit, but sometimes I like to be a bad girl." She gives a sly grin, then directs her smirk at Lucas. He gives her this grin back that says he knows just what she means, and he likes it.

"Wow," Mandy says. "I had no idea. I'd be indebted to you. And I love finding out that you're badass under all that cheerleader." Her whole demeanor changes and gone is pissed-off Mandy, and now she looks like Lily's greatest fan. Mandy's face spreads into this ginormous grin. She really likes this new development about Lily.

"Will you share it with me, then?" Lily asks, with a bit of seduction in her tone. She glances at Lucas who is now scowling. "Don't worry, lover, I'll brush my teeth." She pats his knee, and he rolls his eyes.

"Doesn't work, I can still taste it." He crosses his arms across his large chest in a huff. "How about you sit on this nice warm lap?"

She dodges his reach for her. "I'll eat jalapenos then, that kills it." She smirks at Mandy. "Or a lemon wedge." Lily clearly doesn't care, she gets what she wants, and Lucas gives in to her...that much is clear. They are such a great couple, which I already knew, but it's still mind-blowing to watch them in action.

Mandy looks in love. I can practically see her heart racing.

Lily straddles Lucas and kisses him hard, open-mouthed in front of us all. I hear her whisper, "I'll make it up to you." She gives him a direct look into his eyes, and he smiles, nods.

"I know you will, baby," he says mirroring her lust.

Wow. Just. Wow.

Kian goes, "Get a room, you two."

Lucas smiles and shoots Kian a look. "Got one." He chuckles like a devil.

Lily and Mandy pile on all their outdoor clothes, hats, gloves, and zip out into the cold. All I can think is it's not worth going out into the frigid air for that. But at least the snow seems to have stopped for the moment.

The whole Lily and Lucas exchange is still sending chills down my back. They are hot as ever. It flusters me how hot they seem for each other, but it's like on steroids from what I've seen at school. I'd give my whole diary to my enemy for a relationship like that.

I gasp when Kian touches my hand; it's shocking to have him touch me right after I was imaging Lily and Lucas together. I struggle not to blush.

"Oh, sorry, it's just your turn." He smiles at me, clearly, he likes the reaction he just got. "See, I can make you react."

My mouth falls open. I'm rendered speechless. Kian looks quite happy with himself.

"Well, I think this game is a bust," Lucas says. "Half the players are leaving. I'm out. Kian, you win. You have the most properties."

"Thanks, man. That's generous of you." Kian nods. "Was a good game, while it lasted."

"I'm taking a nap," Lucas announces with a wave back to us, then saunters down the hall, slightly swaying. "In my room." He glances back at Kian and smirks, keeps on walking a bit bowlegged like a cowboy. His swagger is delectable.

Kian calls after Lucas, "You're a lucky bastard, ya know that, right?" Kian glances at me. "Yeah. 'Taking a nap'...that's code for 'I'm waiting for Lily to join me,'" Kian says as he winks.

Whoa. I'm beginning to think nothing embarrasses this boy. But, of course, what do I do? I fricking blush.

Kian points at me. "Ha! Gotcha. I did it again." He snickers. "I need to start keeping a tally."

I fume, but ignore him and keep putting away the game pieces, the fake money, the houses. He gathers up the property cards. I want to throw something at him to wipe the smug smirk off his face. But I also sort of love it. I'm a goner.

"I see a smile there at the corner." He teases. "You can't stop it."

I refuse to look at him as I try like the devil to not allow the full smile. "Am not." I fail and it slips out, big and wide. I sigh, try to hide my face from him, but I'm powerless. I bite my lip, but it does me no good. I'm flat out smiling in plain sight, helpless.

"Ha! I'm the master. I can make you feel anything." His tone sets up a challenge. He leans back against the puffy beige couch, puts his hands behind his head. I almost gasp as I see his thick defined arm and chest muscles under his thin shirt. The clinging fabric hints at his sculpted abs beneath.

This boy is beyond hot. There's no one like him on Earth.

I focus on my fake anger to get my mind off his muscles, glare back at him making eye contact, then pull my gaze away as fast as I can. "Cocky much?" Shit. The second I say it, I know I'm in big trouble. Not only did I say another phallic word, but I also said the ultimate phallic word. "I'll take that challenge, and you'll lose." I'm not sure where that confidence came in my saying that to this sexy boy. I wait on edge wondering where he will go with what I said. Is it really possible to cringe on something but love it at the same time? I look away so he can't read the mixed emotions in my eyes, but somehow, he keeps reading me like a dang book.

He glances back at me within a second. Out of the corner of my eye I see him lean forward and put his elbows on his knees. His expectation is practically palpable. "You're just full of the phallic analogies today, aren't you?" His words are dripping with the smart grin I just know he's wearing, if I dared to look. "I'd give anything to know what you're thinking right now."

I must know, so I steal a glance at him. His eyes are mocking me, drilling me hard with his teasing. Ah, those eyes, they slay me.

"Ah, geez." I put my face in my hands to try and hide my red cheeks. "I'm such a perv." Ugh! *Now* why did I say that? I want to scamper from the room at lightning speed like a mouse.

He cracks up and rolls on his side curling up on the couch, his laughter crumples his athletic body into a ball, and he crashes down onto the rug. He's laughing so hard he can barely breathe, meanwhile I want to die, just blip out of existence. He can't speak for, like, three straight minutes he's cackling like a mad hyena, slapping his thighs, then coughing, sputtering, laughing again.

This is torture, but I can't not laugh at him. He's so damn cute. And those biceps he has bunched up while he laughs are killing me something rotten. He looks so strong it stuns me. His hands are huge, I just imagine them on me, and I blush even stronger. Hot damn, I want him touching me so bad it actually hurts me. I bite my lip in attempts to mute my own laugh as he rolls back and forth, but it's useless.

I fight a severely strong urge to jump on him, tackle him. My fantasy careens, and I can barely breathe I'm panting so hard. What is this?

Finally, he regains control of himself and sits up, puts his arm on the seat of the couch behind him, giving me a new view of his shirt clinging to his seemingly scrumptious rippled abs beneath. My eyes travel along his torso, imaging what he must look like without a shirt on. Thank God for whoever invented thin fabric. Bless you around the world and back. I'm fearing drool might leak from my mouth, I'm so turned on by him.

He sighs. Coughs. Shakes his head. "I totally fucking love that you just said that. I'll never forget it the rest of my life." He smirks as his grin is off the charts huge. "Wow. I'm seriously impressed."

This delights me. But I'm also terrified. What do I say next?

I try not to react with too much glee. "Ah, geez Louise," I say, unfortunately using my mom's phrase, and run my hands through my hair. I finger twirl two curly strands from each side of my face all the way down to the front of my chest. Playing with my hair is a nervous habit. He watches every little move I make with an amused expression. I fail at my meager attempts to remain stoic and smile back at him, my hands still fingering the tips of my hair in front of my boobs. Oops. I hadn't meant to direct his gaze to my chest, but that's right where it's at. I feel my cheeks flush again. Dang...is he really checking me out? My heart pounds, I feel sweaty and dizzy, and confused all at once. So this is what an anxiety attack feels like.

He raises his eyes and locks them on mine, which sends a shiver through me. I'll be damned if I don't see something there that has me a bit puzzled...it almost looks like desire. I shudder again. My heart quickens further. No. It couldn't be. Could it? I'm way too shy to snag a hot outgoing popular athlete like him. He starts laughing again as Melissa and Liam walk back in the front door, chased in by torrents of snow and frigid polar vortex gusts of air. We get bathed in the chill of it, which maybe is a good thing, at least for me. Maybe it will cool down my blushing and freeze my wildly beating heart, if I'm lucky.

Melissa takes one look and me and grins, tips her head to the side. "Everything okay in here?" she asks, her voice loaded with suggestion.

I nod. Cover my heated cheeks with my hands. "It's good. All good." I smirk, shake my head. "Nothing but good." Shut up, Ashley.

"She's highly entertaining," Kian says in a voice full of suggestion. He releases another short laugh. "In ways I never expected."

Oh, I'm surprising? I feel his eyes fixed on me. I might explode if something doesn't happen in the next second to calm things down.

"I'll put this away." I stand up in a rush and carry the game over to the stack on the table and add it to our pile of already played games. I need something to do before I combust. It works and I feel calmer being further away from Kian. "I like our goal to play every game on the table at least once before we leave this cabin. It was a great idea, Kian."

Melissa says, "Yeah. She's really funny, when she's not being shy."

I glare at her. Really, Melissa? Time to change the subject off me. I shake my hands, hoping to break all of their direct stares at me. "So, what happened with the heater?"

"Well, Liam looked at it and it seems we're out of propane somehow, which is odd because we're on a regular schedule for it to get filled. But now I don't feel so bad because it can't be construed as my fault." She nods like she's golden, not the bad girl here so there will be no pissed off parents directed her way. "I'll text my parents and give them the heads up so they can try and arrange for more propane. In the meantime, Liam is a genius."

Liam pulls off his jacket and hat, ruffles his sexy dark brown hair, and grins that winning irresistible smile.

Melissa looks doe-eyed. "He thought of the idea to set up all the space heaters we have around the cabin to keep it a little warmer in there so hopefully the pipes won't freeze. He found windows open a crack in my brother's room, so that wasn't helping keeping it from getting too cold in there either. He added blankets and duct-taped the leaky windows to keep the cold air out. He's totally my hero." It might just be from the hard-biting wind, but this girl might be glowing. "He saved the day." She shrugs. "It may have been out of propane for longer than we thought with how cold it is."

He scoffs. "Yeah, guess my dad taught me a few useful things before he become a full-on raging alcoholic." He nods at Melissa who looks a bit shocked. "And we'll keep checking on it throughout the night for safety. We'll keep it warm enough in there so hopefully the pipes won't freeze. Melissa, you and I could hang out for bit over there and start a fire to warm it up even more, if that wood-burning stove still works, too. I'll check with Lucas to see if they have any heaters to add and I'll run them over." Hero looks good on him, his face is beaming. He makes a beeline for the garage. "I'll check in the garage first." He slips his coat back on as does Melissa and they both head out to the garage together.

"Whoa," Kian says as his eyes sparkle. "Haven't seen him look like that, like ever. What's up? They are tight, huh?"

"Right?" I fan myself. "Something's going on there."

Lucas comes out of the bedroom. "Lily didn't come back in yet?" he asks with impatience in his tone. He's wearing a robe that is open all the way to his belly button. Mandy would most certainly melt seeing that.

"Nope," Kian says nonchalantly. "Hey, do you know if you have any space heaters? They're using them next door to try and keep up the temp, so the pipes don't freeze. Heater's out of propane."

Lucas scratches his head. "I think there's one or two in the rafters of the garage. I can go check."

Lily streams into the house all snow covered, looking like a beautiful white banshee. She looks flustered and confused as she runs down the hall towards Lucas's bedroom, her coat, boots, and hat still on. Her silence as she flees seems odd.

"Oops, gotta go." Stoked, Lucas grins as he tears off down the hallway after her.

I shake my head trying to figure out what's going on; it's like everyone's libidos have soared.

Mandy comes in with a look of bewilderment on her face, too.

"I'm getting dizzy with all this going on." I laugh and Kian nods, raises his eyebrow.

"Same," he retorts.

"That cold hurts. Damn, it's really bad out there," Mandy says as she unpeels all her winter clothing layers off. She looks a bit off, but calmer, and I can't wait to find out why. She rubs her hands on her thighs then fidgets with her sleeves. Scratch that, she's not just off, she looks super weird.

"I'll go and tell them in the garage to look for the heaters up in the rafters." I hop up as Mandy plops down on the couch, our opposite actions like we're a seesaw.

Mandy runs her hands through her hair before a smile appears. I give her a questioning look.

She shrugs, but still smiles. Her eyes tell me something is up, and then she mouths "later".

I slip on my coat, my mind pondering the possibilities of what the heck happened between Mandy and Lily. I can't find my boots, and I need them because the garage floor will be like ice. With my boots MIA, I stuff my feet into Mandy's huge boots. Her feet are two sizes bigger than mine so the boots flop when I walk, plus they are wet so now my socks are, too. I wrinkle my nose as I open the door to the garage. I hate wet socks.

As I get the full sight of Melissa and Liam entwined, I gasp. They are in a hardcore lip-lock on top of the hood of the car.

They stop kissing and look my way, their faces set in steamy passion. "Holy shit. I'm so sorry." I whip around. "I'll leave."

"Wait, Ash. It's okay. What is it?" She slips off Liam and sits on the hood.

I turn back around and, yep, my girl is glowing like a candle in a pumpkin on Halloween, bright and shiny in all the right spots. And a smile bigger than I've seen in months, maybe years, stretches across her face. It warms my heart that she's getting this with someone she's been infatuated with for years.

"Okay, Lucas said there are a couple of space heaters in the rafters." I try hard not to overreact and giggle as I talk. "But it looks like you two don't need that in here."

I hear them both chuckle as I go back inside. I'm not wrecking this for her, not when she's waited so long. I lean against the shut door once I'm inside. I'm right in the line of sight of Kian and he shoots me a puzzled look. I don't move a muscle. "Do not go in there," I say with a laugh. I peel myself from the cold door and shed my jacket and Mandy's boots.

"Why is that?" Kian asks with a straight face. He seriously doesn't get it.

I raise an eyebrow and my hands. "No space heater needed in there, it's pretty hot with those two."

"Got it," Kian says catching my drift. "Wow."

"What? Wait. No way," Mandy says with widened eyes. "That's Liam and Melissa in there?" she asks incredulously. She slows her expression in a slight pause before the ends of her lips turn up. "Shut up. Are you being serious right now?"

"Um, yep, dead serious. Lips and bodies smashed together, on the hood of the car that Lucas's dad works on in the summers." I take a deep breath as I watch Kian's face spread into a grin.

"Well, shit, that's awesome. He deserves a good girl for once." Kian rubs his hands together. "He usually goes for the wrong girl. Every damn time."

"Shoot, you mean Melissa isn't his type?" I ask, my heart sinking for her as I walk back into the living room. I'm instantly worried for my friend. She wouldn't survive getting hurt by Liam. I plop into the chair on the far end of the living room and lean my head back on the soft green throw blanket folded at the top.

"In appearance, yes, but he usually picks girls who break his heart, so he breaks theirs first. I don't think he would have ever even thought to try with a girl like Melissa, if she hadn't eyed him up like she did earlier," he says with laughter in his words, "and then touched his thigh."

"Fascinating," I say, hoping he's right. "Utterly fascinating." I'm jealous of her lip lock with Liam, but still happy for her. I shake my head and fold my hands together, lay them on my stomach. "So, like you and Liam have been friends forever, huh?"

"Yep, since first grade. He's had a hard life." Kian grimaces, looks at the rug before taking a swig of his drink.

"Melissa is a total good girl. She does everything right, everything by the rules. She makes herself miserable trying to be so perfect. I love seeing her with a guy like Liam, and doing what she's doing, totally not her norm, either. But, truth? She'll kill me for telling you this, but she's been in love with Liam for like almost a whole year."

"In love?" He snorts. "Serious? Why didn't she say anything?" Kian runs his hand through his hair as he looks perplexed.

"She wouldn't dare. She was petrified to come over here with Liam here, even though her cabin had no heat." I clear my throat. "And I'm not kidding. She's the best at everything, tries her ass off to be perfect all the time."

"Sounds too hard to live up too." Kian looks at his phone.

"It is, but that's her parents, and she buys into it one hundred percent." I sigh, wishing she didn't. "It causes her a lot of stress."

I glance at Mandy, who's silent through all this, which is totally unlike her. I watch her texting something. The text hits my phone and I read it: *Lily and I kissed.* My jaw drops.

Chapter Seven

I glance up, give Mandy my most shocked look. I text back. *WTF?* It's utterly agonizing waiting for her to type back her response.

Mandy sends a text back: *We were talking & I told her I'm bi she's always wanted to kiss a girl so she asked. Oh God, Ash it was fucking amazing.*

I text back. *Wow just wow. Is that why she flew in here like a mad woman?*

I watch her type madly, her face determined and satisfied looking.

Her next text hits my phone: *Yep. I told her I thought Lucas was hot too. I'd just die I mean really truly die IF*

I mouth "holy f" to her.

She mouths back "right?".

I glance at Kian, he's staring at his phone, too. Good. He missed Mandy and I mouthing words to each other.

"Finally, those jackasses get back to me. I've been trying to find out if our other friends are gonna make it up or not, but they aren't. Too much snow and they started too late." He sighs. "Better they don't though, we don't have enough sleeping spots unless we pile up in the rooms." He grins lewdly. "Wait, what am I saying?" he asks with a laugh, then shrugs. "We're having fun without them, anyway, right?"

He can't mean me, but I'd die if that happened. "Who was supposed to come?" I ask, my heart flies to my throat threatening to choke me as I think about sleeping anywhere near Kian's vicinity.

"Joey, Jack, and Alexa." His eyes are still on his phone as if those boys' names mean nothing.

I freeze in place, a shudder overtaking me as fear floods me. God no. Please, God...*no!* Not Joey and Jack of all people. Memories threaten to take hold, but I keep them shushed. My attempts to stay calm include trying for a steady voice. "They aren't coming, then?" I ask as I stifle another tremble, then glance at Mandy. Her fighting face comes on, her eyes go hard and mean, her fists clench at her thighs. This is the worst possible news ever, and I refuse to let my brain plummet into those awful memories again. Not right now. I can't, especially in front of Kian.

"Nah, they aren't coming." He stands and stretches his arms straight up. "Better this way anyhow." He saunters to the kitchen. "They will wreck our vibe."

Wreck our vibe. He's not fucking kidding, and he has no clue how right he is. The overwhelming urge to puke invades me, so I take a few breaths, nice and slow and easy to try and relax. I can't deal with my emotions right now so I shove them into my dark spot where I wish they would stay forever, shrivel and die so I didn't ever have to feel them again. As I walk past Mandy, she grabs my wrist and pulls me down to sit next to her on the couch. She slips her arm around my shoulder and whispers in my ear, "It's okay. They aren't coming." She lifts my chin and locks her eyes with mine. "Not coming. You hear me, right?" she whispers.

I nod, though my hands are now shaking. "I need a drink." I stand up, waver a bit, my nerves threatening to flare on high alert as I almost topple back on to the couch. I force myself to remain standing and will my legs to move. Terror has settled in me and it's feeling too hard to fake normal.

Kian returns. "Hey, you okay, Ashley? You look off." He cocks his head at me. "Why don't you sit? I'll make your drink."

The boy has a decent, kind heart; he's even showing that for *me,* which I guess doesn't surprise me because he's amazing. "Thanks,

Kian, but I need to move around right now. Muscles are cramping up a bit." Liar. I'm such a dang liar and I fear he sees it in my eyes.

Kian does look worried and I see him glance at Mandy in my peripheral vision before I walk away. Could Kian really care about me? Seems like an impossible thing; he wouldn't even consider me. But he's nice to everyone. Tears fill my eyes as I begin to think the unthinkables I'm trying not to think, and the kitchen blurs before me. Chin up. I can do this. I stuff my bad feelings down, way down to the tips of my toes and stomp them down in there by sheer force of will. I grab a drink and a bag of cheese curls off the counter. I'm going to drink and eat away these feelings until I can get back to where I was before he got that horrifying text Kian got. I firmly set my jaw as I walk. I force a smile as I sit on the bean bag, almost spilling my drink.

"Whoa, let me help you." Kian hops up and takes my drink so I can sit and not spill. There he goes again, being his nice self. How considerate of him. Boy is gaining even more points, not that he needs that. His quick rescue move helps to soften my nerves a tiny bit. I pep talk myself, see Ashley... hot boys can be kind. It's just that hot boys don't like me. Old habits die hard. My mind flips to the fact that Melissa and Liam are still in the garage, which helps me because I need a distraction, plus, I'm so excited for her.

I get situated and open the chip bag and shove a cheesy curl into my mouth. The junk food works. Cheese makes everything better. I even manage a small grin back at Kian. He hands me my drink and I point the open mouth of the chip bag at him.

"Thanks, Kian." Melt my heart much? If someone had told me I'd be sitting in the same room as Kian sharing a bag of chips, I'd have told them they are crazy.

He takes a handful of cheesy curls from the bag—confirming for me that this boy is always eating. "Are you sure you're okay, Ashie?"

He gives me this delicious skeptical look that makes me want to touch his lips.

I smile, a real one. He just called me "Ashie". Giving me a nickname is a huge thing, and my brain can't grasp that he actually gave me one. No one has ever called me that before. This really warms my heart. "I'm good." I can't stop my face from beaming. "Promise."

He smiles, looking relieved. "Ah, there she is. Much better." He sits down with a plop on the couch closest to me and stuffs the whole handful of chips in his mouth in one pop, a satisfied look overtakes his face as he munches with full cheeks.

Mandy gives me a look of intrigue with a raised eyebrow. I give her a short, discreet nod. Yeah. This is epic. Kian next to me. It's like my dream. I try to suppress a smile, chewing helps.

He reaches for more chips, and I pull the bag back. "Oh, don't make me come get it, Ashie, you'll go down." He slips his short sleeve up to the top of his shoulder, then flexes his biceps with a huge teasing grin. "See?"

I shudder. I'd give anything in the world for him to take me "down". Holy crap, his muscles are incredible. That flex he keeps holding sears something visceral in my gut. Like a legit, even bigger lurch of yearning launches inside me, and that is not something I need to add to my existing want for him. It's already huge enough.

"I could lift your little body up with one hand any day. Football and weight training have given me these babies." He smacks his bicep with his other hand. "Years of hard-fought-for threads of muscle, right there." He shakes his head with a cocky grin. "Better hand it over, sweet cheeks, or I'm coming for you." His muscles are bigger than any high school boy's should be.

A hot shiver of excitement rushes through me as I consider letting him come for me. If only! I set my drink on the table because he has this mischievous look in his bright eyes that I don't trust for a second.

I hide the chip bag behind my back. I fully intend to tease the poop out of him like he's been doing to me. I gasp as he charges at me, my heart explodes into mega rapid beating. He lunges for me as I squawk in protest as he proceeds to tickle my sides. I squeal, scream, "Help, Mandy! Help me!" I can't get over the fact that he's touching me. I might faint, but I'm so grateful for the lightened mood, and it feels so good to laugh. For once I'm not stuck on worry mode.

"No can do, he'd whip my butt too. I'm tough, but not that tough." She snickers. "You're on your own, babycakes." When I gaze back at her, her eyes are filled with delight.

I can't stop giggling because he won't stop tickling me. "Stop!" I scream and wiggle trying to avoid his fingers. His eyes are lit like fire. "You're gonna make me spill them! Stop! I give up! You win!" Thank goodness I had set my drink down before he came at me like a raging barracuda. I don't want to have to change my clothes because of a spill.

He grabs something on the side of the bean bag and stands up with the chip bag already in his hands.

"What the...?" I look behind me astounded. "How did you do that? I had it behind me."

"No, you didn't. I already had the bag, in like in the first three seconds, I just wanted to keep tickling you until you screamed for mercy." He chuckles, stuffs an impossible amount of chips into his mouth. His smug expression is intolerable. "I knew I'd get you to cave," he says through a mouthful of chips. He chews, smiling triumphantly.

I fume, my competitiveness flaring a bit. I search and find a pillow to throw at him. He just laughs at me as I hurl it his way. He easily deflects it.

I fake pout. "Oh you—you. Meanie."

He looks aghast. "Meanie? Me? You were the one who wouldn't share the chips. You're the meanie." His eyes are laden with flirty teasing, practically dripping with it, like he's a devil.

I stand next to the coffee table and glance at my drink right next to the decks of cards and cribbage board, noting Kian was likely the one to set up more games to play. Then I allow my gaze to float up to his face. It's like that stupid phase of my brain where life is in slo mo because I can't process what's happening fast enough because shock is also filling me. His full-on smirk sets a blazing fire deep inside my gut. Well shit. I've never wanted this boy more. And I didn't think that was possible.

He lifts the chip bag up higher when I reach for it. But, being I'm almost a foot shorter than him at five-feet-two-inches, so there's no way on this green Earth I'm getting that bag. I must jump to even remotely get my fingertips near it, but I try anyhow, much to his delight. I fail miserably each time, but keep jumping regardless like I'm in denial. He tilts the bag and shoves his hand in for more. He slips too many chips between his smiling lips once again, to taunt me, and chomps down hard on them making exaggerated loud crunches. "Mmmm," he mumbles.

"Pig," I sneer, but my smile ruins my intent.

He's chewing obnoxiously, but he still talks with his mouth full. "Yum, these are damn delicious. Like crunchy cheesy bites of heaven." His eyes mock me hardcore.

I glare at him, my body shaking with a wild urge to tackle him. I put my hands on my hips and tip them to my right as impatience floods me. I stifle the urge to stomp—good gravy I want to stomp—but I know he'll laugh at me, so I don't. I'm tempted to climb him and grab that bag. I smirk at him, narrowing my eyes. With a confidence that comes out of nowhere, I state, "I'm not afraid to climb up you to get to that bag, ya know. I could do it, too. I'm a dancer, and I've got strong legs." I wiggle my fingers on my hips for emphasis as my eyes explode with determination and grit.

Mandy lets out a single, "Ha!" Followed by an avalanche of laughter. "Please do. I wanna see that!"

Kian chokes on the giant mound of chips in his mouth, his body doubling over in hysterics as he struggles to chew through his laughter. He rises to straighten up above me. Then to my absolute horror, he guffaws wildly, and spits out the whole mouthful of chips, it sprays in the air above me. I watch as I scream, bracing for the chunks of saliva-soaked orange cheesy chips that are launched my way. I yelp and raise my hands up to shield myself from the disgusting incoming barrage. I can't move away fast enough to escape the rainfall of them, and they land on me in wet little splats. I'm utterly coated in slimy chip pieces in mere seconds. I stare at him in disbelief.

"Oh my god!" I scream. Orange specks litter my arms, and are scattered all down the front of my shirt. My face is coated in them too, clearly all are sticking to me because of the actual gobs of spit on them. "Oh! Fuck-shit nuggets! Disgusting! Ugh!" I scream again, totally aghast.

This sends Kian into complete hysteria, as if he wasn't already there. He falls back onto the couch as he cracks up like a crazy person, chips spilling out onto the floor from the open bag as he and Mandy get a roaring good laugh at me.

"Real mature," I spit, my cheeks redden and my anger flares hotter.

My face is red, and getting redder, this time it's from pure anger, not embarrassment. My fists are balled. I throw my arms in the air as I'm feeling wretched and enraged. Then I cringe as I notice something weighing slightly down on my hair, damnit! I shudder, soggy chips are in my hair too. I grimace as I touch my hair and, sure enough, there are sticky gooey cheesy grains.

"Ugh, it's in my hair too! Oh! I'm taking a shower right now," I say in a high-pitched wail. I run for my bag, but I can't move fast enough. I'm covered in Kian spit. I once thought that sounded awesome, but it's not, it's completely disgusting. I find my bag, feeling like a chicken with their head cut off as both he and Mandy are still laughing at me. This might be funny, unless you're me. But I'm me, and I'm really pissed. This is so not funny.

"Ungh," I grunt as I run into a chair.

"Need help?" Mandy manages to say between her laughs.

"No." I'm stomping as I walk. I can't stop myself, this sucks big time. "This isn't funny," I blurt.

Kian manages to stop laughing for a moment and he calls after me, "I'm s-s-sor..." He's laughing too hard to finish. "Sorry, Ashie, I'm sor..." He falls into a banter of uncontrollable heckling and laughing on the couch.

Geez. I want to scream.

I scramble into the bathroom, and slam the door behind me. Only once I'm safe inside, a laugh slips out. Did that just happen? I can still hear them laughing through the door. What's so funny anyway? I sure as hell could have climbed up him. Damn right I could have got that chip bag away from, easy peasy. I will get my revenge, I have no doubt. And enjoy every stinking second of it. I don't know what the hell is going on, but my life just got a whole lot crazier.

Chapter Eight

The hot shower feels amazing. I run my fingers through my hair to comb out the bits of chips; this also requires the use of my fingernails. I squint as I cringe. *Ew!* Kian, you are so effing hot, but I don't want your spit in my hair. This is not the way I wanted to experience his mouth on me. I glance at the shower floor hoping the chip chunks don't clog up the shower drain. The hot water streams down my body and I sigh, letting the debacle of what just happened wash away. I smirk because I'm finding the humor in it all now, but only because the crumbs are coming off. *Ick*, some even landed in my cleavage...geez! I laugh out loud as I swipe them away. Oh gosh! I actually said I'd climb him! That's hot. I giggle at myself. I'd love to climb him. That's damn yummy and really, I have to admit...it is funny.

There's a knock at the door. "Ash, it's me, Mandy. Can I come in?"

"Hang on. It's locked. I'll come unlock it." I tiptoe out, dripping water everywhere, and unlock the door, scurrying back to the shower so no one in the hallway sees my naked butt.

"Thanks," she says. I hear the sound of her pee hitting the toilet water, then she sighs. "Gosh. Thanks. I had to pee so bad." She flushes and I get a burst of cold water which makes me yelp. "Sorry for that," she says with a snicker. "Ash, I think Kian likes you. I mean really, really, likes you. The way he looks at you. Teases you, like, relentlessly." I can't see her, but I'm sure she's nodding. "Listen to me on this. I know this. I see it."

"I don't buy it," I blurt as I'm scrubbing my hair, but I stop as I consider what she's saying. Then, I shake my head. "No way." I pause and recall that look in his eyes. That was tough to deny. I smile. *Hmm.* A glimmer of hope births, but I squash it right away. I'm a fool. "Do you really think so?"

"Yeah, I do. He's not doing any of that crap with me." She laughs. "And that was fricking hilarious, by the way. He totally loved it. He's still laughing out there. He's told the story to everyone in the cabin now."

I can't believe a hottie like him would like me. I'm a shy little nothing. "I just don't believe it."

"Hey, trust me, I know these things. I watched him with you, he's loving teasing the crap out of you. There were practically sparks flying off you two just now."

"I thought we had a moment earlier, but then I thought it was just in my head because I want him so damn bad." I rinse the soap out of my hair and smooth in some minty conditioner. It tingles the flesh of my scalp, and it feels soothing, amazing. I sigh deeply. "He would never go for a girl like me though. I'm just a no one."

"Not true." She rips open the shower curtain and nods, her eyes alive with zest. "Sweet baby cakes, you are hot! Way hot. Just look at yourself. Of course, he'd be into you. Any guy would be. You're a nice girl, but with hidden a rebel streak." She raises her eyebrows at me, then wiggles them. "You have amazing waves of luscious hair, your face is gorgeous, and those tits," she says shaking her head. "Your little hour-glass curves, your smoking hot ass. Come on, Ash! You're amazing!"

I smirk at her. Only she can say such things to me and not cause me to blush. "I'm leaving that open only because you've seen me naked before."

She grins, then shuts it. "Now, listen to me. He's into you. No fucking doubt about it. Trust me, I know how to read people. He's hot. He's sweet and kind and he seems like a really good guy. And, Ash, he *so* wants you. I'm serious. One hundred percent serious."

"And he's so funny," I gush. "And those biceps, did you see those? Good God. And, those eyes, that ass of his...I mean...come on! And I can imagine what he looks like under that shirt. When it lays the right way, I can see parts of his abs." I sigh. "Ah, getting hot, I might need to switch this to a cold shower." I flip the handle to the blue line for cold water and then shriek because it's way too cold. I quickly turn it back to hot.

Mandy laughs. "Too cold?"

"Yes, way too damn cold." I rub my legs with soap. "Tell me more about what happened with Lily." The fan is going and with the shower running too both together make for good sound buffers—so we can talk freely without anyone hearing us. I hope.

"Well, we were smoking, ya know, sharing the cig and we got to talking about our exes. And she told me how good Lucas is to her compared to other boys, who treated her like a whore or worse, bastards...anyway, I mentioned how hot he is and at first, she was like 'back off, bitch', and she almost got out of the car. So, to simmer her down I told her I'm bi, and that I think she's so hot, too. I mean we were smoking and blowing it out the cracked car windows, so we weren't outside, the car was running but it was frigid still and we were both just shivering like crazy, on edge, ya know. I mentioned to her how I liked that our lips kept touching the same spot on the cigarette, and she just asked me to kiss her. She'd never kissed a girl before and she was just curious to see. And I was like hell yeah, I've only thought about that about a thousand times."

"You told her that?"

"Yes, I'm forward, remember, and apparently, so is she. Then, we kissed." She sucks in a full breath. "Ash, it was fucking amazing, like better than I ever imagined it would be." I peek out at her. She hops like she's going to launch a basketball into the hoop.

"That's when she raced in the cabin, all hot and bothered?" I drop the curtain and caress the rest of the soap off my flesh in the water.

"You think she was?" she asks, I can hear the grin in her voice.

"Um, yes." I nod even though she can no longer see me. "Absolutely."

"Wow, I didn't expect that at all." Hope is laced in her tone.

"I hope Lucas doesn't get pissed. I mean, that's technically cheating, right?" I thread my fingers between my toes.

"Yeah, but who knows? That's subjective. It was only a kiss. I don't think it should matter. I mean, she's not bi, at least I don't think so, which means Lucas has nothing to worry about." The downturn in her voice kinda breaks my heart.

I turn off the water.

"Okay, I'm heading out so you can get dressed," she says. "See you in a few."

I slip on my tank top and throw on a button up shirt over the top. This shows off my chest nicely. Digging in my bag is a gift because at the bottom are my best jeans. I slip them on, slap in some hair product and slather on a bit of makeup and I'm out the door in six minutes flat.

"Wow, you shine up quick." Kian happens to be in the hallway when I open the door, as if he were waiting. I catch my breath as I think about what Mandy said about him liking me. My heart begins to beat faster, though it's not possible.

My tank works. His eyes go right to my chest and, *ack*, I blush again.

His lips spread slowly into a really big smile as I squirm. "Ready to play a game? All seven of us are going to play."

"Sure, I'm in. What's the game?" That smile of his could be the best precursor to a kiss on the planet.

"It's called Taboo and we're all in teams, so one team will just rotate between the three people. It's Liam and Melissa," he says with a juicy smile. "Lily, Lucas, and Mandy. Then that leaves you with me." The suggestion in his voice gives me way too much hope.

"I'm last?"

"No, not at all. I chose you first." He smirks and places his hand on the small of my back and I startle. "Sorry," he whispers.

"It's okay." Umm. Holy crap. So okay. More than... I want to scream.

He nudges me forward and we walk into the living room. Everyone is set up with a drink. Everyone is smiling and it feels like a dang sitcom.

I stifle my giggle and sit on the couch. Kian sits next to me. He hands me a drink.

"Thank you, Kian." He made me a drink! I love that he thought of me. It gives me the shivers. I can't breathe normally. I try to not hope for too much.

Melissa raises her glass. "Cheers," she says to me.

"You're feeling okay then?" I widen my eyes at her.

"I am. Liam made me a drink." She grins his way.

I laugh. "That's supposed to make me believe it?" I give Liam the evil eye then smirk. "I'm skeptical, but happy you are feeling better."

She nods aggressively, her eyes are honestly telling me just how good she really is.

"Hey," Liam says. "I don't want her feeling bad like that again." That smile of his could win him money, and likely, someday it will, to a crowd of women at one of his concerts, no doubt.

I stare in disbelief as Melissa crawls into his lap. I can't get used to seeing her on a boy's lap, she's never been on one to my knowledge. Ever. She's all pink and shiny and loaded with grins. This new thing with Liam suits her so well. She whispers something into his ear, and he chuckles. She looks like pure magic. I glance at Mandy, and we smile at each other. We both know this is Melissa's first boy-everything and it's so fun to watch. My girl is practically glittering.

We start the game, and it goes on for forty-five minutes. Kian and I are killing it.

"How are you two doing so well?" Lily asks, eyes wide. She adjusts herself between Lucas and Mandy, she flips her hair into a messy bun in mere seconds, but a few stranglers fall which make her hair look tousled and sexy. She strokes Lucas's thigh, pats Mandy's hand and gives her a look. "We'll step it up, right team?"

Mandy nods and Lucas says, "Yep, baby. We will." His hand slips behind her and he must be grabbing her rear the way she's moving. She wiggles against his hand and Mandy's fingers flinch.

I smile at her. They're cute, especially Mandy who looks ready to pounce at the two at the slightest chance.

"No chance, I'm afraid. We rock." Kian stretches and his arm lands behind me, resting on my shoulders. I don't squirm away, but I freeze. This is the cheesy move that every girl secretly wants from a boy like Kian. Butterflies erupt in me as he secures arm upon me with a slight press down.

I glance up at him. "We will win." I nod his way emphatically.

"Damn straight." He pops up and grabs my drink. "Refill?"

"Sure, but I need to eat soon. What time is it?" It's getting dark now. I glance at my phone. "It's six, so we should eat soon," I say. "I'm gonna need to eat or I'll wind up repeating the Melissa show." I wrinkle my nose.

"I'll never live this down, will I?" she asks with a roll of her eyes. She sits up straight and edges herself along, scooting towards Liam's knees. "I need the ladies' room." He hoists her hips up, a hand on each side of her. She turns slightly towards him. "Thanks for the boost."

He releases a single laugh. "No, thank you."

Yeah, whew! It's getting hot in here. Geez, they need a room, too. We all might just need a chaperone in this cabin.

Liam's eyes follow her the whole way as she walks to the bathroom, and I can't wait to tell her.

Melissa's eyes are sparkling when she glances my way just before slipping into the bathroom. Ah, guess she already gets that his eyes were on her with that look.

Kian returns with my cup. "After this game, Ashie and I will make pizza," he declares boldly. He sits and takes a sip of his drink. "You all can wash this time since we will do the cooking."

"You know how to make pizza?" I ask him incredulously.

"I'll have you know, I have a famous homemade crust recipe. Yes, that I do." He nods, rubs his thigh with his free hand.

"I'm seriously impressed." I take a sip of the drink and cough. "Any pop in here?"

He chuckles. "It's good for ya, will put hair on your chest."

I scoff. "Jackass," I say snickering, because I can't not laugh at that.

"Sassy ass," he says back.

"Smart ass," I fling.

"Nice ass," he guffaws and points back at me. "Bet that one shuts you up."

I blush. I might as well wear a bag over my head, I'm blushing so damn much. I just sigh and shake my head. I suck.

One more pops in my head. "Asshat."

He laughs and shakes his head, presses his lips together in sudden refusal to speak.

"What? I dare you to say it." I give him a direct stare. "Go on," I egg. "I dare you."

He laughs. "I can't do it," he says shaking his head as he glances over at Liam.

Liam warns, "Don't do it dude." He shakes his head with a smile. "Kian, don't."

"Chicken." I poke the outside of his thigh with my index finger. Damn his thigh is so firm.

He laughs harder, shakes his head as he stares at his lap. "I can't."

I shoot him a naughty grin. Damn...I really wish I knew what he was going to say. I'm almost ready to beg.

He grins back and holy hotness.

"Let's finish the game, guys," Lily says in an airy voice. "I'm starving for pizza."

After a few more rounds, Kian and I win and head to the kitchen to start up dinner. As he works, I become more and more impressed. He's clearly no stranger to the kitchen. He whips up dough from a recipe inside his head and pops it into a bowl to rise. He repeats it three more times for three more bowls of dough, and I watch him out of the corner of my eye, totally amazed at his level of kitchen skills as I cut the veggies.

"You're a force with the pizza dough. I can say I'd never figured you for being a cook."

He smiles, flashes a glance at me. "Wait until you taste it."

I grab a couple of potato chips from the large ceramic blue bowl on the counter and pop them into my mouth.

"Hungry?" he asks. "I can look for more cheese curls since you didn't get many last time, or I mean," he says through a laugh, "you didn't get them the right way." He smirks. "Or, I saw some cheesy corn chips, too, somewhere. Something cheesy." His grin widens.

I shake my finger at him, glaring back in a death stare. "Don't you even go there. And I've had enough of cheesy chips to last me quite awhile." I give him a-don't-you-dare look but it slips into a smile, I can't not smile at him.

"Did you get all the pieces out?" he asks while inspecting my hair, shifting his gaze from side to side above me.

The boy I've had a crush on forever is digging his fingers in my hair. I legit might die. I throw my hands over my head so he can't peer into my hair like he's looking for lice. I growl, "Yes, I did. No thanks to you and your sprayed spit-filled mouthful of chips." I guffaw, then sigh. "You know you even got some down my," I pause a I meet his wide eyes, instantly regretting what's about to spill out of my mouth, "my...cleavage. I'm not sure how you managed that one." I widen my eyes at him as anger resurges in me. The thought of it makes me fume.

He chuckles, clearly he's loving that. "My spit is talented, and it knows the best places to land."

Omigod. I just giggle at him even though I want to smack him, he's such a tease. I have zero response for that one, so I just stare back at him dumbly. He turns around and digs in the fridge for something. My promise to myself for revenge flickers into my mostly bewildered brain. Now is my chance to get even. Without another thought, I rip the wrap off one of the dough bowls and scoop up the giant mound of dough with one hand. Kian has his back to me opening pizza sauce jars.

"Oh Kian? Ever worn your dough?" I ask in a daring tone.

He turns and catches a glimpse of the glimmer in my eyes and the giant dough ball in my raised hand, which I wiggle at him as his eyes go big. I take one step.

"Oh shit!" He takes off across the living room, half tripping over a pillow, knocking over the rocking chair as he plows through the main part of the living room. He falters onward to where everyone is seated on the floor. They all scramble out of his path, which works great for me because not only does it slow him down, it clears the way for me to gain on him.

"And now, back to the show," Mandy says with glee.

I pause long enough to say, "Payback's a bitch and I'm aiming to be a savage avenger."

He remains motionless watching me as I give a loud battle war cry while raising the dough ball high above my head. Everyone in the room busts a gut with laughter, including Kian. I'm the only one not laughing. I ignore them all and keep my eyes on Kian as I zoom after him. He's still in the lead.

I chase him around the circle of couches and chairs three times as everyone's eyes follow us. Everyone is in an uproar, all shrieking and laughing, whooping it up. He does a quick loop through the garage, and I follow, my feet freezing as I pitter patter across the frigid concreate. He trips on the step back into the house and I almost get him. He's got agile fast moves from football, but I've got my swift dancer moves. However, I still can't catch him.

He snatches a quick look back at me, I give him my most determined eyes telling him he's toast. "Fuck!" he yells with the biggest grin on his face when I'm gaining on his heels.

He heads back to the living room after tripping over about eight pairs of boots and shoes by the front door, knocks over the coat rack and flips around, walks slowly backwards.

"Now Ashie, I'm so sorry about the chips incident. It was totally an accident," he can't say it without laughing, and somehow I retain my saucy glare without laughing too "You were so funny...I'm so sor-" It's the same act all over again, and yeah, he's cracking up even harder, which infuriates me more.

"Don't laugh at me!" I holler. I'm about to lose it.

"Those two just need to get it over with and just kiss," Mandy says in a loud whisper.

Yeah, I'll kill her later.

Lily lets out a tiny laugh. "Yup," she says in her tiny voice.

Someone goes, "I know, right?" I'm not sure who, but I'm going rake him over the coals when I figure out who, but I think it was Liam.

"Now, sweet little Ashie," Kian coaxes as I creep slowly over the coat rack. "You don't want to ruin that dough we worked so hard on, plus, we will have one less pizza if you do."

"I didn't work on it, only you did," I blurt. My blood is roiling, boiling, seething with heat. He's within my grasp now. "And don't call me little! Oh, my revenge will be sweet when this dough is all over your face." I raise the dough ball and shake it back and forth causing a small wad of dough to fly off.

He chokes on his laughter. "Really, we need the pizza. You said yourself that you're hungry. Don't make us have one less pizza, us boys need lots of pizza to function." He's smirking, his expression playful. He's still backing slowly away from me. He's backpedaling and failing at it.

"Do it, Ash. We can eat chips." Mandy gives a slow whistle followed by a chuckle. "Give it to him, baby. Right in his pretty face."

"Yeah, I can make another salad," Lily offers, then giggles which eggs me on to do it even more.

Kian deserves it. Everyone wants to see this. I want to see this.

"You guys aren't helping," Kian yells as he shuffles along, almost failing.

Liam busts a gut in hysterical laughter. "You deserve it, dude. You spit chips all over her, you jackass. Take your lumps like a man."

Melissa squeals, "Oh, I can't wait to see this."

I creep towards him as my heart pounds. His eyes are pleading with me to stop, but they are also daring me, telling me he wants whatever I dish out, and I'm so ready to give it. His hands are raised in front of him and he's bouncing them as he takes slow steps backwards. He's oblivious to the dangers behind him. I see the bunched up sleeping bag on the ground before he feels it and I've got him right where I want him. He's mine. In about one second, he's going down and I can't wait. I lunge forward, holding the dough out in front of me as he trips and falls back onto the sleeping bag.

His mouth goes into a giant O, his eyes widening. His leg shifts and hits mine, pushing me off balance and throwing me forward off my feet. I'm launched. I'm falling through the air, towards him. He crashes hard back onto the sleeping bag and pillows. Panic seizes me as I realize what's going to happen. In absolute shock, I land on top of him, with a hard smackdown in a rough thud with the dough ball and my hand sandwiched between the two of us. The laughter behind us is ginormous. They sound like a crowd of people rather than their true number. It sounds like a zoo. Kian is laughing and so am I. I shake my head—I want to smack him, but I'm too filled with some odd form of unexpected joy, even in my embarrassment.

"This is not how I planned this to go down!" I shriek. "*Oooh!*" I slip my hand out from the dough. It's gloppy and my hand is covered in it.

His eyes are lit and excited as I meet his gaze. He stops laughing for a moment but smiles at me.

My entire body is fully along his. I'm acutely aware of every inch of him beneath me and I freeze. At my stomach, there's a very hard lump. My eyes go wide. Oh, it can't be!

He keeps his eyes locked on me as he whispers, "You caught me." This boy is glowing with joy.

I gasp, then scramble off him as fast as I can. I stand, staring down at him with my eyes wide as they can go. Did I really just feel what I think I did? No. It's not possible. It's just not. I shake my head as I take a step back.

Kian is grinning so big his face might slit open. He doesn't move a muscle, but touches the blobs of dough caked on him.

I look down at my chest. A quarter of the dough is sticking to my tank top and some has snaked itself down inside my cleavage. I groan. I'm messy again. How did this happen? Most of the dough is on him though, and his eyes are twinkling at me something fierce while he's just about laughing his head off, a slight red tinge is blooming beautifully across his cheeks. Now this boy is blushing?

I tremble like silk on a clothesline in a slight breeze. Oh. My. I may never recover. I made Kian blush.

He stops laughing for a moment and says, "That was fucking awesome, Ashie. That was totally hilarious. You rock." He tries to pick the sticky dough off his front.

I'm trying not to laugh but I fail as laughter takes over me, too. I roll my eyes, giggling. I gaze down into my cleavage at the wad of dough wedged there, shake my head, and, yeah, I'm effing blushing again myself as he catches me looking down there. I sigh. "Ugh. Dammit! I need to shower again. Not fair, and all you need to do is change, but it's all over my skin. Again!" I throw my hands up in the air then try to peel off some of the dough off my chest. "Yuck, this sucks!" I clench both my fists and throw them down along my sides. I know I must look like a toddler throwing a tantrum, but I can't help it. "I'm taking the hot water, screw you all, I need it. I'm coated in food." I pause as my anger flares higher. "Again!" I repeat as fury fully claims me.

I trudge off as everyone is laughing at me, cracking up, cat-calling after me. Someone is clapping. Ugh! Who made me the entertainment this weekend anyway?

Kian calls after me. "Don't worry, I'll make another ball of dough while you shower. But hands off this one, you little kleptomaniac."

Refusing to respond, I slam the bathroom door in a huff behind me, drop my bag on the ground and slide down the door to sit on the floor. I silently crack up, my smile stays as a permanent grin. Oh. My. God. My hand goes to my mouth as I gasp. I take a deep breath and hold it. I'm flabbergasted, but maybe, just maybe, Mandy's right. The thought sends shivers all through me to the ends of my dough covered fingers and to the very tippy ends of my tingling toes as I let that breath out. Wow...just wow. But I'm one hundred percent sure I'm just imagining it all.

Chapter Nine

I gather up my bag and my dough covered tank before I exit the bathroom. Everyone is in the living room but Melissa and Liam, who are probably checking on the cabin next door, and getting distracted by other things, steamy things, no doubt.

I call out to Lily and Lucas, "Hey, can I use the washing machine? I have two outfits full of food now that need to be washed." I hold up my clothes with a smirk as evidence.

"There's our own private comedic movie star," Lucas retorts. "Good show, my love. Good show."

"I'm so glad I could entertain you all," I say drily with an eye roll. "I might be swearing off food for the night, just to be safe."

"At the end of the hall," says Lily pleasantly. "Laundry detergent is in the cabinet above. Stain remover is there too so you can spray it." She gives me a look of sympathy, then a smile. "I hope the dough comes out."

"Yeah, me too." I sigh and trudge down the hall but turn back towards the kitchen as Kian's clothes enter my thoughts.. "Kian, you want your shirt tossed in too?"

He's in the kitchen working on the pizza. "Yep, thanks. That would be great. I'll bring it," he calls.

The laundry room is tiny. It has a utility sink with a paper towel holder above it. There is a drying rack on one wall and a cabinet on the other. I lay out the chip-coated clothes and the dough covered tank on the washer. I pick off as much dough as I can with my fingers and roll it in a paper towel; it has to go somewhere. I sense someone behind me, and I startle, then fling myself around. My hand hits something solid. I'm surprised to see Kian is only about a foot away

94

from me. I flush as I wonder what part of him my hand smacked. I look up at his smiling face and he's holding his doughy shirt up.

"Well, I've officially worn dough now," he smirks, his blue eyes are bright under the laundry room lights. "I'm halfway to your status."

"It was supposed to be on your face!" I spit. I put my hands on my hips and tap my right foot, furrow my brow. My hair is up in a bun and the few curls that have fallen bounce on my chest as I exaggeratedly move my foot.

Kian's fingers grasp one of my curls and I flinch, then stop moving, my eyes are glued to his. He flicks the curl back and forth between his fingers while he holds my gaze. It's almost too intense and while I love it, I'm scared to death.

"You're so beautiful when you're cheesed off," he says when a grin. "When you're coated in cheese, and when you're not," he adds with the sexiest grin I've ever seen in my entire life.

His sentence slowly sinks into my reluctant brain as my jaw falls slack. My heart comes flying up from my chest threatening to beat itself right out of my body at hearing those unbelievable words come out of him. My heart is so jittery it literally wants to burst out of my mouth to take flight. He leans toward me like he might kiss me and my pulse pounds like a speed boat going wide open on a boat-free lake. His hand moves to stroke my cheek, and when he dips his head, our lips achingly closer. Our eyes are locked and I'm afraid he can see the fear in my eyes, but I hope he sees my excitement, too, my acceptance, my desire for him. The painful years of want. His lips are parted, they are full and a deep rose, not pale pink like mine. And I can't wait to feel them on me.

Someone rushes into the room. "Ash, can you add this shirt to the load, too, I—oh, crap, my bad. So sorry," Mandy stops in the doorway, grimacing as she backs away. "Really bad timing."

Kian steps back from me, disappointment flooding his handsome face. He's flushed. I feel my cheeks go red, too.

"Damn. I'm so sorry, oh frick, I ruined it." Mandy hands me the shirt. "Carry on." She whips around and rushes off.

Kian and I glance at each other and it's too late. We can't get that moment back.

Someone yells from the kitchen, "Kian, better come check these pizzas!" It's Melissa. "I think they're done."

He smiles at me and nods. "I'd better go check since I'm the pizza chef tonight. Thanks for washing that." He sounds so sincere, and when he touches my arm before turning to go, I melt inside. He drops his head, then walks out the door.

My heart is beating so hard it feels like it's about to rip a hole through my chest. He almost kissed me. Oh, wow! He almost kissed me! Right? Or am I insane? My breathing is rapid, and I can't slow it as I spray my clothes and Kian's with the stain remover. Kian had apparently already picked the big dough chunks off before he brought it to me because his looks way better than mine. I finger the neckline of his shirt, smooth my hand down the front of it wishing I were touching him in this shirt. I bite my lip. I can't believe he almost kissed me. My heart is singing and I'm praying hard that he will try to kiss me again. Or, maybe I'll have to try kissing him if he doesn't try again, though that scares the absolute shit out of me. Would I dare?

I start up the washer and head out to the living room. Kian is cutting pizzas with a giant wheel pizza cutter. He glances up as I come near and gives me a little knowing smile which causes a swirl of desire to flip inside my abdomen.

"Hungry?" he asks me.

I nod. "Very." I look directly into his eyes and try to will him to know I really wish he had kissed me. We keep our eyes locked, both of us smiling like we have a secret. It's damn delicious. "I'll get you a drink. What would you like?" I ask.

"Anything." I should have known that one.

"I'm on it." I get him a can from the fridge and mix myself a drink.

"Yum," Lily says as she gets the plates out. "This smells amazing, Kian. Thanks for cooking for us. I love your cooking." She sets the stack of deep blue ceramic plates on the counter. "Liam and Melissa, you two are clean up duty tonight."

"Yep, it's our turn. We've done nothing for meals," Melissa agrees.

Liam comes up behind her. "Let me at that pizza. I'm ravenous as a bear." He starts grabbing slices and piles four on his plate. He adds a giant handful of chips and grabs an apple out of the fruit bowl on the counter. "I'm famished."

Melissa takes one piece of pizza and an apple. She smiles at me, I'm sure she's hoping I've noticed she took some food.

I nod at her and give her a smile. I won't say anything to embarrass her, but I'm so glad she's eating.

Lucas and Lily grab slices next, then Mandy. Kian and I go last.

Everyone sits scattered around the living room, plates held in our laps or to under chins. All of us are silent for like three minutes as we eat.

"This is really amazing pizza, Kian," I say. "You're a good cook."

"See, told you," he says with confidence.

Everyone agrees with me and thanks Kian. A boy who cooks, that's so hot.

"I still can't believe school is closed two days in a row. And who knows when this repair guy will come. I'm sure he's super busy right now. So, what's everyone's parents saying about all this? Are they mad?" Melissa asks. "I'm hoping this polar vortex stays and we get yet another day here. I'm having a blast with you all."

"Me too," Lily says with a grin. "This has been awesome."

"We're making food, cleaning up, having fun, kinda like some sort of cabin crew." Melissa gives a sweet smile to me because neither of us wanted to come here at first, but, clearly, we're both very happy we did. I return her smile. Calling this lucky doesn't even come close to the truth.

"Well, my parents are fine with it, but they think we're in your cabin, Melissa." I smirk. "And I'm not correcting them. Hell no." I take a giant bite of pizza and chow it. It's damn delicious. Once I get the bite down, I say, "They'd be pissed though if they knew I was in cabin with boys." I grin and glance at Kian.

He smiles back and winks at me. "But you're eighteen, right?"

"Yes, but it wouldn't matter."

Kian snorts. "My parents think I'm at Liam's house," he says with a grin. "They're fine with it since school is closed. I'm always over there so it's not weird in any way. I texted my dad, told him we've been lifting weights, so he doesn't get pissed at me that my training is slacking in this weather."

I blink as concern fills my eyes. I spy a pained look enter his normally happy jovial eyes. He recovers quickly though and erases the evidence, grins at me. Oh, what was that all about?

"I told my parents about the heat going out in the cabin," Melissa says. She grins. "But I lied about where we're staying. They think the three of us girls are staying there with the heaters going. They are freaks about me driving in storms, so they want me to stay put. Plus, we have the whole no gas issue, too. The little gas that's left in the tank is probably frozen by now."

"No doubt it's frozen. And, wow, I'm rubbing off on you, Liss, you're lying to the parentals. Good work, I'm proud of you." Mandy pops a chip in her mouth, crunching it as she smirks.

"How about you, Mandy?" Lily asks, licking her fingers.

"My dad knows I'm at the cabin with Melissa and Ash, but honestly, he believes whatever I say. I could tell him anything and he'll buy it." She flicks her hand. "My mom is off in another state with the bastard she cheated on my dad with. She never checks in with me. She probably doesn't even know I came up here."

"Yeah, your dad believes you, wrongly so most of the time," I pipe in with a tease. "You have him wrapped around your little finger, girl."

"I know, right?" She throws her head back and gives an evil sinister laugh.

"You're a good liar, too," I say to her. I'm seriously envious of her abilities. She should win an award for her acting in how she's pulled the shades over her dad's eyes through the years. Being an only child to him as a single dad has made him worship the ground she walks on. She can do no wrong in his eyes, but sometimes it makes her into an entitled brat. Other times it makes her strength blossom, like when she's standing up for someone she loves, she's all in for that person to the max. Like she did for me recently. I can barely stop the bad feelings as memories start to intrude on my thoughts. I swallow hard and freeze so the tears forming behind my eyes don't leak out. I take a deep breath and pull the denial around me like a cloak.

"Yeah, I've had lots of practice. Plus, my dad wants to believe all the good so it's easy, quite honestly." Mandy scoffs, shrugs. "I'm a rebel at heart, but my dad thinks I'm a sugary sweet pea. I'm not about to mess with that."

"Ashley, you look really weird. Are you okay?" Melissa looks at me with concerned eyes.

I quickly swipe my face clean of any trace of my bad feelings encroaching again, and sigh. "Nope. I mean yep, I mean, I'm good." I glance at Mandy then sweep my eyes away to look at Lily. I need to change the subject like right now. "How about you, Lily? What do your parents think?"

She's sitting on the floor. She pulls her knees to her chest and places her hands on top of her knees, sets her chin on top of her hands. She tilts her head to the side making her gorgeous hair fall like a cascade of grace. "They know I'm with Lucas here at the cabin. I think my parents are the only ones who know the truth besides Lucas's."

"You told them?" I stare at her aghast. "Wow. My mom would freak if she knew I was with my boyfriend alone in a cabin."

"Yeah, well, we weren't going to be alone, Kian and Liam were going to be here, and possibly others."

I cringe at the mention of the "possibly others".

She continues, "And it's not a big deal, really, because my parents love Lucas. He saved me, he's my hero and my parents know it." She smiles. "Plus, they also know we are pretty much committed to each other." She puts her hand on Lucas's thigh, and he smiles back at her. "Both our parents are pretty cool about us."

There's clearly a story there with Lucas being her hero and I'm wondering if she's going to ever share it. I try not to look at her too expectantly.

Lucas rubs her arm, runs his fingers down her arm to hold her hand. She sighs and straightens out her legs, places their folded hands between her thighs making a thigh-hand-thigh sandwich. "Remember Alex Sonderman? He moved away at the end of last year when we were sophomores."

I nod. "Yes, he was one of the most popular guys in our class last year, so yup, know him." I do remember Lily dating him last year. He was hot, really hot and he knew it. He played football, hockey, baseball, and was voted hottest boy by class vote last year by the junior girls.

Her expression turns sad. "He used to hit me." Lily's eyes drop to the ground. "A lot." She glances up to see if we're looking at her. Tears flicker into her eyes and she blinks them back. Lucas releases her hand, rubs her back and she leans back into his hand. His free hand forms into a fist at his thigh.

My eyes go wide. Mandy stops chewing and gets a super pissed off look and Melissa looks scared. Neither Kian nor Liam react; clearly, they knew this already.

"Oh, no," I mutter softly.

"We were dating and one time at a party, Alex dragged me to a back room when I didn't want to go and beat me up bad. Real bad." She wipes her eyes. "He wanted sex and stuff."

"You don't have to tell us this, Lily," Mandy says with great concern infused in her voice. She looks like she might cry, too.

"No, it's okay. I want to tell people, so no one goes out with him. I want it spread around. He was very deceiving. Popular, but really, he was a monster. He hid it very well. I didn't want to tell people at first, but now I do. I mean, he's at a different school now, but it's not that far away. I wouldn't want any of you girls to fall for his charms, because believe me, he is charming. He fooled me for months before he started to hurt me." She takes a sip of her drink. "Anyway, at the party, he grabbed me by my hair, caveman style, and dragged me down the hall as I scrambled my feet along trying to keep up. People thought it was a joke and laughed." She stops for like twenty seconds, chokes on a sob. She clears her throat, then continues. "Alex was smiling the whole time, shooting his smile my way and to the whole crowd, charming them as he always did, but he was hurting me, like real bad as they all laughed. It was awful." Her eyes tear up, and she coughs. She shakes her head. "Um...he was so popular, everyone thought he could do no wrong. I was really scared but I couldn't say anything because I knew if I did, I'd get it worse. When we got back to the room, I was petrified when I saw his eyes. He demanded I suck his dick. I didn't want to. I was having fun and it was a great party and I wanted to go back, so I refused. He grabbed me by my hair, again, and pulled out a fistful, I watched it fall to the floor as he demanded I suck him. I was a fool, thinking he wouldn't hit me too bad at a party, so I tried to crawl out of the room. He grabbed me, beat me up so bad, I couldn't move. Lucas found me in a pile later that night. I have no idea how long I had been there, either. And it was Lucas who carried me out to his car and drove me home. Then, he went back to the party and beat the ever-loving piss out of Alex. Warned him to never touch me again. I've been with Lucas ever since." Tears bubble out her eyes, she wipes them away, gives us shrug, and a weak attempt at a smile. "That's when Alex was gone from school from school for a while, if you remember, then he moved."

I did remember, but I had never dreamt this horribleness was the cause.

Lucas's fist clenches and unclenches, as it had the whole time she spoke, but relaxes now that she is done, but his eyes still look hard and mean. He looks scary, not like the Lucas I've come to know today. He softens his features and pulls her onto his lap, hugging her tight.

I'm stunned. I can't believe she went through all that. "Oh my gosh. I always thought your life was so easy because you're so beautiful and so popular. Everyone loves you. I'm so sorry, I shouldn't have judged you like that." I want to give her a hug. It feels awkward, but I still ask. "Can I give you a hug?" I feel like dog shit because I used to hate her, and she was going through all of that.

She nods and I crawl towards her from my spot on the floor. She leaves Lucas's lap and crawls towards me. We hug. She lets out a sob. I rub her back. Oh, this poor girl.

"I'm over it, I really am, I'm just emotional when I tell people about it sometimes." She leans back and smiles at me. "Thank you. I may be popular, but most girls aren't nice to me. They just want to be with me because of my status. No one is genuine, not like you three. You three are really, truly nice. I'm just not used to that. I really hope we can hang out more, I really like you guys." She smiles so sweetly it buries all my past hate for her.

I nod. "Yes, I'd like that, too." I smile back at her. "I'm so sorry, I used to think you were so mean, and I'm sorry, but I hated you."

She smiles a sad smile. "I know, lots of people think of me that way."

"I'm sorry," I say. Geez, I'm a piece of shit for judging her. "I'm just as awful as they are."

"No, you aren't. What you just said proves it." She smiles weakly at me, her eyes raw and vulnerable, but grateful.

Melissa and Mandy appear. Mandy wraps her arms around Lily too, and we all pile on in a girl group hug. We all giggle. I feel silly and sappy, but I don't care.

Kian goes, "Aw, how cute is this." It's a mocking voice, but when I glance at his eyes, I see he's really serious, he means it. "Nah, I'm joking. It's pretty damn cool."

We all release our group hug and go back to our spots.

"I always thought your life was a piece of cake, too," Melissa admits. "Being popular and a cheerleader, I thought all that made your life easygoing, a breeze." She sighs. "And all that time last year you were going through absolute hell."

She nods. "I was in hell, yeah. He hit me almost every time I saw him towards the end. He'd even hurt me at school, he'd pinch me under my shirt on my back until I'd bleed unless I smiled as we walked down the hall together." She shudders. "So, I caved, told my parents everything, like I told them everything. And now, my parents know Lucas and they love him for the good man that he is. He's a big tough guy, but you should see him with his younger sisters, he's sweeter than apple pie." She grins. "He's a lover, but a bad guy fighter when life calls for it." She smiles at him and he returns it. "He's my hero."

"Aww, I love that," I say in a high-pitched voice.

Melisa pipes up, "Yeah, I guess I've seen that sweet side of you, Lucas, being at our cabins through the years." Melissa looks at Lucas, then she looks sheepishly at Lily, but says nothing. "Well, mostly," she mutters under her breath.

Maybe I'm the only one who caught that, but my heart fills with admiration for Lucas. What he did took guts.

I had always envied Lily for her popularity, I had thought just as Melissa did. In fact, Melissa, Mandy, and I had often whined about how unfair it was that the popular ones had an easy time of everything. I guess it's just not true, we can never know what someone is going through by looking at them.

"I never saw you with a shiner either," Mandy says. "I would have never known."

"That's because he usually hit me where my clothes would cover it. He was smart with his abuse." She raises her shirt to show us a scar.

Melissa gasps.

"What a cruel monster," Mandy says angrily. "Pure evil."

"Oh my gosh, Lily." Melissa gets tears in her eyes. "I'm so sorry. I judged you, too, I thought your life was the best and I've so often wished I was you. I'm so sorry."

"Hey, how could you have known? My own parents didn't even know for months, and they live with me. When he beat me up at the party, he was drunk and careless, he hit my face and made evidence. I couldn't hide it from my parents even if I had wanted to. That was right before Christmas break, so I had time to heal before going back to school. By then, I was able to hide it with makeup so no one at school knew."

Lucas nods. "I wasn't going to let him do that to her anymore. And, honestly, I'd been in love with her for months. When I found out he was hitting her at that party, I went fucking ballistic on his ass." He frowns, his brows deeply furrowing.

"Did you go to the police?" Melissa asks in a shaky voice.

"No, I wouldn't do it. I was scared he'd come after me. My parents fought me, but I told them I wouldn't talk if they brought me in." Her eyes hold her feet in their glare. "My fear of him is still very real."

Liam clears his throat. "I can totally understand that, Lily. My story, as long as we're sharing our shit shows, is somewhat similar. My dad's a drunk, a raging alcoholic. I'm lucky when he notices me at all. He probably doesn't even know I'm gone. He rarely leaves his office in our basement. He only leaves to get more liquor." Liam stands up, takes steps towards the kitchen, turns back to face us. "That's been my life since I was twelve and my mom took off with another man. The end." He looks surly. "And no, my life isn't easy either because I'm popular. And. It would fucking suck ass, without my friends. My friends are my family, especially Kian and Lucas. And I have my music, my band. *Mi amigos.*" He turns back to face the kitchen, his head down, and motions for Melissa. "We doing dishes now, babe?"

"Yes," Melissa says as she hops up, and races off to be by Liam's side. She wraps her arm around his waist, and he leans his head down to the top of her head. She turns her face up towards him and he leans down all the way, she kisses his cheek and whispers something into his ear. He nods and kisses the top of her head again. It was such a sweet exchange, it brings tears to my eyes. Wow, am I emotional. I smile as my gaze meets both Mandy's and Lily's. We clearly all saw Liam and Melissa in the kitchen. I nod towards the kitchen, blink my eyes, and Mandy mouths "I know, right?"

"Okay, I think once dishes are done, it's time for cards," Kian announces rubbing his hands together. "The funniest damn game in the world. I think we all need to indulge in some laughs right now."

I nod, totally in agreement. "I've never played," I say. "Never even heard of it."

"You're gonna love it. Get your drinks ready, friends, it's gonna be a hilarious ride. You will laugh your pretty little arses off." Kian nods. He clearly knows.

"It's fun," Lily says with a smile. "Though it can get a little offensive at times, so be prepared."

"Great," I say sarcastically, but smile. I can feel the blushes warming under the skin of my cheeks already. "Maybe I should just wear a bag over my head."

Kian grins at me and says, "But then I won't get to see you blush."

I roll my eyes and throw a pillow at him. Gawd, really? "That's the point, dumbass."

He pouts and says, "Aww! But that's my favorite." He smirks at me chuckling.

Geez. What can I say to that?

Chapter Ten

"No." I flip to my next card, which is about doing it. "Never." I look at the next one and it's about dicks. "Nope. Oh my god. No. Taboo." I bust out laughing as I turn the card face down.

"Oh, I want to see that one!" Kian tries to swipe the offensive card out of my hands.

I shift away from him and scramble the cards, so he won't know which one I referred to read. "Ha. No way, Kian." Me bringing up dicks again is not what I need.

"You have to pick one," Lily says. "You can do it." She smiles at me. "Just pick one. It will be okay. We're all adults."

I sigh and read another. "Geez, but okay, this one." I toss the black card at Liam.

He scrambles the cards and reads them each aloud. Several of them create uncontrolled laughter. Mandy snorts at one. Liam picks mine. Again.

I hide behind my cup and blush.

"Damn, girl. You are killing it," Kian counts my cards. "She has ten cards. I only have five. What does everyone else have?"

They all call out numbers and no one has more than six. I'm winning. I'm not sure if it's a good thing or a bad thing to be winning this game, but I grin through my blush and get ready for the next round. Though, I'm really not ready. I know I'll get another penis card of some sort. That's just my luck.

"My turn." Melissa reads her card.

Everyone quickly decides and they all toss their cards to her.

I have a hard time deciding, again. Snagging a long drag of my drink I take my time reading my cards once more.

"Today, Ash," Melissa coaxes.

"Wait, read it again, I need it again." I don't know, they are all bad, naughty, and I don't know what to pick.

She reads it aloud again.

"Okay." I flick to the next card. "Nope." I giggle at the next one. "That's just wrong, but maybe it might just be perfect." Kian snatches it out of my hand before I can pull it away. I drop the rest of my cards and scramble to try and get it from him without spilling my drink. "Hey, cheater! Kian!" I whine. "Give it back."

He reads it and his face erupts into amused shock. "Oh gosh, Ashie! You're naughty! You picked this one?" He teases me relentlessly with an irresistible smile followed by an eyebrow raise.

I slap his arm and chest with my free hand. His muscles feel so freakin' hard even under my light slaps.

"Should we just look the other way, let you two get your kiss on?" Mandy asks. "You both need that, and bad."

I shoot her a glare then widen my eyes, which was dumb because almost everyone sees me do this. I'm red in the face, instantly. 'Cause, when am I not? Kian hands me the card with a huge smirk. He pulls it back when I reach for it, two more times.

"Kian!" I shriek. He hands it to me with a big guilty grin claiming his mouth. I down the rest of my beverage to avoid that grin. "I need another drink. Anyone else?" I toss the card, the exact one Kian just had, at Melissa. I hop up and practically sprint to the kitchen.

I glance back for a one second. She didn't bother to mix them up enough, clearly, because mine is the first one she reads and every damn person busts a gut, including me, but no one sees me do it because I'm facing the kitchen. Of course, they all know it's mine. Maybe I am a pervert; my brain chooses the funniest most outrageous ones, the cards that make everyone laugh the most.

"Me, I want a drink," says Lily. "But I want to make it myself."

I sigh as I mix my drink. I don't want to go back to the living room. I'm too ashamed. Maybe I'll hide in the kitchen.

Lily comes up next to me and gently nudges my arm. "Kian loves to tease you. I've never seen him tease anyone as much as he teases you, just so you know." She grins at me. "I'm being serious. You should be flattered. He just doesn't do this." She pours clear soda in her drink and stirs it.

"Really?" I ask. I find that hard to believe, but that doesn't seem to erase the happy look I know I'm displaying on my face. Her words make me downright giddy.

She nods with a pleasant smile. "Ready to get back to it?" She urges me with a stretch of her arm towards the living room.

I nod. Shrug. "Okay, I guess. If I have to."

She chuckles. "You never have to."

Lucas arrives next to us before we take one step. "Changed my mind. I need something." His hand goes right around Lily's waist. As I leave, I see him slip it down to her cup bum. What I wouldn't give for Kian to... Lucas's hand goes further. Yeah, looking away now. Wowza.

I take my seat next to Kian on the couch feeling a bit hot and bothered which causes me to blurt out, "You didn't touch my cards, now did you?" I narrow my eyes in mock anger.

He holds his hands up. "Nope, hands off. I swear."

Uh huh, the Mr. Innocent act, my butt. However, he gives an innocent grin.

"Which one did you pick?" I ask Melissa.

"Oh, yours of course. We figured it out by process of elimination and Lucas knew what Lily had, so it had to be yours." Melissa smirks at me.

Terrific. I feel heat flare in my cheeks as I take the card from her to add to my winning stash.

"My turn," Kian says. He rubs his hands together. "I can't wait."

He reads his card aloud and we all look at the ones in our hands. Liam starts laughing.

Mandy coughs. "Wow." She shakes her head. "Raunchy."

It takes a lot for Mandy to say that. I grin at her and she shoots me a look like *holy crap*. I'm intrigued—I want to know what she has. I give her a silent giggle.

People start tossing cards to Kian.

I have no good cards, so I just choose one with the words "Ginormous Boobs". No one will be able to tie that one to me. Right?

I hand it to Kian, while avoiding eye contact, and make sure he scrambles it in with the others, so he doesn't know which one is mine.

Kian reads all the cards. People laugh or scoff or gasp at various phrases. They're all really funny on some level. He hasn't read mine yet and he has two cards left. He reads another and it's not mine, either. Mine is last, apparently. He reads mine and grins. I don't have ginormous boobs, but I'm clearly the most heftily endowed female in the room, so he can't possibly think it's my card.

"I pick 'Ginormous Boobs.'" Kian nods like he likes that card.

"What? How?" I shriek. I bet he did look at my cards. "You did look at my cards," I accuse.

"Well, Ashie, it's the funniest." He gets a big cocky grin across his face. "I had to pick it."

I start laughing, cover my face with my hands. First, we all talk about phallic stuff, now we're on to breasts. "Yes, it's mine! Alright, yes. I don't know what to say."

Everyone rolls, they're all laughing so hard.

"What is wrong with me that I'm so good at this game?" I bury my face into my folded arms, then cover my eyes with my hand.

"I love it," Kian says as he whoops it up with an uncontrollable laugh. "Ah, that's so good." I spread my fingers and peek through them at him. He's grinning as I'm dying.

Hot damn, this sucks.

I shove on. Sit up straight. I can do this. "Okay, it's my turn. At least I can't win this round."

"Ash, you should be proud." Kian nods at me. "You rock at this game. You are a rockstar. You're funny."

I ignore him, because, this is not a talent to be winning at this dreadful game. I'm like the taboo queen. I read my card and they all whip their cards at me. I choose Lily's card. We play for another half hour before people start drifting off. Mandy and Lily head out to the car for a quick smoke. Melissa and Liam go to check on the cabin next door. Kian and Lucas raid the kitchen for snacks. I sit on the couch and stew in my drink, contemplate my unexpected and bizarre ability to win at this game. I've got nothing. I don't get it.

I text my mom to give her an update. Why I think of my mom right now, I don't get that, but she'll appreciate it. She's super grateful for the update which makes me feel better. I feel a twinge of guilt that she doesn't know I'm sleeping in a cabin with three barely eighteen-year-old boys. She'd just die if she knew. Then she'd certainly kill me or ground me until I'm twenty-five. Then my dad would kill me all over again.

Mandy and Lily burst in the front door. "Damn is that frigid." Mandy shivers and she shakes out of her coat. "It's not snowing anymore, though."

"I need a blanket," Lily says as she scurries across the room and dives onto the big poufy chair and snugs the blue soft blanket around her waist and tucks it under her thighs. "I see it's snack time, huh?" She nods towards the boys in the kitchen. She and Mandy don't seem the least bit awkward with each other this time. Interesting. I watch Mandy stroll to the bathroom. I'll have to grill her later.

"Yeah, they've been eating since you two left." I shake my head. "Damn, they never stop eating, do they?"

"Never. And it just soaks into them, never creates a bulge, they just burn it right off like it's a glass of water." Lily shakes her head.

"Lucky bastards," I say with my eyebrows furrowed. "I have to watch what I eat. Dancing helps, but still, I have to watch it."

"Yeah, I do, too." Lily nods. She gets it.

Mandy comes out of the bathroom and joins us. "Are we done playing, or just taking a break?"

"I'm game for whatever." I stretch my legs just as Kian appears in the living room.

"You trying to trip me or something?" he asks, with an accusing playful sneer.

"I took you down once, boy, I can do it again." I pop my eyes open widely at him as I smirk.

He scoffs. "That you did. You took me down hard."

At the mention of "hard", my brain goes there, my cheeks heat as he gives me a look that confirms he knows where my brain just went. Ugh! Geez. Seriously. What *is* wrong with me? I'm such a hormone freak show. I bite my lip to keep my words in. I try to get over the blushing though, but it's useless when I catch Kian staring at my chest and adjusting in his seat. To my utter shock, he grabs at his jeans at his belly button and shifts his jeans back and forth. I almost audibly gasp. Is he doing that because of me? I can't even look at him, thought I bet he's starting right at me. I jump up and go refill my drink. I need to get out of here and fast.

The boys shift to another game and I'm out. I don't think I can handle it, I'll be a pile in twenty minutes if I play such a game now. Mandy comes over with a bowl of popcorn. She passes it around and I take a handful; I'm getting the munchies now. I'm craving cheese. I smirk, no chips, though.

"Thanks," I say before I pop some popcorn into my mouth. "I needed this."

Lily grabs a handful. "Yeah, I really need this, too, I'm feeling woozy. I may need to go to bed soon. I've about had it."

I check the time on my phone.

"Melissa and Liam are sure taking their sweet time checking on the space heaters." I giggle. "Right. Ha! Checking on the space heaters, that's a good one. But seriously. I'm just so thrilled she's getting with Liam. Lily," I give her a look, "she's been crushing on Liam from afar for literally months, like severely so. She's been obsessed with him. Not stalker-like, but hardcore wanting for sure."

"She's just adorable, right? I'm loving watching them, too. Her parents are going to go ballistic, though." Mandy shakes her head. "He's got the 'bad boy' image going on."

"Why? Liam's a really good guy." Lily frowns. "He's not bad. Not even remotely."

"He's a bad boy though, think about it with his clothes, being in a band. Melissa is a total rock-solid good girl, a strict rule follower." Mandy crunches some popcorn, flops her hair back over shoulder. "They're opposites. He's a rebel and she's an angel."

"Yeah, like her parents expect her to marry a doctor or a lawyer, an engineer or someone ultra-professional. They have very high expectations of her. And she buys into it all." I raise my eyebrows. She's screwed for getting in with a bad boy image. Her parents will hate it. But do they ultimately have that much control?

Lily nods. "Ah, I get it. But Liam is truly a sweetheart. He looks like a rebel and acts like one, but he has a giant heart. I've gotten to know him. I can fully vouch for him. He's really not as much of a player as he portrays himself to be."

"That's good. That might help, but her parents are still gonna freak, even just at how he dresses. They aren't in today's world by any stretch of the word."

Liam and Melissa come through the front door with groans.

"Uh, that just plain hurts to be out in." Melissa removes her hat, gloves, jacket, and boots. "Ow, it just burns your skin and lungs to be out there for even, like, two minutes."

"We'll have to shovel tomorrow. We keep trudging through the deep snow in the driveway, maybe we should shovel now that the snow is slowing down." Liam shakes his head and his hair flops back into place effortlessly.

"Is it done, though? I thought more was supposed to come tomorrow." Melissa grabs her phone and starts tapping.

Liam nods. "I think we're supposed to get a little bit tomorrow."

Kian shouts, "Liam, come back and join us!"

"Be there in a minute." He touches Melissa's back. "You wanna play or sit with the girls?"

She smiles and nods our way. "Sit with the girls."

He nods, kisses her on the cheek.

Aw! He's so sweet to her, it melts my heart. I grin at her but she's looking at him, but glances our way as he joins the boys.

We motion her over to come sit with us. I want to hear what she's been doing over there at her cabin for so long. I bet it's a yummy story.

"How's the cabin?" I ask with an intense look, which she catches.

She grins enormously. "Good. The space heaters are working and it's not so freezing in there anymore, so all is good." She settles next to Mandy and grabs a handful of popcorn, which I'm proud of her for doing because she usually avoids carbs like the plague.

"That's it? Oh, come on. It sure took you a long time to check them out." I smirk at her as I giggle. "What else did you two do? Make a lasagna? You were gone long enough to make one." I give her teasing eyes as she blushes.

"Oh my god!" She whispers. "I can't even...he's so amazing. His kisses light me on fire." She gushes, ending with a big sigh.

"Uh-oh," I gasp, and my hand goes over my mouth. "Yes!" I exclaim, and Kian looks my way with interest.

"No, not that, not that far. But far enough. Oh my gosh. I'm just getting lost in him. I can't believe this! Let's just say I needed that stroll through the frigid polar vortex air to shake those feelings out of me." She sighs and her muscles look like they're melting as she sags back in the cushions with a seriously satisfied look on her face.

"Love seeing you like this," I say as I hug my legs to my chest. "I'm so happy for you, Liss." Finally, my friend was hooking into something with a boy.

"Thanks. I never thought this would happen in like a billion zillion years. This is the best thing having this cold weather hit now, and Ash, thanks for forgetting your phone, and being irresponsible, and Mandy, thanks for forcing me to come over here. Thanks to myself for forgetting to get gas." She snickers. "None of this would've happened without those dominoes all falling into the right place at the right time."

"It's destiny," I say returning her happy look.

Chapter Eleven

We girls are heading to bed. The boys are staying up to play games. We all lament we have to head home in the morning, and I'm depressed because even with all our flirting, Kian and I still haven't kissed. Who am I kidding anyway with that? A boy would kiss any willing girl. I chastise myself for even coming close to thinking it's more special than it is.

There are four bedrooms. Lily and Lucas will be in Lucas's room, Liam is in Lucas's parents' room, Kian will take one of Lucas's sisters' rooms, and the three of us girls will take the other sister's room, and pine for something else, something more that we can't have right now. Which is what we should be doing though. Right? Waiting. But...it...seriously hurts me badly to not consider flinging myself through Kian's bedroom door in the middle of the night, because it's right damn there next to our room. How will I sleep?

I stare at the stupid popcorn finish ceiling as I lay on the bed in Lucas's sister's room. Mandy is next to me asleep on the bed. Melissa is on the air mattress on the floor, because she insisted. I'm pretty sure they are both asleep based on their breathing patterns.

All I can do is think about Kian. His laugh. His eyes. His large hands. His massive shoulders I wanted to climb up to for that chip bag today. Geez...*his ass*. He seems rock hard, every inch of him. He's a damn machine. So much so, I'm dying to touch him. Everywhere. I want to run into his room and let him envelope me in his arms. But I know I can't do that. And he may not even want that, which would be mortifying to be rejected after flinging myself at him, and I'd embarrass myself so bad that I'd never be able to show my face

116

at school again because he'd see me and laugh, and I'd die a painful death—a hot black choking death.

I sigh.

Goodness, I want him so much that it hurts in every speck of me. I thought I wanted him before, but after interacting with him today, that's a joke. I want to scream from the absolute agony of it; it's worse now than ever. My heart pounds all by its lonely self, alone in my little makeshift bed. The memory of his eyes from today taunt me. His words caress me as they replay in my head, but they also confuse me; does he want me? Am I making it up? No. I can't be. Even Mandy said so. I felt him grow hard beneath me when I fell on him with the dough. Guys can't fake boners, right? It's not like how you hear about girls faking orgasms. Guys can't fake one, right?

I wish I knew. Why can't they teach us this stuff in sex ed instead of just how not to get pregnant and how not to get a disease? There's so much more to it.

Maybe he was thinking about someone else when I landed on him and his hardness was just a coincidence, or a simple act of friction. But what if he does want me? I want to scream out a giant loud fucking squeal if he does like me. Oh, God, could it be possible? My heart begins to race with hope. That amazing boy wants little shy me? Chills drill through me; I can't stop them. But, I can't imagine why he'd want me. I mean, I'm no one. I'm just Ashley. I'm just a girl who dances, loves animals, hates meat, loves pizza, but I love him. God, I love him. I have loved him from afar for like...ever. At least, I think I do. I can't *not* think about him. Every time I try, I fail. He seizes my thoughts every moment and I can think of nothing else.

I want to shake Mandy awake and ask her if she's sure he likes me. I can't do that; that would be mean of me because she's out cold. Geesh. This hurts. It stabs me like a thousand thumb tacks are being slammed into my thighs and ass all at once. I want him to kiss me so much that I want to cry. Ugh, am I pathetic or what, thinking I need this so desperately, I'll cry? But somehow, it's the damn truth, and weak as I am about it, I sink into the yearning as it fully consumes me so much that I can't even fall asleep.

I'm gripped by the intense urge to pee. I jump out of bed; Mandy stirs, and I freeze. Shit. I woke her. She breathes like she's still asleep, so I creep out of the room. I step out into the hall and it's dark and silent. I glance at Kian's door, and I actually take a step that way as my heartbeat rages. I chastise myself. I can't go in there. No matter what. I just can't. Hell no. I can't throw myself at him. I can't assume he wants me. I just...need to wait. Watch him for signs. Gracious, I need to pee. I cringe as I turn back towards the bathroom and I run smack into a rock-hard body, as if I hit a wall. I gasp. My whole self is in full contact with someone.

"What the—?" I exclaim. I almost pee myself from the shock of it.

"Where are you going?" It's a boy's deep voice.

I freeze. Oh, dear, help me. It's Kian. My heart drops to my toes as both panic and elation overtake me.

"I got lost. I was going to the bathroom," I say, knowing it's so lame of me.

He sighs. Our fronts are still touching, he's not moving, I'm not moving. I might melt into him and not ever leave, like ever, but then he takes a half a step back, which makes me want to cry out for him to take a step back towards me.

"The bathroom is that way." He points down the hall in the dim light from the hall nightlight, in the opposite direction of his room.

I nod. "Ah, yes. I got turned around." I still have not budged. Our fronts are still near almost touching, we are still within mere inches of each other. I quiver. All I'd need to do is reach up and touch him. So, I do. I can't help myself.

He shudders as my hand touches his chest. I hear him draw in a quick breath and it doesn't come back out.

"It's so dark here, I'm sorry," I say, but of course, I'm not sorry, because I sure as heck did it on purpose.

He lets that breath out. "It's okay, Ashie." His voice comes as a husky manly whisper that makes me want to jump him right here, slam him into the wall and ravage him like someone I don't know myself to be. He's turning me into that, and I don't know what the hell to do with it. He takes another step backward away from me.

I melt when he again says, "Ashie."

His nickname for me is so endearing, it tugs at me in deep spots, making me want to do things I never thought possible. Just him talking to me makes me want to kiss him. Who am I thinking like this? Who am I to consider kissing a boy like him? Who am I to like a boy like him? I sigh and shake my hands, hoping I will flick off these crispy hardcore sexual feelings. I'm so wound up, I'm ready to spring.

"You okay?" he asks, his voice as brittle-sounding as I feel.

I take a step towards him, and I reach out and touch his side and he gasps, then groans like I did more than simply touch him.

"Oh, God," he says as my hand drifts to his rock-hard rippled abdomen. I don't know who I am anymore as I feel up his abs lightly, gently, yet with great urgency that feels more like trepidation in one second, but like hot sex in the next as my breath comes hot and fast. His breathing churns up to match mine.

"Yes," he murmurs, then he groans. "Oh, Ashie, please don't stop, I..." He moans again so loudly that it grips me hard in my pelvis without him even touching me, and something lurches inside me. He keeps his arms all proper at his sides as I still caress his body. I swear I felt some kind of real lurch in my groin area when he moaned, yet I'm not even sure what it was.

I sigh. I can't help it. His abdominal muscles feel amazing under my trembling fingertips.

Just then, my bedroom door opens, and Mandy comes out looking confused, her eyes half open, her hair all mused up.

"Ashley? You were gone...is that you?" She shakes her head and rubs her eyes like she can't really see me, even though I'm right in front of her.

Jarred, I stand stunned like I've been slapped. "I'm here, Mandy." I yank my hand from Kian, and he startles, jerking like he's been stabbed.

"Come on, it's the middle of the night." Mandy grabs my hand and pulls me towards our room.

"Good night, Kian," I say helpless as Mandy pulls me along behind her. She's going to kick herself in the morning when I tell her what she interrupted.

Kian remains silent, and he doesn't move, until I hear him say in a weak voice just before Mandy drags me into our room, "Good night, Ashie. Sleep well. I can't wait to see you in the morning."

My heart hits bottom as the full crushing loss of what just happened fully hits me. "Me too," I call as Mandy yanks me into our room by my arm. Damn. And I still need to pee.

She throws me onto the bed which almost makes me pee myself. She hugs me, tells me she "loves me" and then rolls over. Geez, I think she must have been sleepwalking and she screwed up a major moment for Kian and me, again. I try to swallow my desires and slam my eyes shut forcefully. Maybe sleep will come if I...don't think about Kian. Well, I might as well not breathe, then.

Chapter Twelve

I'm spreading cream cheese on a bagel at the kitchen counter and I'm blushing like a freak as Kian walks into the kitchen. I can't even look at him, but he's so sweet. I inwardly cringe as I recall how I felt up his abs in the middle of the damn night in the hallway. What kind of person am I? Who does that?

I try to smile at him, but it comes out only as a weak smirk. School has been canceled again, so we get to stay. In fact, we must stay and wait for the propane man to come because he can't come today anyway. It's exactly what I want, another day around Kian, but I can't handle standing beneath his fixated confused gaze. He looks as if he doesn't know if he should talk to me or run off.

Panic rises in me, and I spew out everything in a rush. "School is closed again. We have to stay another day. The repair guy is going to check it all out, whenever he ends up coming, and do a full maintenance check and make sure it all works, so Melissa's parents want us to stay to let him in the cabin. Is that okay with you guys? I hope so and I'm glad and if we can play more games and stuff."

He smiles hugely. "Good morning, Ashie." He says it like I didn't just splat a diarrhea of the mouth word salad at him, like I didn't come on to him in the middle of the night with touchy-feely hands all over his chest, like everything is normal.

I want to fall into a hole and die, but he acts just like he did yesterday towards me and if he can do that, I can, too.

I give him my smile as I try to calm my frazzled nerves and booming heart. "Good morning, Kian."

He looks at me like I'm still me, even though I no longer feel like me. But he's doing it, so I feel okay. "I hope you slept well." He says it like he's just a friend and my heart sinks. He doesn't want me. I knew it. I'm getting my hopes up for nothing. I'm a damn fool.

I glance at his eyes, then snatch my gaze away. I sigh and grip my plate so hard I expect I will break it. "Yes, I did. How about you?" Heartbeat, slow the F down.

"I slept amazingly well." He grins.

Ah, he feels something for me. Maybe? Right? I see it in his eyes perhaps, and it cuts deep into me that he's okay with what happened in the middle of night between us. I sigh and glance for one second at his gorgeous eyes. Am I making that up? I want to thank him for not making a huge deal about it, but, of course, I can't do that because everyone would notice and wonder why I was thanking him. I take a seat at the table where everyone else is already seated, and he joins with his own bagel.

"Did you have sweet dreams?" he asks me. Could he be any more genuine?

Oh, wow! That look in his eyes is killing me. I'm so jumpy I feel like a freak.

I dare to meet his gaze. There it is, that sexy look that says he knows I want him, and he loves it—a lot. I smirk and try not to giggle. Mandy smacks me on the back and I almost spit out the coffee in my mouth. She's laughing silently as I glance at her. She knows. Ah, she remembers last night, too...she wasn't sleepwalking. I turn a deep shade of red I don't think I've ever reached before and I almost get up and run from the room, but the look on Kian's face stops me. He looks...satisfied.

Wow. I mean, totally wow.

"Have a good night?" Mandy asks sarcastically with a knowing snicker.

I ignore her and smile at Kian, knowing all the others can see my face blazing like a red rose, but I don't care because Kian's hand grasps mine. This hurls me into unchartered ground that quenches something in me. I...whoa. He's okay with what I did? Perhaps, more than okay. I fail at suppressing a smile.

His jubilant smiles back matches mine.

I need a new topic, and fast. "What's our first game today?" I ask with chills running through the hand Kian is grasping. He lets go of my hand and I instantly wish it were back there, but his eyes tell me not to worry, there is more to come. And, please? Will there be?

"How about the game you put your hands and feet on colored circles? What's that called again?" Kian asks, but he can't keep a straight face, and a laugh escapes his lovely lips.

Mandy snorts. "Whoever invented that game loved sexual tension, because hot damn. It's a game of weird mandatory awkward positions for a group of people that basically eggs on a group orgy? I mean, really?" Mandy scoffs and swings her free hand in the air.

I glare at her. Is she really trying to kill me?

"Though, it's a pretty damn funny game to play," she adds. "If you are the one spinning the game wheel, that is." She grins like she wants that role.

Liam snorts. Grins. Clearly, he agrees with her. "Well, I'm not opposed to playing naked." His smile is pure as the devil.

"I'd be in," Lily says with a chuckle.

"Same," parrots Lucas with a lecherous grin.

I nod. What else can I do? Liam's comment has knocked me out damn stupid and I have no idea what to say. I'm already hotter than an inferno, though, and this discussion is feeding my fire. I need to step outside into the polar air or throw my body into a cold shower. And it's only breakfast.

I get an idea how to get myself out of this hot seat. "I'm gonna shovel the drive this morning. Anyone in to help me?"

"Yeah, we gotta do that." Lucas nods before taking a bite.

Ah, the voice of reason. Thank you, Lucas.

"Yeah, and if several of us do it, it won't be so bad. And we should do your driveway too, Melissa." I nod towards her cabin. "For the repair guy."

She looks as flustered as I feel. "Yes, because at some point, he's coming, and he needs to be able to get into the driveway, I'm sure."

"Right." I nod, grateful for something to do that needs to be done. A release of this tension plaguing me.

After our breakfast, we all suit up to brave the elements, and the idea of naked game-playing has died off. We leave our phones inside on the counter, so they don't freeze solid and we trudge out into the garage to arm ourselves with shovels of some sort. Me, Kian, Lucas, Melissa, and Liam are on snow shovel duty while Mandy and Lily handle the breakfast dishes. There aren't even enough shovels for more to help anyway, so we trek out like a battle team to fight the fierce thick blanket of snow that has trapped us in this cabin. I'm armed with a small dirt shovel, but it's still a shovel.

Kian holds a real snow shovel, which with his muscles this shoveling will be easy. He will be a powerhouse, no doubt. His eyes above his neck up satisfy something in me, and draw me in. I can't even explain it other than that. We all pick a spot and start to shovel. We lift. We fork it all onto the yard. We clear it like pros. The five of us work amazingly fast. Then we head to Melissa's cabin driveway and do the same. We aren't so helpless as our parents make us feel at times. We can be responsible. Sometimes my parents treat me like I'm still eight years old and it pisses me off. I mean, I'm now an actual adult, but they don't treat me like one at all.

"Hearty work. Good for the body." Kian nods at me with warm appreciative eyes. He got his workout, which will likely please his dad.

I nod back. "Yep. We worked hard and got it done fast." I stand my shovel up and lean on its handle giving Kian the best accomplished eyes I can. He clearly values hard work, and I admire that in him, too.

We pile back into the warm cabin in a rush. I spy Lily and Mandy at the table and quickly strip off all my winter clothes. I approach my friend with a smile. Lily and Mandy have made us hot chocolate with whipped cream and a side of chocolate chip cookies.

The boys are extremely appreciative and dive into the snack immediately. They start to devour before I even claim a cup. I snag one cookie. Melissa takes a hot chocolate only and I gaze at her wistfully, wishing she'd just let herself enjoy life a bit more, but I'm still glad she took the cocoa. Liam will help her with this eating thing, I'm thinking. He holds his cookie to her lips and urges her to taste. She does and smiles as she chews. Good girl, Melissa. He kisses her lips, and it melts me a bit. He will be good for my friend, for sure.

Kian catches me watching them and he smiles back and nods their way. I grin. He seems to like it, too. Our friends are becoming a solid, yet unexpected, couple right in front of our eyes.

We all lounge about the living room with our big mugs of hot chocolate and I'm okay with it all. It's like being at a party where you're actually comfortable in your pajamas, like a girlfriend sleepover. It's like buttered warm French bread slices, comforting, filling, delicious. Only with hot sexy boys.

"So, what is our first game of the day?" Mandy asks with a flick of her last bite of her cookie into her mouth.

"Not the naked playing one," I say as I eye Kian, and he does a pout with his yummy lip out. I smirk. I cringe. Damn. Now why did I have to bring that up? I seriously have no control.

"Okay, how about Clues?" Kian asks with a silly face as he opens the lid of the game box.

"Yes, perfect." I smile. This one isn't sexy, I mean Miss Red is hot, but no one else is, so, it won't turn me into a useless mush pile. Well, being near Kian does that already. But I'm in. Kian's eyes drop to my chest, and I startle. "I'm Mrs. Whites."

When you're the most gifted chest-wise in the room, you don't choose Miss Red, you choose Mrs. Whites. But Mandy swipes her from me and hands me the red Miss Red game piece. I acquiesce but squawk, "Mandy!"

I shoot her a gaze loaded with daggers. We will be having some words. I shrug at her. Way to screw it up for me, friend. I know on some level I'm more Miss Reds than Mrs. Whites. But then again, Mandy isn't Mrs. Whites either, but it's just a game, right, so why do I really care anyway?

Chapter Thirteen

The afternoon slides by so fast because I'm enjoying myself. I'm so thankful we need to stay to let the repair guy into Melissa's cabin. The guy is proving to be elusive. Yay universe for giving us this! We play so many games and it's so much fun. I don't think I've ever had this much fun in my entire damn life.

Liam and Kian want to switch to their games now. Mandy is showering, and who knows what Lily and Lucas are up to. They're just gone. Just one guess needed for what they are likely up to.

Kian slides a red plastic cup towards me. His grin taunts me. "You know you want this..."

"After yesterday, I'm not so sure I need any more. I don't need to go there again." I fold my hands and place them on the table, shake my head, and stare intensely right into his electric blue eyes. I unfurl a smirk as slowly as I can and end it with a lasting half-smile. I gape at my cup then flick my eyes up to his. They are still full bore fixated on me. It sends spears of delight through my pelvis.

He nudges the cup towards me again with his index finger, his eyes begging me to grab it. "Dare ya."

I really do want it because it helps me talk to him. I want to talk to him, but I feel mega nervous and not in control of my mouth, I'm so on edge. All I can think about is almost kissing him. I reach for the cup and his grin goes giant and his eyes light up. He watches me as I take a sip while I hold his gaze.

"Hey, you two in this game or what?" Liam asks, staring at us, impatient for our answers.

"Yeah," I say. "I'm in to play. What are we playing again?" I glance in my cup. Crap, I drank half of it already. Seriously? I'd better slow down. Shifting in my seat I notice Kian peek in my cup.

"Thirsty much?" His eyes are teasing me something fierce as he runs his hands through those dark blond locks.

I yearn to touch them so bad I almost groan.

Liam deals us the cards. "Lush Uns. I'll repeat the rules. Okay. Every time you lay down an odd card, you must take a drink. If you lay down a wild card, you must drink while we all count to five, like one-one-thousand, not 1-2-3-4-5. The player to your right inspects whether you actually drank or not. They are judge and jury, no arguments. Skip means you get to pick someone to take a drink and a draw two card means you have to take two drinks of your own drink. Reverse is just reverse, you get a new master." He gives us his classic naughty snarled bad boy look, the one that has always given Melissa the chills. I glance at her and she closes her eyes, savoring, then pops them open, visibly sighs like she's in the hot shower as she stares at Liam. She grips the wooden arms of her chair like it's the only thing preventing her from oozing into a puddle on the floor. I snag her in an eye lock and she tells me with her eyes that she liked that look of Liam's, like a whole lot. I giggle. She once told me if looks could give pleasure, she'd be in it constantly just by watching Liam's naughty grins alone. When we saw him sing at his show a few months back, his facial expressions kept changing, reacting to the words of his song like he was acting it, thrilling Melissa to her horny little core. It's so funny to watch her when she talks about him now, her good girl persona disappears like a wimpy ghost. Her comments make me laugh so hard because she never usually says naughty stuff, except if it's about Liam. Melissa and I exchange smirks. This is the best thing that has happened to my friend.

"What's so funny?" Kian asks. "I'm the funny guy, I want to know." He's smiling at me, he wants in on our joke, nope, not happening pal. When Melissa and I are both silent, he shakes his head, softly chuckles, says, "Only girls get to know? Huh? No fair." He pouts, sticking out that luscious lower lip of his and giving me puppy dog eyes.

I stare at his protruding lip. Gawd, I want my lips on that thing so bad, I'm almost salivating. I start to get lost in my own fantasy, but he catches me staring too long, so I quell it. No matter. I'll save that image up for later when I'm in bed. Yeah, and I feel my cheeks heat again as I blush. I can't control it. I laugh at him because, damn, he's so cute I can't stand it.

He stares back at me. He seems to like seeing me blush. How embarrassing.

The game begins and I need to snap out of my fantasies and get in the game. It's my turn. I have to drink because I lay down a five. I sigh and glance at Kian.

He seems to love it that he gets to be my sip patrol. He leans over towards me to peer in my cup and I can smell him, he smells like freshly washed clothes and mint, and it takes my breath away. I take a sip of my drink to comply.

"You call that a drink? That sucked. Try again," he says with a devilish look. "Master says so."

I sigh as I chuckle with my cup in front of my mouth. "What? I drank. A big sip too!"

Liam gives me a stern look. "No arguing with your judge, Ashley. Penalty drink, take another. Oh yeah, forgot to mention, and the dealer is a dictator and gets to hand out penalties at their discretion." He clearly loves this power and fist pumps Kian across the table.

"Boys," I say with a roll of my eyes. "I see how this is going, you two are in this together, keeping all the power." I glare at them in mock anger, each in turn. I pretend to be offended, but my smile tells them I'm not really, at least I hope so.

"Everyone gets to be the dealer, it rotates, so you girls will get the power, too." Liam nods. "It's fair, everyone gets a turn."

Now I see why we're sitting boy-girl-boy-girl.

"Oh good, we get to give you penalty drinks, too, thank goodness." I sigh as I flutter my eyelashes. Kian waves his hand at my cup. "Okay, okay, I'll try again." I take a sip and glance at Kian for approval, blinking my eyes in mock obedience. "That good enough for you, oh master of me?"

"Umm...I like where this is going." He chuckles, peers into my cup and nods. "I guess that works, but next time I'd better see the bottom of that cup, or else I will sick Dictator Liam on you."

"Wow, you're a harsh driver." I lean back in my chair, toss my curly blond locks over my right shoulder feeling feisty.

"You have no idea, I've got a whip in my back pocket for later." He laughs this despicably evil laugh, and throws his head back. "I'm evil Batman when it comes to following the rules of drinking games. And I'll bring you to justice real quick." He gives me a direct stare down, his eyes playful as he puts his palms on the table with his elbows pointed up like he's ready to pounce at me.

I drop my jaw in mock horror, put my hand to my chest in pretend shock. What a naughty brain he has! That direct look of his grips me hard right in the center of my lower gut. And it's not letting go.

"He is evil. It's no lie," Liam says with assurance. "Asshole made me repeat a full cup chug once when he was dictator because he thought I didn't really drink. He's ruthless. Gotta watch out for him."

Kian laughs. "Ah, I knew you did it, I just wanted to get you back. Payback for the time you fed me that awful concoction you cooked up, ya jackass."

Liam laughs heartily. "Damn, that was a good night. And your payback is a bitch."

"So happy I could cooperate for your entertainment." Kian slams his hands down on the table, making both Melissa and I jump.

"As you well know, I needed the laughs that night." There's a hint of sadness in his voice. It makes my heart hurt for him. "Now take a drink, ass munch."

"Selfish dick," Kian says, though he's clearly joking. "You're a jackass, ya know that, right?"

Liam laughs at him, runs his hand through his thick dark hair, another move that makes Melissa turn to warmed jelly. "Back at ya." He nods at Kian.

I glance at Melissa and we share a smile. We both love their banter and razing of each other. Her eyes are lit, soaking up all of Liam like he's a real star. She grabs his arm. He locks eyes with hers, and she grins like his groupie girlfriend.

"Isn't it your turn?" I ask Liam. "I get to be judge and I'm ready." Oh, this game could get really nasty. I like it.

Liam lays down an eight and eyes me like a savage. He's safe, for the moment.

I say, "Hmpf, not fair."

I can feel Kian's eyes on me, so I swivel my gaze his way.

He says, "You're mine on your next turn, Ashie. All mine." He points at me, then at himself. He laughs like he's crazy.

"Well. You can try, but I'm gonna resist." I grin.

"You just try it, baby, you'll see." Kian flares his eyes wide at me, stacks his cards and lays them face down before him. He aims his gaze at Melissa. "Melissa, you're up," he says.

I don't know why I'm watching every little move he makes because he can clearly see me doing it. I'm just itching to grab him, I guess. And I seem to have lost all semblance of restraint.

Melissa freezes. I can see her heart beating like a million disturbed butterflies. Breathe, Melissa, breathe...I will these thoughts to her across the table with my eyes, but she's staring at her cards. She glances at me and takes some comfort from my eyes as her shoulders visibly relax, her eyelids flutter. She takes a deep breath, lets it out slow as she lays down a nine. She looks absolutely petrified.

"Drink," Liam commands with an intense direct stare at her.

I almost laugh out loud as I see his words send shivers down her spine as she first sits up straight, then wiggles, probably to loosen her tense muscles. She sighs, tries to smile and takes a long drink, way exaggerated, which makes Liam crack up.

He touches her arm. "Slow it down babe, no need," he says in a voice full of compassion.

"Okay." She obeys, looking less nervous.

"There ya go, girl, now you've got it. Just one drink for an odd card." Liam holds up his hand for a high five and she reciprocates. It's so cute how he's taking care of her.

She said last week that she would have given up romance novels for a full year just to touch him, now she gets to touch him all the time, and all it took was for her to pet him. I can't not smile at that thought. She will never live that moment down.

"It's me now." Kian rubs his chin while eyeing his cards. It's such a nice chin attached to such a sexy jawline, stretching up into a manly cheek peppered with a sweet dimple, attached to...

Crap. I'm staring and he catches me.

He lays down a wild card with a smirk.

Melissa is on him. "Drink up," she demands. She touches the rim of his glass as she tries to peer in. He lifts it up too fast. "Whoa, slow down bub, I need to assess this first." She nods. "Better finish it." My girl wields her power freely and I love it.

I laugh. Oh, the power of this game. I'm hoping someone lays down a reverse so I can be Kian's master. A girl can hope, right?

"Yes, ma'am." He nods, then guzzles down the rest of the cup in like three seconds.

"How do guys do that?" I ask. "You all seem to be able to drink something in like no time at all, like you breathe it in or something."

"Us guys have mad drinking skills. I can do that with anything, you name it, milk, soda, energy drink." Kian flashes me his pearly whites. Damn. How are his teeth even sexy? That doesn't even make sense, but I know I want my tongue running across them. He peers into my cup. "What's your card, little Ashie?"

I raise my left eyebrow to his smirk. "Little?"

He chuckles like the flirty devil that he is.

I look at the cards in my hand, I have nothing good to lay down. With only evens being the safe cards, I'm screwed, I have none, nothing, diddley crap, jack squat. I haven't had a single even card all game. My dumb luck. I lay down a draw two card. Kian peeks in my cup and nods to me. He eyes me intently as I take my two sips.

He looks into my cup. "Not enough, sweets. Try again."

I sigh. I love this; his full attention is on me. I never thought I'd get off on a boy telling me what to do. He moves closer as I take another sip. His closeness sends chills through me, and I feel a slight blush sneak in. Dammit! Here I go again.

He nods with a grin that won't quit. "Yeah, you'd better finish that sip good, not do a crappy job like you did washing dishes yesterday."

I slam my hand on the table as I shoot him an aghast look. "Are you kidding me? I washed those damn things spotless. You don't know what you are talking about."

"I saw egg on one and I just wiped it away with the towel," he accuses with a saucy look. He is in full flirt mode, his eyes are lit, his dimple is out and I'm just a pile of hot messy mush because of it.

"You did not! I inspected every dish before I put it in the drip tray. They were all perfect, spotless, no egg." I shoot him a fiery look.

"I know what I saw, and I saw egg." He grins. "It was yellow and crusty."

"Liar."

"You'd better wash again today to get some more practice. In fact, I'll inspect your work." He grabs a handful of chips from the bowl and shoves them all into his mouth at once.

"You most certainly will not," I protest. I slide my chair away from him moving closer to Liam. "Why do you put so many in your mouth? I don't trust you. I'm not going anywhere near you today when you're eating those cheesy chips."

His eyes are impish as he opens his mouth like the old joke of "seafood", which is basically see-food. And gross.

"Ew, Kian!" I frown at him. "Keep that crap in your mouth, and keep it shut when you chew," I scold, frowning and adjust my shirt. "I seriously don't trust you with cheesy chips in your mouth."

He heckles me with this nasty grin as he chews, mouth appropriately now closed though. His jokester mode is at full blaze.

"You two done flirting yet?" Liam claps. "Let's get on with it, I laid my card a minute ago." He sighs. "It's like playing a game with four-year-olds with you two. Focus."

Liam plays an even card, again. He gets all the damn stinking luck. I'm beginning to suspect he has all the even cards in his pockets or something, and he keeps feeding them to his hand. I decide to watch him more closely to catch him in the act, in case he's cheating.

He nods but takes a sip despite his even card and then throws his gaze Melissa's way. She looks into her cup, shudders making her breasts bounce a bit. Liam's eyes fall to her chest, and I'm dying. Can't wait to tell her later.

She lays down a draw two card and her porcelain white skin shines with a light pink blush. Poor girl is having a hard time. This is all so out of her comfort zone.

"Down it, baby. Wait, I need to see inside your cup first." Liam peers in, nods. "You have my permission to drink."

I know that look of hers and she's savoring his attention, loving every second of it. She's the good girl, as usual, and does exactly as he dictates, which he clearly likes. Liam's looking a bit hot and bothered himself. How delicious for her. She does look really sexy today and I need to whisper that in her eat.

Kian selects a card from his hand, lays down a skip. "I choose Ashley to drink."

I scoff. There was zero hesitation there.

Mandy comes up behind me, touches my shoulder. "Hey baby cakes." I glance back at her with a happy little smile and try to convey to her with my eyes how good this game is going, how much fun I'm having with Kian. She reciprocates with a big smile, rubs my upper back. It's such a comfort to have her near.

"No fair to give me the skip," I say in a pouty tone, eyeing Kian directly, and sticking out my lower lip.

Kian shakes his head. "Them's the rules, sweets. You've gotta do it or I'm pulling out my whip." He raises his fist and jerks it abruptly in the air in a whipping motion. So naughty. "Maybe you'll get lucky and draw an even card next."

Yeah, unless Liam has them all in his pocket. "I haven't had an even card the entire game, Kian." He watches me drink, inspects my cup, nods his approval. "I think this game is rigged."

Kian scoffs. "No way. Liam wouldn't do that. You're just unlucky."

I scan my cards. Kian laid a red skip. I have no red cards and no skip cards, only odd cards and a wild card. I reluctantly lay down the wild card because I have no choice.

His face spreads into a grin. "Don't worry. I've got you covered."

"Well, poop." I sigh watching him watch me. I sigh again for emphasis. "Okay. I can do this." I shake my whole body, prepping myself like I'm about to do a super hard task.

I've been the entertainment on more than one occasion in this cabin, and here I go again. I roll my eyes at them, each get a turn.

I raise the cup to my lips and only get a few sips in and I need a break. This sucks. I just can't chug.

"You ain't done yet," Kian moves closer to me, so close I might choke because my throat has such a lump in it from him being near me, I can't seem to swallow right. He comes an inch closer, and I hear Mandy cough behind me, she knows what's going on in my head right now. "Come on, give me the payment for your wild card, honey little sweetie Ashie," he says in mocking sweet tone. He licks his lips and gives me a hard, direct stare.

I drink too fast and choke, spit out the mouthful back into my cup.

Everyone is laughing at me as I gasp and sputter. "I'm done."

Kian laughs. "What's the penalty for spitting it back out, oh master Liam?"

Damn. He has me over a barrel. I'm screwed. I plead with Liam giving him puppy dog eyes to go gentle on me.

Liam gets an evil look which ends in a naughty grin. "Full cup."

My eyes widen, damn, I need to work on my puppy dog eyes apparently. "Well, I didn't need that." I give them a pained face.

Kian is laughing so hard, he loves this and I'm loving that he loves this. But, yeah, I need to be done with this game.

"This is going to take me awhile." My hand is trembling. I drink for as long as I can before I need a breath.

"You gonna make it, Ash?" Mandy asks through a laugh. I glance back at her and shake my head. She tosses her silky brown hair over her shoulder. She looks extra beautiful today, too. Dang, I have hot friends. I give her a silly grin. "I'll carry you to the bathroom if you need me to." She pats my shoulder.

"Oh, I was hoping I would get to do that." Kian folds his arms across his large chest. He smirks at me.

"Be my guest," Mandy says with glee.

Chapter Fourteen

I stare at Kian. Wow. Did he just say that? Or am I just hallucinating? Terror washes over me. I dismiss it in a flash. But not wholly. I'm sure it's innocent, right? Not malicious, hurtful, mean.

"Drink, baby." His eyes dance with a sparkle and a tease. It's like a warm bath I want to stay in. "You owe it. Give it up. It's payday for me."

Yeah, I cannot deny that face.

I down another one-third of the cup before I need a break. This is tough. "You are trying here, aren't you?" I accuse him with a direct stare while grinning. I want more of his attention and I want him to know I want it.

"Well, yeah, how else am I going to get you alone in a cabin full of people?" He unleashes an evil chuckle while rubbing his hands together.

My heart stalls dead like it's been thrown in the snowbanks outside. Gone is the playfulness as I fill with fear and dread.

Will he do to me what they did? I'm frozen in place, I can't even shudder. No. He's not like them.

"I'm a professional when it comes to sweeping girls off their feet who need assistance to the bathroom. And I've got the pipes to do it. I can whisk you right off your feet like nothing and run off with you. Caveman style." He grins, flexes his biceps, ever the joker, which should have been sexy to me, but it's not.

I'm gripped with dread. I'm terrified and I know I'm being irrational.

His words repeat in my head. Maybe he means to get me alone just for a fulfillment of our missed kiss, but everything stops, and I'm suddenly dead weight. I feel sick in the pit of my stomach, and I need air, like now. I need to get away. Oh, please, not this now. I slow my breathing and try to think rationally. But then, I want to be alone with him, don't I? Yes, I do. But what if he hurts me like they did? I need to go...I can't be here.

Need. To Run. Now.

I zone out as the room spins. It seems oddly silent as my heart beats too fast, and I can barely breathe. I close my eyes as my mind floats back. I'm flung into what happened two weeks ago, as if I'm really there. I freeze as the horrid memory floods my whole brain, completely consuming me.

I was alone at a party in the living room with three boys: Jack, Henry, and Joey, three boys from school. I had thought Henry was sexy back then and I was excited that he was flirting with me at the party, even though I really wanted Kian more, it was fun to flirt with Henry. I knew they were friends. It was a tiny party and everyone else went off to rooms or to the basement to play ping pong, including Mandy, who'd found some girl to latch onto and sneak off into a room with, much to her absolute pleasure. That left me alone with the three guys.

They were flirting like mad with me. I liked it. There were calling me "beautiful, hot, sexy," and I had liked all the attention they were giving me—that is until they decided it was time to take my pants off. They said so. It was time. I knew it wasn't.

I had stared at them as they talked about me like I wasn't even in the room. They never held me down. They never held my arms back, but there were so many strong boy arms man-handling me, I was struggling to deflect them. They took turns messing with me. While one was distracting me, teasing me, flirting with me, the other one tried to wiggle my pants off. I had worn my mega tight skinny jeans, which turned out to be my saving grace because they couldn't just easily strip them off. I had thought they were joking around at first. But then they'd successfully wiggle my jeans down a bit, I'd wiggle them back up as I laid flat on the floor. It was on repeat. I had to wiggle my hips to yank my jeans back up. My writhing about only served to get them to try harder, to want me more. Too mortified to even take the time to cringe, I swerved and bucked their attempts.

For a bit, I played along, still thinking, hoping, they were joking, and this would end as a silly tease. Just be a joke, albeit a cruel one. I hoped this was a simple flirt session that went too far, and they'd stop, apologize. They were good boys. Right?

They complimented me profusely as they tugged on my jeans, pulling them down again and again after I snuck them back up, but the look in Henry's eyes changed—his eyes didn't look flirty anymore, they looked really hungry, and angry, and it scared me as he then managed to forcefully, and a bit painfully, yank my jeans down enough to see the full lacy crotch of my pink underwear. He had whistled, ran one hand through his gorgeous hair while he held onto the waistband of my jeans with his other. I had watched as the hand from his hair went to his crotch, where he adjusted his jeans with a sigh over an obvious bulge. He brought both of his hands to my jeans to have a go at them again after I had successfully yanked them back up a bit. That's when I got really scared and I realized this wasn't a joke, it was really happening.

Joey unbuttoned my top and I couldn't stop him because my hands were grasping my jeans as I tried to yank them up as Henry tried to pull them down once again. Jack sat back and watched, he neither helped, nor stopped the other two; I was too busy to glance at his face. Did he want this, too? Or was he as gravely horrified as I was? As frozen in shock as I felt? Or was he just taking in the show, patiently waiting for his turn? Joey's hand slipped into my bra. I felt his hand fully cup me, his thumb ran over my sensitive tip, and I wanted to scream but I couldn't. I knew these guys, they were nice, but they were out of control.

They would stop, right? Panic had filled my mouth with silence as Joey began to remove me from the shell of my bra.

That's when Mandy saved my life. She came out of the room and screamed, "Hey! What the fuck are you doing to her?" Mandy held her fists up ready to fight if any one of them made a move.

Her new friend rushed over to me, her face full of concern. I recognized her from school, too. She helped me collect myself as I fixed my clothes. Then she and Mandy ushered me out of the house so fast. I'd never been so grateful to see Mandy in my whole life.

I avoid looking at Kian. I'm projecting but I can't stop. Did he really mean that? Would he really do *that* to me, what those boys almost did, when he got me alone? Or, was he just kidding, flirting? Wanting to kiss me only? Part of me knew he wouldn't.

I stand up and the urge for flight seizes me. Panic percolates in my gut. My heart pounds. I push my chair back from the table, ready to take off. It's hard to breathe.

"Whoa. Ash, you okay?" Kian asks. I notice the concern in his voice, but it doesn't calm me.

I stare at the front door. My vision blurs. I need to go. Now. My eyes are stinging, tears are about to spill as I sprint for the front door.

I hear chairs scrape the floor. "Ash, what happened?" He sounds scared.

Before I reach the door, I hear Mandy say in a disgusted tone, "Shit. Nice job, fucker. Wrong choice of words. She was alone with some guys and was almost gang-raped two weekends ago..."

I shut my ears. I don't want to hear her say any more about that awful night. I don't want it to exist. I skip my boots, don't even look for my jacket, and I throw open the cabin door. I charge out into the frigid cold air, my first steps on the frozen ground already sending jolts of jarring pain through my feet, but I keep going anyway. I can't stop.

The frenzy of swirling snow flies before me from the strong wind gusts that blast across the driveway. It's cold, really cold, but I don't care. I need to get away. The snow flies around like white sheets of diamond bling as the cold bites me hard with its ferocious teeth on every inch of my exposed skin. It stings like a multi-thronged whip on my flesh.

It's beautiful though, in an eerie ominous way, as I rush out further into its glittering whiteness, made brighter by the large moon above. I'm almost tripping on nothing as I trudge over the freshly shoveled driveway, almost vomiting as I start to fall, but catch myself. I somehow garner the will to stay upright in the blustering wind that thrashes my body, threatening with cold sheer force to rip my skin open. I stop once I reach the end of the driveway and hug myself.

"Self-hugs mean good self-care". That sentence I'd read online the other day, and I repeat it in my head as I twist my body back and forth in the biting wind.

The cold snow-covered concrete is stabbing my feet like I stuck them in an ice fishing hole on the lake. It hurts so bad, almost like a rash chemical burn, but I can't go back in there. There... where boys could hurt me. No way. The cold wind violently wrenches the last bits of warmth from my body as I shiver and begin to crumple. I gasp, hunched over as the bitter night wind whips me raw.

After what feels like an eternity, I hear multiple footsteps rushing to me.

"Ash! You've got to come in." Mandy is touching me somewhere, gently pulling my arm. I stand firm, not moving. I watch the wind carry the snow in a wild dance. Its beauty does not escape me even now.

"You're going to freeze to death out here!" Melissa is pulling on my other arm now. "It's dangerous. Come on, Ash. Please! You'll get frostbite. We should all just carry her." She sounds terrified and I should feel guilty, but I can't feel anything.

A hand presses on my back. I don't know whose hand it is. Why is it so hard to think?

"Please, Ashley, come back in." It's Lily's soft feminine voice, even she is out here. Wow.

They all plead with me, they sound like purring, mewing cats as their words slur into a single hum.

It's like I can't comprehend, or act, or move—I'm frozen. They seem far away, but yet, they're all next to me.

Someone is yanking on my arm, and I yank it back. My head is down. I don't look to see who it is. My cheeks hurt, my whole body winces. I feel ready to cave in on myself. The wind is slapping me, roughing me up from the outside in, reaching into me with its ice cold fingers, but I can't move. My knees weaken and I'm on the verge of collapse.

The wind beats me as a beastly gust hurls a massive blast of snowflakes at my face, a crystalline wash. My teeth are chattering, my whole body is convulsing as I lose control and fall to the ground, the bitter cold scratchy concrete wants all of me.

In the distance, I hear the guys yelling to get me inside. More footsteps, yells. Deep voices ring out. They cut through the whirling storm with ease, yet I can't place where they come from. Are they out here too?

I want to stay here. I can curl up in the fetal position, curve my body to itself, fold myself up into nothingness. I can live in the shell of the absence of everything. There's lots of room here.

I stare at the snow in the air. It's so fluffy and pretty, like billions of floating crystals. I let the wind freeze my tears to my cheeks. Am I really just wearing a tank top in the middle of a polar vortex?

Lily starts to cry and screams, "Oh my gawwwd! She's gonna die!"

There's way too much screaming, way too much swirling snow, all the cold, the sounds, the bad feelings are whipping me so hard, harder than the wind, and I still can't move.

"Let me." It's *Kian*.

Oh, Kian. Hi, Kian.

"I'll carry her," he says it with such a loving tone, I must be dreaming.

Is this a dream? I don't know what this is.

But I don't want him to carry me. What if he carries me to an alone place in the cabin and hurts me? But I don't want to believe that about him. He's not *like* those boys. Right? Wait. Maybe I do want him to carry me. Oh, I'm so confused.

I don't fight him as he lifts me. He's so warm, I soften against him, snuggle into his warm body. It feels so good to be held, especially by him.

I fall limp as he hoists me up for a better grip; my face is near his neck. I slip my arm around him. His warm skin feels so good on my cold cheek. I nuzzle my face in because I can't stop myself, cold seeking heat. He stops walking as I nuzzle. My tears come harder as I lose the fight to not sob. I begin to calm slightly as I realize he's helping me, not hurting me. I feel his heart beating so fast, he snuggles me tighter, shifts me higher up on his chest, which presses my lips against his neck.

"It's okay, Ashie, I've got you," he murmurs like a beacon of comfort.

I move my lips slightly, almost in a kiss because his skin feels like electric warmth beneath my cold lips. He gasps. I feel a shiver ripple through his body as he starts walking again. I am hyper aware of every inch of myself touching him across his hard chest, my hip against his hard abs. My feet are painful and numbish all at once. My fingers hurt so I put my free hand on his chest and he flinches.

"I'm so sorry," he says, his voice is full of regret. He drops his chin lower towards me. "I didn't know. I didn't mean it like that," he whispers, and I believe him because I want to. Even softer he says, "I would never..."

I hear his words, and I want them. Call me a fool, but I hold them in my heart like they're pure gold.

He steps up the front step and I feel heat grab for me; the cabin door must be open and sharing its heat. The brutal biting wind chases us inside and the cold and warm air mingle in a battle for a second, until someone slams the door behind us and the heat wins. I'm shivering violently despite the warm cabin air. But it feels like the sun, flooding me with life-saving heat.

Kian carries me into the living room. I still have my lips on his neck. I'm not moving. He keeps shivering as do I and I cannot tell if my shivering is from the cold or being this close to him. He sets me down on the couch, and I want to cry because I want his skin under my lips again, my body against his. He grabs blankets and starts piling them on me. The heaviness is as comforting as the warmth of the cabin.

My lips feel like they must be purple. My cheeks feel red, scratched raw from the bitter wind. I can't feel my fingers or my toes. Everything hurts.

"Oh my god, what are we going to do?" Lily sounds super panicked. "Is she frostbitten? Does she need to go to the hospital? We can't drive in this!"

"Shh...it's going to be okay, Lily," Lucas says. "Don't worry, we can warm her up."

She says, "Okay, if you say so." She whimpers like a puppy.

I glance at them. He has his muscular arms around her, snugging a blanket around her even tighter before he kisses her forehead. They look like they stepped off a magazine cover, her white porcelain skin against his deep brown flesh is so stunning. I need to tell her this later. They are so beautiful. Blindingly so.

Everyone is rustling around, but it's like they are all muffled. I can't hear them right. I try to wiggle under the blankets, but it's too hard so I just lay still, and close my eyes.

"I'll make her some hot chocolate," Mandy says. "Or soup, maybe she needs soup." It's so un-Mandy-like to think about food fixes. She must be out of her mind.

I feel someone rubbing my feet.

"Don't worry, Ashley, it's just me." It's Melissa and her hands are lathering up my feet. It feels kind of good, but kind of hurts too because she's doing it so hard. "We'll get you warmed up in no time."

"Maybe put her in the hot shower?" I hear Liam say, though I can't see him. "That would raise her body temp quick."

I don't want anyone to make me naked so I hope no one takes his suggestion, though it is a good one and it would probably work. But the thought of someone other than me removing my clothes makes me want to vomit right now, and I don't think I can do it, so it's gotta be a no. There is no laughter in the cabin, and I hate it. We've had so much laughing in this cabin and I've ruined it, completely trashed it with my stupid excursion into the dangerous cold. The room is spinning and puke is creeping up my throat.

"Bucket..." I manage. Someone scrambles, trips over something, there's sounds of a ruckus and curses. I'm holding the puke in and I'm doing a bad job because I'm about to spew it all over. Mandy arrives with a bowl, but the vomit comes out of my mouth as a spray so only half goes into the bowl and the rest goes onto Mandy.

She screams. "Ugh! Shit!" But then immediately she soothes me, "It's okay, Ash. It's okay. Don't worry sweet cheeks, I'm here."

Ah, Mandy. No one is like you.

I start to sob. "Mandy, s..so...s...sorry." I am shivering, my body is quaking from the cold, from puking, from remembering those boys' hands on me trying like demons to de-pants me. The whole room is swirling. I close my eyes. I need the memories to stop.

Mandy comforts me more. "It's okay, Ashley. I'm washable. I'll just take a shower and wash the clothes. I'm just so worried about you, that's all I care about right now."

She's always so nice to me. She loves me. I love her. We are friends.

Someone dangles a wet rag in front of me, but I can't get my hands out, so they just wipe my mouth for me. I love you, too, whoever you are... I look and it's Kian. He's wiping my vomit off my mouth, my chin...he's touching my barf. *Oh my gosh*...and he's still smiling at me. He touches my cheek with his other hand. I hope he isn't touching my puke. A shiver rocks me.

He cringes as I shiver. "I'm so very sorry," he says again so sweetly. His eyes are so soft and caring, and they look sorry, they really do. "Ashie, I'm so very very very sorry." His face is gentle, his joking eyes are gone now, but I want them back. I want him to make me laugh right now. Please...

I muster it out. "Laugh?" I ask. "Please, make me...laugh, Kian?" *Please*...I beg silently.

He smiles really big. So cute. Sexy. He chuckles. "Plenty of time for that later, Ashie. We need to get you warmed up right now."

But that's what I want, him making me laugh again, but it's too hard to repeat. The others are there but I only see Kian as my eyes close. I'm so very tired.

Chapter Fifteen

I wake up to hands on my forehead, then they travel to my cheeks, two hands cup my face, and they feel big. Warm. I open my eyes. Kian. Blink. Kian again. I smile.

The room is dark except for the lamp across the room. I try to sit up, but I have so many blankets on me it's hard to do. Kian pushes them off me so I can sit.

"What time is it?" I ask looking around. "Where is everyone?"

"It's three forty-five." He hands me a glass of ice water. "They're all in bed."

"Thank you," I say as I take the glass from him. I cringe. It's cold. And I'm embarrassed. I lost control. Everyone in the cabin knows my attempted rape story now. This hits me hard, and I want to crawl back under the blankets and hide. My throat is super scratchy, and vomit-coated, so I gulp the water fast and it caresses me with its lovely cleansing coolness. "That was good." I sigh. "I needed that."

He takes my glass, hands me a wrapped peppermint candy, and I pop it in my mouth. "I'll get you a refill. Of water," he whispers the last part.

"Thank you." I'm still cold so I pull a blanket up to my neck. The mint helps me wake up more, but I crunch it. I'm always too impatient to suck hard candies down to nothing.

He returns and there is a lemon wedge in the water. He sets it on the coffee table. "Crunchy mint?" He smirks at me. I love the amusement on his face. He pulls a chair close, and sits in it.

I nod. "It's good. Thank you." He picks up the glass and extends it towards me. Our fingers slip past each other as he hands the water to me; the light friction of our touch sends a jolt down my forearm.

148

I want to touch him again, so very much so; that was way too short. "Lemon water, huh?" I smirk back.

"Yep, it's the best for a scratchy throat, according to my mom." He holds his hands up. "I even used a knife to cut the lemon wedges myself."

"Kitchen skills are good in a boy." I give him an approving look. Flirting with him will tell him I'm okay, I hope.

He just stares at me, no smile appears, and he almost looks as if he's in pain. "Are you okay?" he asks. "I can get you anything you need. Grilled cheese? Soup? Hot chocolate. Another blanket." He pauses as I shake my head. "How do you feel?"

"You should be sleeping."

He gives me a look that says "are you kidding me?" and then he relaxes.

I nod slowly. "I'm okay. You've helped me so much with just this water." He has the same clothes on still from earlier, not pajamas. "Have you stayed up all night with me?" More guilt piles on top the guilt.

"Yes. I told everyone to go to bed. I wanted to stay up with you, watch you sleep, make sure you stayed warm. You know, make sure you were okay." He touches his lips. "That's what I was doing when you woke up, making sure you felt warm enough."

Oh my gosh. He watched me sleep? How sweet is that! My heart sends butterflies to my extremities. He's going over the top and it's melting me into a puddle.

"Listen," he says with downcast eyes as he runs his right hand through this hair. He freezes with his hand on the back of his neck for like ten seconds before dropping his arm to his side. He raises his eyes to meet my gaze.

I realize I'm holding my breath, so I let it out.

He begins again, "I'm so sorry I said that earlier. I had no idea about what had happened to you. I was just trying to be funny and

I didn't mean anything bad by it. I swear. It's no secret, I like you. And I just wanted to be alone with you, but not in that way, never in that way." He looks so guilty, and that makes me sad. He didn't do anything wrong, he shouldn't have to feel so guilty. But it's my fault that he does, because I ran out of the cabin like a freak show not letting a single soul in the cabin help me until I hit rock bottom.

"It's okay, Kian. How could you have known?" My hand is trembling despite the pile of blankets on me as I raise the glass towards my face. I'm so shaky, the water spills out the top like crazy, generously soaking the blanket as I bring it to my mouth.

He winces as he watches my hand wobble. He reaches out towards me. He looks so caring and compassionate. I've never had a boy look at me like that in my life. Girlfriends, yes, but a boy? Never.

"Need help?"

I shake my head.

"And these guys who did this to you...they're friends of mine?" He cocks his head to the right, his eyes go wide and more concern consumes his face. "Mandy said they are, but she wouldn't say anything else."

"Yes, they're friends of yours. You're on the same teams for sports." I swallow more lemon water.

He grits his teeth, clenches his big hands into fists on his thighs. "Are you going to tell me their names? Because they're no longer friends of mine. Because I'd like to beat the shit out of them."

My eyes go big. I didn't expect that out of this funny boy's mouth, he's always so jovial and happy. I shake my head. I remain silent, because, no, I don't want to talk about it. I sip the cool lemon water instead. I don't want violence to stem from violence.

"I'm serious, Ashley." He leans towards me with his elbows on his knees. "Which of my friends tried to rape you?" His angry tone flares at the end of his question. His voice is very strained as he's clearly trying to cover up his anger, but mostly failing.

I grimace at the word "rape" as it falls out of his mouth. It's such a horrible ugly word to come out of such a beautiful mouth. It's shocking to hear this tone in his voice. I can't process it well. I've never heard him sound this way before, and I don't like it.

I shake my head again. "I can't talk about it." He'll have to respect that. I want to forget all about it and go on.

"What they did wasn't okay, it was complete shit. Weak. Monstrous. They need to pay. That is unacceptable to do to a girl. Shit. I can't even believe this." He puts his head in his hands, rubs his temples. "Did you go to the police? You should go to the police." The look of determination on his face is unarguable.

"No." Then everyone would know. Why would I do that? My parents would find out. Hell no, fucking no fucking way. I'm not embarrassing myself like that. "They were drunk." I shrug even though I don't believe what I'm saying either, there's no excuse.

"So! That's no excuse to do that to a woman." He punches the arm of the chair which makes a crack sound, he probably cracked the wood. I jump and he flinches. "I'm sorry, this kind of stuff makes me livid." He sighs, looks across the room.

"I know." Clearly. And I love him for it.

"Then I go and say that to you. What the hell is wrong with me?" He stands up and paces. Hands going through that thick blond hair again, hair I so desperately want to rake my own fingers through. "Ashley, all I meant was that I wanted to spend time with you alone, ya know, like just you and me, but now you probably hate me, and I don't blame you. I was an insensitive ass." He lets me see those bright blue eyes of his and they are filled with regret. "Dammit."

I shake my head. "No, please, Kian. I don't think that about you. I don't." I take a deep breath. At least I don't fear that anymore now. I was a bit irrational. "I...I want that, too, time alone with you, that is, I mean. I really like you, too. Like, a lot." My hands are shaking as I allow my thoughts to be spilled out in front of him, alive in the world. Real. I'm overly emotional, and I'm about to let something secret fall out of my mouth too easily. I can't seem to stop it. "I really wish you had kissed me in the laundry room yesterday." My heart pounds as I watch his reaction.

He comes over to me and kneels on the floor before me, peers into my eyes, his own so hopeful, the anger gone. "Really? You do?" His eyes are lit up and the joking smile returns. "Would you go out on a date with me sometime? Just you and me?"

I nod. Smile. "I'd love to. I want that more than anything." I can't believe he's saying this to me. I want to squeal!

"That's so awesome. Okay. This is, wow. I'll take you wherever you want to go, you name it."

How can I not love this boy? He's gorgeous, wait—love? Not love, but wow...dang, is he hot. I can't love him, I barely know him, but somewhere in me I feel the birth of the bud of love, of what could maybe be the start of something fabulous. Even through the blanket his touch makes me tingle and want to squirm. I shove the big load of blankets off me a bit because his intense gaze is making me hot for real.

I bite my lip. "You really watched me sleep?" I giggle. "I hope I didn't toot or talk in my sleep, or snore."

He laughs and the sound is so wonderful. His laugh is so rich and hearty it makes me smile all through my body. It warms me up better than the pile of blankets.

"You're golden, no such indiscretions occurred." He laughs again. "Though I'd pay big money to see those things happen," he teases.

I want to swat him, but I roll my eyes and chuckle instead. "Would you tell me if I did?"

"Maybe, or I'd use it as blackmail to get you to go on a second date with me."

I laugh. "No need for that, I already want that."

"Ah, you say all the right things," he says and bats his eyes like a southern belle, tips his head to the right, rests his chin atop overlapped hands on the mound of blankets on the edge of the couch.

I giggle.

"Now, how about that grilled cheese? I make a mean one. As you know, I'm the master of all things cheesy." He bats his eyelashes at me trying to convince me he's innocent.

I burst out with a short laugh. "Right, that's not exactly how I'd put it," I smile at him, loving being back to playful with him again. "But yeah, that sounds wonderful." I sip more lemon water. "Are you going to have one, too? I don't want to be any trouble."

"I'm eighteen, I eat 24-7 and then some. I'm always hungry." There's a no-nonsense look on his face.

I watch his butt as he sashays to the kitchen.

"I'm just the best damn grilled cheese maker you ever did met," he says with a southern drawl, bad grammar clearly on purpose. He looks back and catches me watching him walk away. He winks. "How's the view?" He peers down his body, trying to eye his own backside.

I bust a gut laughing at him as I blush.

He's pure magic. He swings his hips as he walks, saying "Mm...yeah...um-hmmmm. I'm working it, uh-huh." He flicks imaginary long hair, bats his eyelashes at me. "Now, don't ya'll go anywhere, right suga?" he screeches in a southern accent. His showmanship is over the top and hilarious.

"No, ma'am, I'm not moving off this couch. I swear I won't dare."

"Good girl, honey. Good girl. I'm happy as a clam to hear you say that, I'm a ma'am. Yes, ma'am. Most folks think I'm a sexy boy, but I've got them all fooled, I'm really a southern ma'am, no boy." He nods his head, a smile plastered across his goofy face.

I burst into giggles. He's got me laughing pretty good to where I can't even sit still.

He says, "And I can whip up a can o-tomata soup better than Martha, any day and every day."

I crack up. He's priceless.

I want to cheer and say, "Thank you, Kian, for making me laugh!" But I just watch his southern cooking show imitation with delight instead. He's so funny as he makes a show of flipping open cupboards for pans, soup, digs in the fridge for cheese and butter, narrating his every move like he's a chatty southern chef. He's the best thing for me right now and I can't believe I get to spend time with him. Alone. And I'm not scared at all. I smile. He did get his wish.

I almost cheer thinking about our conversation. I'm so excited because I get to go on a real date with him when we get back home. Two dates planned already! I could just die. He wiggles his butt at me as he wraps a pink cooking apron around his waist and ties it. This might be the sexiest thing I've ever seen, a big strong sexy man in a pink apron making me laugh and about to make food for me. If I wasn't a goner for him already, I'd be one now. I crack up and scream inside because wow, that butt, hotter than a sweet potato pie pulled from a southern oven in July, not that I know being from Minnesota. His southern roleplay isn't wasted on this northern babe. Yum-*me!*

After Kian's mock cooking show is done and my gut hurts from laughing, he carries the soup and grilled cheese to the living room and places them on the coffee table. He slips off the apron and tosses it behind him like it's rubbish. I giggle, then slide down to the ground. We both bring our bellies to the edge of the coffee table. I keep one blanket wrapped around me as he flutters his eyelashes at me again.

"Now, for grace. Fold your hands, love. There ya go. Now, Dear God, thank you God for this yummy exquisitely prepared amazing as the sun itself grilled cheese and tomato soup, made by yours truly, amazing outstanding stupendous, Chef Kian. And thank you for Ashley being safe and smiling at me and laughing at me because that made my whole night, if not my whole year. Amen."

My jaw stays open as the full weight of his prayer hits me. If perfection exists, it's right now.

He smiles at me. Nods at the food. "Dig in." The hilarious southern belle is now gone, and I get the wonderful Kian back.

"Thank you, Kian. For this food, and for making me laugh. You've made me feel so good and I can't thank you enough." I don't know how my life got so magical, but I feel like I'm glowing.

He chuckles. "Eat it first and make sure I didn't ruin it."

"I wouldn't even care if you did, you entertained me so much. You're so funny."

"Thank you, love!" he says with the southern drawl again. "You're sweet as a North Carolina peach."

I laugh at him, how can I not? He's priceless. And gorgeous. And sexy and wow, after my first bite of the sandwich, he can really make a delicious grilled cheese. I take a bite again and chew to confirm it. "This is really good, Kian. I'm impressed."

He flashes his eyes at me. "Learned it from the best cook I know, my mom."

Ah...this boy could not get any better, he's like a dream. "She taught you well." I dip my sandwich in the soup again and take a giant bite. The warm sandwich and the soup are the best things I've eaten in my whole life. They taste that damn good right now.

He grabs the lighter from the table and lights the candle in between us. "This is kind of like our first date right now." He grins.

My eyes light up and I show him the joy in them. "You're right, this is our first date. We are alone." I blush and hope he doesn't notice in the candlelight, but when I look at him, he clearly sees it, and he smiles. Relief floods me. He likes it, which makes me blush deeper.

"You're so beautiful," he says. "And I really like to make you blush. I must confess." His gaze is one hundred percent focused on my face.

Wow, my cheeks feel like they get even redder under his intense gaze, which seems completely impossible. I manage a weak, "Thank you." Then I smirk. "You're the hottest southern belle guy, um, ma'am, I've ever did met."

He smirks, says bringing back the accent, "Bad grammar and all. Likewise, suga, you hotter than eggs on a hot Florida sidewalk, sizzling louder than the sound o' the semi-trucks passing by the sea-lon where I get my hair did, with juicy oranges being squashed together as that big ol' truck bounces into and out of the giant man-sized potholes through downtown Tallahassee."

I laugh so hard...hmm...what is sea-lon? Salon? Maybe. "So very creative," I say nodding. "You should do improv, Kian."

He's back to Kian again. "I try," he says, "That I do, ma'am." He looks me right in my eyes. "I'm so happy, thrilled to see you laughing. You're even more gorgeous when you're laughing, so I guess I'm selfish; making you laugh is all for me."

"Oh, I doubt that," I say.

"It's true." His eyes say he's joking. "Thank you for eating my grilled cheese and not telling me it tastes like a piece of cheesy cardboard."

I laugh. "Kian, it's really good, and I'm being totally serious! You rock at making grilled cheese."

He smirks. "You were just really hungry."

"No, that's not it at all. It's really very good."

"Mandy made cake. Want a piece?" He raises an eyebrow at me.

"Yes, she's the best cake baker I know. She doesn't make much more, but her cake is heavenly."

"Yeah, like I already ate three pieces after everyone went to bed. She's gonna kill me in the morning when she finds out."

I chuckle. "I'll just ask her to make another. She will. She loves me."

"I can see that. She's a really good friend. So is Melissa."

"I know, I'm so very lucky to have the two of them in my life. They make my life so good." I sigh. Dang. I forgot I puked on Mandy. "Oh, gosh. Was Mandy able to get herself clean? I feel so bad I puked all over her." I sigh. "Guess Melissa and I are the puke twins."

He laughs. "She did. She hopped right in the shower, and I washed her clothes."

"You were so nice to me. I felt you wipe my face. Thank you. You didn't have to touch my puke." I pause, smirk. "And, you know how to wash clothes, too? How can you get any more perfect?"

"Yes, I do. And you just wait and see." His face goes serious. "And, Ashley, I fish and clean them myself, I'm not scared of gross stuff. Plus, I change my little nephew's diapers, and he's spit up on me more times than I can count. It's not a big deal. Really, I'm a boy, I used to play with dirt and worms. Also, I'm not afraid of soap and water."

I grin. "Wow, I'm impressed. You can cook, do laundry, clean up puke, and you change diapers? I think I've hit the jackpot for a good guy."

He chuckles. "You have no idea. I'm totally amazing." He rolls his eyes and flicks fake long hair over his shoulder. "I'm the best, darling." Now he's a classic Hollywood movie star.

I crack up. "Kian, you are priceless, incredible."

"The cost of admission to The Kian Show, priceless. Can I quote you on that?" He doesn't even grin as he says it, he's totally serious.

"Yes, Kian, absolutely. You are priceless." How does he not crack up? He's a dang natural.

"Oh, thank gawwwd! I'm worth it." He uses a Boston accent, wipes his eyes as if he were crying. He's like watching a comedian live in-person.

I giggle. "You're making my stomach hurt I'm laughing so much." I pause. "Seriously, you should do comedy. You'd kill it."

"And my dad would kill me." He goes all serious, then shifts his facial expression again quickly. "I'm just happy to make you laugh. It suits you." He beams a grin at me. "I said it already and I meant it, you're so beautiful when you're laughing."

I blush again. Geez, he gets right under my skin and makes me feel like a million bucks. He's amazing.

"It's almost five, I guess we should get some sleep, huh?" I suggest. "Well, I mean you should, I clearly got some already. I can't thank you enough for staying up with me, for cooking for me, for making me laugh." I hug myself. "Best first date ever."

His face lights up. "Really?"

"Really. The best." I'm on cloud nine, all rolled up in delicious fuzzies.

"I'm just going to sleep on the floor out here. I'll make a bed with the sleeping bags."

"Oh, you should take the couch, I'll move to the floor. I've been here hogging the couch for hours."

"I can use the camping cot from the garage, or just a bunch of sleeping bags. It's okay. I want you to take the couch. I want you to sleep and get some rest so we can play more tomorrow. All these days off of school for cold weather must be a record, huh?" He arranges a sleeping bag and pillow. "You go ahead and use the bathroom first, then I can go second."

"No, you go. I can go second," I insist.

"Go ahead, Ashie. I'm fine to wait." His face softens. "Ladies first."

"Okay, thank you, Kian." I stand up. I feel a bit unsteady, but I quickly get my bearings.

"You need me to help you walk?" Of course, he noticed my unsteadiness. Dang, he's attentive.

"No, I'm okay, but thank you." I smile his way. I turn, knowing full well he's probably looking at my butt. I grab my bag and head to the bathroom. I look at myself in the mirror and my face looks makeup-less. Probably got washed off by tears, snow, and when Kian wiped the puke off my face. Well, I guess if he still likes me after all that, he must really like me. My cheeks are rosy, and I do have a happy glow. I smile as I brush my teeth, which is a little hard to do while smiling, and the toothpaste foam keeps falling out of my mouth, but I can't suppress the smile.

I slip into my pajamas and wonder if I should leave my bra on because this fabric is really thin and I will be near Kian, but then I decide that my bra will be too uncomfortable to sleep in, so I remove it. When I open the door, Kian is right there and I immediately regret the no bra because I'm jiggly as I walk and, naturally, his eyes go right to my chest and widen as he sucks in a breath.

"Whoa," he says under his breath.

I blush...dang it, I hate being shy. My heart races. "Your turn." I try to move out of his way, slowly, so as not to make my chest jiggle too much.

He sighs as if enjoying. "Yeah, my turn." He takes one step towards me and my heart flutters like the last dry leaf on an oak tree in a brisk late fall breeze.

I lift my face up as I close the gap between us with a step towards him.

He lowers his head closer to mine. I'm afraid to move. My heart stalls as he whispers, "Is it okay if I kiss you now?"

I put smiles in my eyes for him, and one on my lips, too, as I nod. "Yes. Please do," I say.

He presses his lips to mine in a peck and my heart explodes, sending a shock wave throughout my whole body. I wrap my arms around him in a flash, and crash against his chest, smashing my bra-less breasts right into him. His arms envelope me. He moans against my mouth as his lips coax mine open more. He sucks my upper lip in between his and I moan, too, as I welcome his tongue into my mouth, caressing it with mine. I'm erupting into explosions inside and feeling comfort in him all at once and I think I'll never be the same ever again in my life. Kissing him is way more delicious than I imagined it would be, and I never want it to end, but he suddenly pulls back. I want to lunge back at him and suck his mouth back onto mine.

He's breathless, as am I. "We'd better stop now." He winces. "Not that I want too, you're... an utterly amazing kisser."

I swallow hard, bite my lip, and try to reign in all control because I really want to slam him into the wall and kiss him again, smother him with my hot mouth. I sigh and follow his gaze to my chest, which is, oh-so-awkwardly alert in my tips at the moment. My cheeks heat.

"Oh, whoa!" I say. I laugh as I try to suck myself into the bagginess of my pajama shirt. "Yeah, I'll just go over there, now." I point towards the living room. My cheeks are flaming bright hot red.

He releases a quick soft scoff. "Right. That's probably a really good idea. I could use a really cold shower after that," he says with a suggestive chuckle laced in his words. He walks into the bathroom, and within seconds, I hear the shower come on.

I start to crack up, wishing I could slip into a cold shower, too. I'm so hot from our kiss, but after all that cold earlier, that's the last thing I need. I slip under the blankets and wait for Kian to come back out.

He saunters out of the bathroom, whistling.

"Have a nice shower?" I ask in a teasing tone.

"Yes, it was very... exhilarating and calming." He's grinning pretty huge. "And damn cold."

"Ah, I see." I sigh. "I could have used that myself."

"No more cold stuff for you right now. We just got you warmed up."

"Right." I wish I could sleep right next to him, it kills me to know he's going to be sprawled out just a few feet away from me and all I'd have to do is walk over and I know he'd welcome me, but that would lead to things we aren't ready for yet. "Kian, thank you again for all you did for me today. You truly are so very wonderful."

"You're very welcome. And I'd do it all over again. Any time. And every time."

I quietly sigh inside, but in my chest, where my heart is doing jumping jacks, my soul is dancing. "Good night."

"Good night, Ashie."

I chuckle. "I love that nickname."

"Good."

I try to relax and wait for sleep to come, but I'm so worked up after that kiss that it takes me a while before sleep takes me. All I can think about is Kian.

Chapter Sixteen

In the morning, I suck down a coffee and nibble on a breakfast burrito that Lily made as Melissa brazenly charges me, hands on her slim hips.

"Are you doing okay, Ashley?" she asks with copious concern in her voice. She rubs my shoulder. "I'm so worried about you." She does a little stomp and the look in her eyes flares to impatience.

That stomp means something. "I'm okay, thanks Melissa."

She raises both hands in the air and boldly announces, "Girl meeting time. All girls...get your asses moving in ten minutes. Our bedroom. Haul butt." She leans towards me. "I'm super fucking pissed you didn't tell me about all this, Ash," she whispers as she shoots daggers at me. Her eyes flicker between anger and flashes of concern. She wrings her hands.

She very rarely swears. She's lethally livid with me, angrier than I've ever seen her. Her eyes tell me I'm not forgiven, and I'd better cooperate with her little meeting or she's caging me up forever. But this isn't about her.

I swallow hard and nod. "Sure thing, Liss." She's gonna chew me a new one. Seriously so. Yeah, I screwed up by not telling her about what happened at that party. Everything about it was fucked up, though. I'd be furious with her if she did that to me. We're friends and I denied her the truth, for the both of us. I stripped her of the best friend right to help me when in a crisis. This is gonna be a hard battle to win. I just need to get her to know it's not about our friendship at all, more about my own embarrassment. If I can get her to understand that, then I'll be golden. When three guys make you feel like a slut, you kind of believe it for a bit. And you feel like a

162

piece of worthless shit, existing only for their pleasure, because my pleasure was nowhere in what happened. Which seems the opposite with Kian, who is all about my happiness and pleasure. I'll have to make Liss understand. All I really want is to just forget it, shove it somewhere to choke it out of existence and die.

I sigh and mow down the remainder of my breakfast and I'm the first one to get my butt into the room. I'm sheepish as Melissa charges in, her eyes are flaring wide at me. She plants herself next to me and gives me this look that screams at me how-dare-you-not-ask-me-to-help-you-with-this. It's surely a friend betrayal in her eyes. But it's so much more to me.

"I'm sorry," I say as Lily and Mandy slide into our circle. "I should have told you, Melissa." Tears sting in my eyes. "It was wrong of me not to tell you."

Her anger softens immediately, and her eyes fill with sadness instead. "It's okay. I just wish I had been there for you, and I feel like a loser that I wasn't. You've been suffering and I haven't been a friend." Her eyes fill with tears, and I realize my silence has not hurt only me, but her, too. "I'm so upset for you. Worried about you." Her eyes look like she's in pain as she timidly asks, "Did they...hurt you?"

And, I'm crying, just like that. No restraint as I all out sob in front of them. It's still living just under the surface of me and it still hurts so bad. *I was almost gang raped,* by boys I know. I can't even think it without crying profusely, right? Let alone say it out loud.

"I...I...didn't..."

"Hey..." Mandy starts.

"Don't." Melissa pulls me into a hug. "What you went through. I'm so glad Mandy was there to protect you."

"Damn fucking straight I was," Mandy says. "I was ready to fucking rip their dicks and their nuts right fucking off, but I wanted to get you the hell out of there more." The anger in her voice makes me feel good. It's good to have friends who profess the desire to fight to the max for me. I have zero doubts she would have pulverized them. She's that fierce.

I gasp, wipe my eyes. My whole body hurts.

"Tell me what you can. No pressure. But it always helps to talk about it, ya know?" Melissa releases me and I sit back. The four of us are sitting in a circle on the floor. I reach for a pink fuzzy pillow from behind me and hug it like it will help me talk about how three boys almost fucked me without my permission. Boys all four of us know. That's something I may never be able to assimilate to make sense.

"Only tell us what you're comfortable with though," Lily nods, her eyes are so chocked full of concern. She gets it, and I know that more than ever after what she shared.

I sigh and look at the pink shaggy rug in the center of us. "I had my super tight skinny jeans on that night, and it saved me." I gasp as a sob overtakes me.

Lily mutters, "Omigod, I'm so sorry." She's almost crying herself.

"We were at Jackson's party and it was small, not many people were there. Everyone had either gone downstairs or to rooms, so I was left alone with the three guys, but I knew them from school, so it was fine. They told me I was beautiful, that I had a nice smile and pretty eyes. Honestly, I was having a good time with them, but then things changed. They moved on to talking about my breasts, how they were 'nice handfuls', which was odd to say to my face, but I was like, whatever. They're boys and boys like boobs, so I didn't care so much. It seemed pretty typical. They said they liked my curves, like a lot." I snort. "What girl doesn't like to be liked by boys, and complimented by them?" I shrug realizing I was a fool. But now I'm so over that false notion. Mostly.

They all nod.

"Three of us were sitting on the floor, one boy was in a chair." I let out a shaky sigh. "Then it got a little awkward as one guy said he's always liked my ass, and I just laughed it off. But they kept flirting with me, so I flirted back. It was fun, a little too far, but still fun. We were all drinking, they were drunk. I was, too." I sigh as a tear slips to my lips and I swipe it away. "Then, it was like I wasn't in the room as they said to each other that it was now time to take my pants off."

Both Melissa and Lily gasp. Then the room falls dead silent.

I glance at Mandy. She knows all this, so she just sits there, looking pissed.

"Oh my god. No," Melissa says as her hand flies to cover her mouth. She shakes her head, making her fine blond hair dance as her face forges into a look of full horror. She keeps her hand over her mouth as she watches me.

"Fuck," Lily says with a pained expression. "And we know these guys?"

I nod, still looking at the shaggy carpet. I glance up at each of them. "You all know them." They don't ask me who they are, so I don't offer up their names. My eyes go back to the carpet; I flick the thick strands of it back and forth with my index finger. "Two of them started working on getting my jeans off, but they couldn't easily rip them off because they were so tight, and my stomach was bloated with beer which made them even tighter. They would succeed in getting them down a bit and I'd wiggle them back up, which I could only do while lying flat...as I was laid out on the floor, I wriggled a lot, which of course made them want me more. They just kept trying, I kept managing to pull them back up each time they got them somewhat down. It was like a tug of war. One...boy...unbuttoned my shirt and slipped his hand in my bra." I gasp and close my eyes as I say, "He rubbed me with his thumb." I shudder. "I couldn't stop him because I was fighting to keep my pants up." I open my eyes and focus on the rug again. "The boy still working on my pants would move my jeans down a few inches, and I'd wiggle them back up, on repeat, like I lost count how many times we did that shit. They didn't hold my arms down, but they didn't have to because there were two of them and I was so busy trying to keep my pants up I couldn't fight them off. Then he got them down enough to see my underwear, like they could see almost all of it. I noticed he had a hard-on and I panicked, and then he became more determined and he yanked my pants to my thighs, thank God my thighs are a little thicker, my curves and my tight pants saved my ass, literally. If Mandy hadn't come out at that moment, he would have got his dick in me in no time, it was like mere seconds away." I shudder and keep shivering. "I just couldn't get over his eyes. You know. They were so mean, hard. Hungry, like a savage." I gasp. "It was like he wasn't even a human."

Melissa is just shaking her head, her eyes terror-stricken.

"What did the third guy do?" Lily asks with knowing dread laced in her question.

"He watched from his chair." I drop my eyes to the carpet again, then flick them back up to my friends.

"Ugh. What a sleazy fucker." Mandy clenches her fists. "He's as bad as the others watching like that and not stopping it."

"Oh, he had zero interest in stopping it. He was just the gang leader letting his friends do the grunt work. Once I heard him say, 'hurry up ya fuckers, someone might come.'"

"What? You didn't tell me about that part." Mandy flares her eyes wide, her eyebrows furrow together in her most angry facial expression yet.

"I couldn't say it out loud, hell, I could barely even think it until now." I sniff, wondering if there are other parts I'm unconsciously suppressing. "So that's it and if Mandy hadn't come out when she did, I'd have been a gang rape victim." I shrug. "I should have screamed, right? But, honestly, I was too busy trying to keep my clothes on to even think of the idea to scream."

"I'm so very sorry," Lily says. "That should never have happened to you. Those guys are the worst kind of fuckers. They should rot in the hot muddy pits of the earth."

"And I'm so sorry I wasn't there for you." Melissa crawls over, throws her arms around me. "I'm sorry I was pissed at you earlier, but never keep something like that from me again, okay? I want to help you, be there for you. You all are my best friends, and it hurts me to know you were hurting so much and I never even gave you a hug." She whimpers. "I didn't know."

I nod as tears stream down my face. The hug makes me feel better and I sputter through a few gasps. "I know."

Mandy and Lily wrap their arms around us, too, and we don't move for like a minute before we peel away from each other.

"I needed that." I laugh, then shrug. "I just didn't want to talk about it, ya know. I didn't want to acknowledge it. Still don't, really." I stare at the ground. "It was kind of like it didn't happen if I didn't say it." I frown. "Only it did."

"Do you see them at school?" Melissa asks with a grimace.

"Yes. They even talk to me like nothing is different. That first day afterwards at school, they talked about my ass as I walked by and they said how they wished they 'had gotten to tap it.'"

"Oh my. I can't even. Omigod. That's effing beyond harsh, and utterly cruel." Lily shakes her head. "The bastards. How could they do that to someone? I just don't get it."

"Yeah, they didn't even care that I heard them. It was like they wanted me to hear it." I rub my temples and then my eyes.

"Did you go to the police?" Lily asks in a rush.

"No. I didn't want my parents to know about this, so I didn't. I mean, how embarrassing. I don't want my dad to know about this. Plus, my dad will probably kill them." I sigh. "*Plus*, I'd been drinking, and I didn't want my parents to know that, either."

"It doesn't matter if you were or not. It's not okay, not at all." She presses her lips tightly together. "You should tell the police, though. Those boys need to be stopped." Melissa stares at me directly. "Do you want to tell us who they are? I'd like to know. But it's your choice, of course."

I shake my head as I meet Lily's gaze because I don't want her to know. She's actually friends with these guys as are Lucas, Liam, and Kian.

"You're the victim. It's not your fault," Lily says in a kind, soft voice.

I drop my eyes to the carpet as I consider telling them. Nope. I can't do it.

"Okay. It's okay," Melissa says with kind eyes. "You don't have to tell us."

"No, don't worry about it. I just wish I knew so I could unfriend them, that's all, but this isn't about me." Lily hugs herself. "Lucas would probably beat them up if he knew. As would Kian for sure, of that I have no doubt. It would be good to have someone beat some sense into them before they do this to another girl, though." She sounds a little hopeful it would happen. And Lucas already stepped up as her hero, so I get it.

"Right, like part of me feels obligated to speak up to protect another girl from them, but most of me just wants to pretend it never happened so I can go on with my life." I hug the pillow tighter to my chest.

"Well, I can tell you Kian is nothing like those fuckers. Like, at all. In fact, he's the opposite of that kind of guy." Lily touches my hand. "Can I tell you something I do when I'm feeling like a victim again after what I went through last year? Maybe it will help you, too."

I nod as I wipe my wet cheeks with my hand.

"Okay. Repeat after me: I decide when. I decide how. I can change my mind." Lily rubs my hand. "Now you say it."

My voice feels like it will come out all shaky because my whole body is shaking. "I decide when. I decide how. I can change my mind." It comes out less shaky than I was afraid it would. I repeat it. "I decide when. I decide how. I can change my mind." It does make me feel better, so I manage a small smile.

"And repeat those sentences in your head, or out loud, whenever you feel like a victim. For me, those feelings still happen from time to time and I repeat those sentences in my head until I feel better. Until I feel empowered again. It won't erase what happened to you, but it will help you realize you have some control about how you feel and your own actions, and what you accept as okay in your life." She shrugs. "It works for me."

"Thank you, Lily." Tears form, heavily filling my eyes. "Thank you so much. This really helps me." I blink and the big heavy tears fall. I cry from the pain and from the relief this meeting has given me.

"Just so you know, there were some days when I repeated those words in my head all day long." A sad look deepens upon her face. She shakes her head as if she's throwing the look off her face. She smiles, then says, "And, again, Kian is a really good guy, I've known him for a long time," she rubs my arm. "And Lucas has known him even longer than I have. He wouldn't be friends with Kian if he were a bad guy."

I nod, smiling at the mention of his name. Thinking of last night with Kian makes a warm feeling wash over me. "Thinking about him makes me feel better," I confess. My smile widens. "I really like him." The sad truth is, Lucas is friends with the boys who did this, too. People can hide their demons even from their closest friends. I guess I did, too.

"Yeah, babes, and I had to stop you from grabbing his dick in the hallway in the middle of the night." Mandy points at me with a teasing accusatory look.

Melissa gasps. "Wait. What now?"

"I wasn't going to grab his dick! I was feeling his unbelievable abs. That's nowhere near his dick. And I wouldn't grab his dick like that in the hallway!" I laugh. "Geez, Mandy!"

"Well, it looked like that's where your hand was going, so I grabbed your arm to stop you. I was afraid for you with what just happened to you. I didn't want you to do something you regretted." She laughs, lightening the mood. "I keep interrupting you two, though, my bad. I'm so sorry. I'll try to step back."

My cheeks flame red. "Oh holy hell, gosh, what if he thought I was going for his dick, too? Oh, I'm so embarrassed." I cover my face with my hands.

Lily laughs in my face. "Yeah, not a newsflash, boys fucking love it when you grab their dick." Lily's eyes tease me.

"Oh, right, but not in the hallway when we hadn't even kissed yet." I grin sheepishly at my friends.

"Nah, pretty sure any time works for them," Mandy grins. "But seriously, I need to give you space. I'm, like, hindering your sparks from flying. I'm dampening your vibe and I'm sorry."

"I know, right? First, we almost kiss in the laundry room and you barge in and then you stop me from touching his abs, which, by the way, are like, oh-my-fucking-gawd incredible!" I giggle, lean my head back, and close my eyes to savor the memory. I open them and say, "They're totally beyond amazing. I'm not lying. And they feel even better than they look." I wiggle my fingers in the air and the girls all laugh.

Lily nods. "Yeah, I've seen him at the beach with his shirt off; his abs are freaking amazing. He's always working out. His dad's a slave driver with the sports, but it's made Kian into a super mega athlete and given him that unbelievable body." She twists her face in disgust. "If you ever hear a guy yelling at the games, it's probably Kian's dad. He's relentless, and way too hard on Kian to be the best in every sport." Lily wrinkles her nose. "He's kind of a jerk."

I sigh. "Oh, poor Kian." I wonder how Kian turned out so good with a dad like that. But I've seen hints of this hardness he endures from his dad already.

"I mean, Kian loves sports, for sure, but his dad, he's just brutal about it and Kian just goes along with it and takes it." She sighs. "When I see his dad berating him after a game, I feel so bad for him."

"Wow, I had no idea." I squeeze the pillow to my chest. "I feel bad for him, too."

Melissa's pretty face becomes twisted with horror. "Oh my gosh, Ash, what if they aren't done? I'm scared for you, Ash. Maybe those boys wanted you to hear them talk about you like that because they plan to come after you again to finish what they couldn't last time."

"No." Lily shakes her head. "If you're with Kian, no one will dare touch you. No way. He's a sports star school, and you all know how popular he is. Like, everyone either admires the shit out of him because they worship him, or they are scared of him cause he's, like, superhero strong. I mean, seriously, haven't you all seen his biceps? He's built like damn brick house and could pound anyone to the ground in just one punch."

"But I'm not his girlfriend."

They all laugh at me.

I frown. "What?"

"Seriously? Ash. Wake up. I'm pretty sure you're about to be," says Lily with a giant smile.

"He already asked me who the boys were. He wants to beat them up, which is exactly another reason I'm not saying it. I don't want him to get in trouble and get kicked off the team over me. Plus, now that I know that about his dad, I'm not risking him getting into deep shit with his dad for beating up teammates. I'm keeping my mouth shut. I'm not letting Kian get in trouble over this."

"Teammates?" Lily says with dread.

"I get that, Ash, I really do, but it's just so wrong. Please, just think about going to the police, will you?" Melissa's eyes plead with me. Her rule-follower heart is aching for me.

I nod. But hell no, I'm not doing that. I saw the look in Kian's eyes; he meant it, he'd go after them and I'm not letting that happen.

"He won't stop asking, you know that, right?" Lily touches my hand. "He's like Lucas in that way. It's part of what bonds the two of them together, and even Liam. They hate abuse, neglect, mistreatment of women. It's, like, deep in the core of them." Her eyes go wide. "They're the good ones. I'm being dead honest here."

I sigh. I believe her. I do. Which is exactly why I'm keeping my mouth closed on their names. I smile. "I like that you just said that."

She holds up her petite hands. "It's true. They're three good guys. Really good."

I shudder as I recall what Kian said yesterday. The truth is, two of those guys who almost raped me were planning to come to the cabin yesterday. I look at Mandy and she clearly knows what's going through my head. I give her a worried look and she gives me a stern one.

"Don't worry," she says. "They aren't getting near you, not with me, us, and Kian on your side to protect you."

I nod with tears in my eyes. "Thank you, Mandy. I know. And that helps." I put my head in my hands as Kian invades my thoughts. I exclaim, "Oh, my gosh! I'm falling so hard for him, and I'm worried he doesn't like me the same way." I throw my gaze up towards the ceiling. "Last night, after everyone was in bed, with Kian, it was incredible."

All three of them burst into uncontrolled squealing and gleeful laughter.

"Oh, do tell," demands Lily in her juicy tone.

"Honey, you're so clueless," Mandy says as she chuckles. "He practically salivates when you walk into the room." Her eyes are laughing at me, too.

"Really?" I raise my eyebrows.

Lily bursts into a belly laugh so hard holds her gut. "Seriously? Ash. How can you not see it?" I like that Lily is calling me "Ash" now, too, like we're really friends. "Wake up, love. He's so into you."

"Oh, I guess I just never thought Kian would ever like me like that, being I'm a nobody. I was too afraid to hope."

"Stop it with that kind of talk," Lily scolds.

I sigh and hug myself. "You wouldn't believe it. He was so sweet last night. He stayed up watching me sleep. How sweet is that? Then, he made me laugh so hard as he pretended to be a southern woman chef, and he made me grilled cheese and soup. He cooks!" I smile as I raise both my hands in the air. "He asked me out, too, for when we get back home." I roll my eyes. "I guess we considered last night our first date."

"See!" Melissa giggles. "It's already happening, Ash."

"Yeah, and we did kiss, last night, and it was so amazing." I smile as they all shriek and scream. "I had just taken off my bra in the bathroom and I walked out into the hall, and he was just right there. Omigosh, he asked permission to kiss me, and I practically mauled him. He took a cold shower after our kiss and he told me he did." I laugh, then sigh. "Best kiss of my whole freaking life. It was so damn hot! Like, it was so super yummy. Better than I could ever have imagined."

"Ah!" Melissa screams and taps her feet on the ground in a series of light stomps. "Why did you take so long to tell us this? But don't stop. Tell us everything. I love it."

"I so love this story too," Lily says with a satisfied grin growing on her face. "Swooning."

I put my face in hands, then pop my face back up and I stare at the ceiling again. "Okay, so, truth. When I landed on him with the pizza dough when we were making the pizza, I totally felt him have a giant hard-on beneath me. That's why I scrambled off him so fast, I was so shocked."

"Whoa," spills Mellisa.

"How can you possibly question if he likes you with all this, Ash?" Mandy eyes me like I'm a freaking idiot. "How much more proof do you need?"

"I don't know. Maybe because it's too good to be true." I smile. "I'm not that lucky."

We hear Kian yell out in the hallway. "Liam, what did you do? Did you fucking die a slow death in there? Shit, it's damn toxic, like putrid, nasty like my grandpa's effing outhouse at the cabin. That's some kind of alien shit odor or something."

We all stop talking and listen during his rant, then crack up.

"You girls okay in there?" Kian calls at the door.

"Yes! Go away, Kian!" Lily screams and we all giggle.

"Oh, shit. Will do! My bad. So sorry," he calls through the door. "And hi, Ashie."

We all laugh.

I'm beaming.

"I guess these walls are pretty thin; his words were pretty clear. I hope he didn't hear us." I widen my eyes. "I'll die if he heard me talk about him."

"Don't worry, I'm sure he didn't hear," Melissa says, but how the hell does she know? "And if he did, then it's a confirmation for him that you like him back." She smiles like it's a simple done deal. "And that would be a good thing."

I sigh. "It'd be like a dream come true if he did."

"If?" Melissa asks in exasperation. She takes a pillow and beats me lightly on the head. "Get it through that thick skull. Kian likes you," she chants, a little bit too loudly for my comfort.

"Oh, girl, for the love of—you better believe it, he does. He does!" Mandy grabs my shoulders and gives me a tiny shake. "Wake up. I ought to shake you! The boy wants you. Really bad. Quit being so damn blind."

I smile at all three of them, then bite my lip. Maybe they're right. I have amazing friends.

Chapter Seventeen

Mandy has brought in a bag of licorice. She rips it open and takes one, then passes it to me.

"Thanks," I say.

"Celebratory licorice." Mandy nods as if it's a thing.

I pass the bag on to Lily, who takes two licorice pieces, then she passes it to Melissa. She looks at it like it's a toxic piece of garbage.

"Liss, just eat one." I urge her on.

"I'm good." She shakes her head.

"Fuck you. Take one. Now." I glare hard at her.

Lily looks at me like I'm a harsh bitch.

Melissa takes one and just holds it up in front of her face and stares at it.

"You can do this. It's good. You like licorice." I sigh. "Go on. I've seen you eat it before."

She takes a microscopic bite.

"More." I point at her.

"I'm not hungry." She sets it on her thigh.

"Please, for me?" I plead with her with my eyes. "Celebration licorice for my kiss with Kian?"

"What the hell? So random. Why do you care if she eats it?" Lily is eyeing me like I'm a nasty dictator.

I sigh. I've had it with Melissa's not eating crap. "She's anorexic and Mandy and I went through hell with her last year and I'm not doing it again, or I'm marching up to your parents and telling them, so they take you to the doctor," I blurt since there's no ignoring all the elephants in the room anymore, not among us friends.

Melissa's mouth goes to the shape of an O and her eyes flare angry at me.

Lily's eyes go wide, and she looks worried again. Lily keeps surprising me. I never expected her to be so caring. I'm legit ashamed of all my past thoughts of her.

"Liss, you want to help me. Well, I want to help you, too." I load my gaze with compassion as she meets my eyes.

Melissa is trembling, then bursts into tears. "I can't go to size three."

"Shut the fuck up right now." Mandy reaches over and slaps Melissa's thigh. "If you're fat, what the hell am I? A fucking hippo? Come on, Liss. Be real."

"Right, for the love of—I'm a four and I don't feel like I'm fat." Lily looks down at her flat stomach.

Melissa stops balling and looks sheepish. "You're right. I'm sorry. Neither of you are fat at all. None of you are. I'm being stupid."

"Yeah, Liss, I'm a size six, the biggest of y'all, so am I a giant fat cow, then?" I raise an eyebrow at her and give her an intense accusatory glare.

"No. Not at all. You're just very curvy, hourglass-ish-y, Ash. Not fat."

I huff, scoff, and throw my hands in the air. "Yeah, well you're making me feel damn fat right now. We've been through this at least a hundred times. I know you freaked out last year when you went from size one to two; don't do that again on your way to size three." I glare at her. "You're growing. That's normal. And, you don't have to be perfect. Why is thin perfect anyway? It's not. Get that out of your head right now. I know your parents push perfection on you, but seriously, you don't have to go along with it anymore. Liam is clearly infatuated with you just the way you are right now and I'm pretty sure he won't care if you're a size three."

"Or more," Mandy states emphatically.

"I know. I'm sorry. I get all that now. But what if I gain weight and he loses interest?" She throws the licorice on the pink rug.

"And you all call *me* a dunce," I say with a roll of my eyes.

"Then he's the wrong guy for you. But, hey, you don't know Liam like I do. He's not like that." Lily shakes her head. "I guarantee it."

Melissa sighs as hope fills her eyes. "Really?"

"Really." Lily hops up. "Let's stop talking about the boys and go join them. And trust me, you will see how Liam is with time. I think you already can see he's not like everyone thinks he is."

"Right, I know what you mean." Melissa smiles a genuine smile. "He's not like I thought he was. I thought he was a total bad boy. Well, he is a bad boy, but in a good way." She blushes as she smirks. "He's so amazing."

I grin at her and rub her back. Yeah, I have to agree. "Bad boys who aren't bad in a mean way are very sexy." We all make our way to the door of the room. "Good girl meeting," I say before Lily opens the door. "Thanks for all your support. It means a lot to me. I have the best friends in the world."

"Yep," Mandy says as she rubs my back. "Here for you. Always. Forever."

"For sure, I'm there," Melissa says, nodding her emphasis as she touches my arm.

"Right. I'm there for you whenever you need me. Just ask." Lily opens the door. "And thanks for including me in this. It was a really great talk."

I nod and give her a little hug. She's not at all like I thought she was. "Thanks, you're all awesome friends. And you, too, Lily."

She beams a happy smile my way. "Same," she says in her little happy voice.

I carry the licorice bag out with me to the living room, planning to offer a piece to Kian.

He's on the couch. I catch his eyes in a glance and start on a direct path towards him. He grins, his gorgeous eyes welcoming me to sit next to him on the couch. I slide in beside him and hold up the bag of licorice. He grabs it, his eyes are lit, a little wild, and from what I'm seeing in them, the girls are totally right. I want to scream with joy as I let him pull me to him, our sides are fully in contact and it sends massive shivers through me. I snuggle into him as he chomps a bite of licorice, then flashes me his amazing giant smile just before he takes another bite. He smells delish as I nuzzle against his chest, like a mix between something citrus and the dish soap from the kitchen, with a splash of strawberry licorice. Yum. I can't help it, I smile like a lovesick fool.

Chapter Eighteen

"Let's play Truth Licorice," Lily says as she plants herself on Lucas's lap where he's relaxing on the recliner. He goes "oof" as she sits, then grins. "We play this at cheerleader camp. It helps people get to know each other better."

"Okay," Mandy says. "I'm in. How do we play?" She settles herself on the floor and pulls a big blue blanket around her waist, tucking it under her long, outstretched legs.

"We pass the bag around and as we each eat a licorice piece, we have to tell a truth about ourselves, or many things—you get to pick. First round is something good or positive, or something we like. The next round is something we hate or something bad. Then it alternates until the whole bag is gone."

Melissa gasps. "I can't eat that much licorice! That's a huge family-sized bag."

"I'll eat yours, too," Liam says with a grin. "But have a few, I really like licorice breath."

Her cheeks go flaming red as she smirks. She manages, "Got it."

"Everyone in?" Lily asks.

All nod. All are in.

"Okay. I'll start. And it can be as simple as 'I like steak', or as naughty as you want." She shoots Lucas a look. "Within reason." She raises an eyebrow that seems to say *behave*.

"I might need a drink for this game," I say with a scoff.

"Ash, that's the best part. Since no one is asking you questions, you get to decide what to say. and you can pick things that don't embarrass you." She takes out a licorice, takes a chomp, chews as she thinks. "I like marshmallows and chocolate. I love it when I'm

180

up here at the lake with Lucas and his family and we roast marshmallows with his sisters." She stops and chews some more. "They love to eat the s'mores in pieces, too, like not as a sandwich, just like me." She scrunches up her shoulders and her nose which makes her super cute. She takes another bite and chews, then says, "I love Lucas, and his family, too. I couldn't have been luckier than when he came into my life." She pops the rest of the licorice stick into her mouth. Lucas wraps his arms around her waist in a hug and nuzzles his face into her hair hanging down her back. Her face falls into an expression of sheer pleasure. She just sparkles.

"Need a room?" Mandy asks with a smirk.

"Stop." Lily smiles at Mandy with teasing eyes. "We're good. We're playing Truth Licorice...we're not going anywhere. It's your turn."

Mandy grabs a licorice and takes a bite while she chews for about twenty seconds. "So, some of you already know this, but I'm bi. I'm fine with it. I've known since I was, like, thirteen. I've dated both boys and girls and I'm not a freak." She takes another bite of her licorice. "I love to play basketball, and I love my friends. And that's it for me for this round."

I nod at her. I'm proud of her for not being ashamed of who she is.

She hands the bag to Melissa, who takes a licorice piece out and stares at it, lays the bag on her lap. "Okay. Truth. Right. So, this will end positive, but not start that way." She gives a big sigh. "I don't really want to eat this. Like at all. But I will eat one for Liam, because he likes licorice breath." She shoots him a glance with a shy tiny smile. "I do like licorice, but I can't seem to easily eat it, because I lean a bit towards the anorexic side of things, and it's been a struggle for me since middle school." She takes a bite of the licorice with a sheepish look on her face. She chews slowly and deliberately as she stares at the rest if it in her hand. "But I'm better because of Ashley and Mandy. They help me ground myself and not get lost in it, so I don't spiral down into not eating enough to function." She takes another bite. "I've had really bad days and really good days since they sat me down for their intervention. I'm so thankful for my friends and I'm in a better place because of them. And that's my positive thing." She smiles.

"Always there for you, Liss," I say with a nod.

Liam rubs her arms. "I'll help you, too."

She smiles at him and her eyes fill with a few tears. "I'm not a freak, either. At least I don't think so anymore."

"No, you aren't a freak." Liam grabs the bag of licorice and slides one out, takes a bite and chews it up. "I'm Liam. I feel like I'm in an AA meeting." Everyone chuckles as he smirks a silly grin. "And I'm in a band, that's my good thing. Other things I love... I love to kiss, and I do love licorice breath, so I'd eat this whole damn bag if you all let me." He passes the bag to Kian with a grin. He pulls it back when Kian reaches for it two times, then passes to him.

"Jackass," Kian says as he swipes it from Liam. "My turn, give me that damn bag." He takes out a licorice and begins to chuckle as a little mischievous grin plays onto his face, his eyes light up. "I really like cheesy chips, and pizza dough, especially when it involves a certain hot mega sexy girl, who shall remain a secret from you all." My heart does a leap inside my chest as chuckles sprout up across my friends. He takes a ginormous bite of licorice as my cheeks flare bright red. I jab my elbow into his ribs. "Ow!" he says with a mock hurt face, but then turns his face serious. "This hot girl is in my science class, and I've watched her walk around the room for months now, but I don't think she ever noticed my eyes on her because every time I looked at her, she'd shoot her eyes to the ground to avoid me." He takes another bite of the licorice piece and chews while he lifts my chin and holds my gaze, smiling while he chews. When he's done chewing, he says, "But now she's not looking away and it fucking rocks."

Lily squeals, then says in a soft voice, "Aww. Wow. That was beautiful, Kian. You're giving me weepy eyes over here."

"Melting," coos Melissa.

My heart might explode into five billion flaming pieces. I hold his gaze as a slow grin spreads across my face. I seriously want to hop up, straddle him and kiss him hard and long and juicy, but I'm not so much into PDA, plus, my face is already flushed and if I did that, it would get worse. Geez, is it hot in here or what?

"Wow," is all I can manage to say, fighting every urge in my whole body to grab him, and plant my lips on his. He's still holding my chin and maintaining my eye-lock. I'm seriously speechless. He's been crushing on me, and I had no idea. Like none; zero. Am I really that oblivious? I always thought he looked at me because he felt my eyes on him, like I was always stare-stalking him whenever he was in the classroom, the hallway, the lunchroom. My eyes never left him during his games. So I figured he sometimes looked back only as an automatic response, nothing more.

He hands me the bag of licorice and I hold my breath. How the heck do I top what he just said? I take out a licorice, trying to control my hand from shaking too much.

"I was going to say I like pizza and pancakes, but I can't follow that up with simple dinner and breakfast foods." I smirk, take a bite of the licorice as there are a spatter of laughs in the room. Kian glances down at me and I hold his gaze as I chew, then my confidence solidifies somehow and I speak, "Okay. Truth. I've been crushing on this guy, this amazing guy, who's a total sports star at school. He's mega hot, mega popular. He's really funny, like real legit comedian funny, and way out of my league. Yeah, for, like, for about," I gulp, giving a pained look, "like, a year." I glance at Kian, ready to wince if he frowns from my confession. I remain silent and hold my breath and let that sink in as he grins, and nods. I allow the breath out...he's smiling...oh thank goodness, he doesn't think I'm a freak show. "And he's the best damn cook the world has seen, which is awesome considering he's a big, strong, kind-hearted, generous, and sexy as fuck...man."

Kian blushes and my heart zings. He shakes his head as if he can't believe what I just said. "Whew. I mean. Hell yeah, I always caught you staring at me, I think that's how I noticed you in the first place."

My insides swirl into a flurry of hormones. Oh, that grin of his does things to me.

I let a forced breath out of my nose. "Zip it, chump, your turn is up. This is my turn. I'm not done." I tease him with my eyes. He gives me a fake shocked face that melts into a giant grin. I turn my gaze away from him as I continue, "I was scared to look at this guy in the eyes for more than a second because he's the most amazing person I've ever seen. He's smoking hot. Yes, I'm saying it again because it's so true," I gush as my cheeks flare redder. I seriously have no clue how I'm saying all this to a room full of people. "He's way more popular than little old shy me, he's basically the star of our school. I never expected him to notice me because I'm no one and he's everything."

"Hey. That's not true. You were going good until that last part," Kian says, frowning as he turns his body towards me. He grabs my face with his big hands completely covering my cheeks. He guides my face towards his before he speaks, "Don't you ever say that again. You're everything. And more." He plants his full lips on mine in a peck kiss. It's sweet, his lips are soft, gentle and he manages to make it the sexiest thing ever.

I could almost cry.

"Swoon," Lily says. "Aw, this is just the best, you guys."

"I know, right?" Melissa says. "So highly satisfying."

"Effing stellar," Mandy chimes in.

I hold Kian's gaze. That was probably the most amazing moment of my entire life and I want to savor it. I cannot believe this is really happening. He pulls me to him. I snuggle into his rock hard chest. Being this close to him is like being in a hot tub; I feel all squishy and warm, yet on fire all at once.

"Toss me that bag, bro. You two keep going doing your own thing." Lucas holds his hand up and Kian tosses it to him like a football. About four licorice pieces fall out as he catches it. "Bonus." He takes all four and holds them together and takes a big bite of all of them at once.

"No fair, I want a bonus," Kian complains.

Lucas chomps obnoxiously as he smirks at Kian. "Too late. Okay. I love Lily and I love to eat. Lily."

Kian, Liam, and Mandy laugh. I just shake my head and Melissa's eyes widen.

Lily smacks him in the chest. "Keep it clean, please, Mr. Potty Mouth."

"What? It's your turn, that's all I meant," he smirks at his own joke.

"Right, that's exactly what you meant, my ass." She rolls her eyes.

Kian cracks up. Liam smirks.

Boys.

Laughing through his words, Lucas says, "I love that, too." She smacks him twice in a row on his chest and then gives him a playful glare. "Okay, okay. I love to eat *food*," Lucas corrects, trying not to laugh as he says it. He shoves more licorice in his mouth as he grins, shrugs, while still chewing he asks, "This is censored truth, then?"

Kian chuckles. "Nope."

"Okay, no, it's not censored. But remember us girls? Yeah, we're here." Lily rolls her eyes as she pulls out a licorice and takes a bite. After she's done chewing, she says, "My turn. Now a round of something we hate or something negative in our life we wish would change. I hate olives and mean boys. I hate math and friends who betray you." A sad expression rests on her face. "And I hate that we have to leave this cabin soon because I'm having so much fun with you all, and I'm so bummed we will probably never get to do this again."

"I know, right? But we could hang out," Mandy suggests. "We could party."

Lily nods. "Right. True. That makes me feel better."

Lily passes the bag to Mandy. She takes one out and gnaws on it. "I hate being an only child. I hate not having my mom in my life. I hate mean boys, too. And mean girls." She gnaws on her licorice as she thinks. "I hate that grandmas die, and I hate the taste of capers."

"I'm so sorry," Melissa says with a frown. "Death sucks."

"Thank you. Everyone has to die someday, right?" Mandy stares at the ground. "Which sucks."

I shoot her an *I'm sorry look* when she raises her eyes up. She misses her grandma dearly. Her loss is pretty recent and still so raw for her.

"So sorry, Mandy," Lily says with sympathy in her eyes.

"Yeah, death sucks." Liam nods.

Melissa takes the bag as Mandy offers it. She pulls out a piece and hands it to Liam, who smiles his thanks to her then takes a big bite. She hands him the whole bag, too. "I hate it when my parents push me so hard to do everything right. It's like it's some big sin with them to screw up. I hate the pressure they put on me to get straight A's all the time, to be a kickass soccer player—though I do love soccer, but I hate it when my parents are pushing me to try to get a scholarship, especially when I already have a college fund. They just refuse to accept anything less than the absolute best out of me, all the dang time." She runs her hand through her lovely blond locks. "It's just so much pressure, you know? And like, there's already so much pressure out there to be the best, I just don't need them ramming it down my throat all the time, too." She pauses. "And I hate how they don't treat me like an adult, even though I technically am one."

"Yeah, I so get that." Kian looks at her with a pained expression. "Parents pushing you to be the best in sports, I mean." He sighs. "I've got that shit, too. With my dad, that is. And them lording over me still like I can't make my own decisions."

She nods. "It's like if I don't try hard enough, or they think I don't try hard enough, they berate me. It's like in everything I do, they have to tell me how I could have done it better. It's never good enough. They've turned me into a goody-two-shoes perfectionist and I'm trying to not be that all the time, because I hate it." She sighs. "And all the while I'm trying to move into being my own person, only they won't let me."

"I can help you be a naughty. Break that image," Liam offers, swinging his licorice back and forth with a lewd look. "And it would be my extreme pleasure to do so."

Melissa looks him in the eyes as she blushes, hard. He smirks then chuckles.

She giggles. "Oh, I have like zero doubts about your ability to do that. You already started."

He gives her thigh a rub as she holds his gaze solid. Wowza, hot sparks flying off those two, or what?

Liam finishes Melissa's licorice piece and grabs another from the bag. "Okay. It's me again. I hate my dad. I hate how he drinks way too fucking much every damn day. I hate when he yells at me," he says with a snort. "Fucker is either ignoring me or yelling at me. And, I hate cooking and I hate school, because it's so damn boring."

Before Liam passes the bag to Kian, he takes another couple licorice pieces. "I need a bonus, too."

"I'm taking a bonus, too, then, ya hog." Kian takes out three and starts to mow them down. After, like, thirty seconds of chewing his mouth is clear, he says, "I hate my dad too, when he pushes me so hard to be the best. I hate when he screams at me in my games and yells at me to score, and all my teammates hear it, plus the whole damn crowd." He frowns. "And I really hate when he nails me to the wall afterwards telling me everything I fucked up, as if I don't already know it." He snorts, takes another bite, and gnashes it between his teeth. He growls as he chews. Then he says, "And I really fucking hate it when he does it in front of the whole team." He sighs. "I'm so ready for college to get away from him."

"I'm so sorry, Kian. That's so wrong." I rub his hand of the arm that is around my shoulders.

"Yeah, he's an asshat sometimes. I mean, I know he loves me and all, but he's such a hardass to me all the time about being the best player in every damn sport I play." He actually looks upset now, and it's a look I've never seen on him before. "It really sucks. It's like I'm supposed to be this mega athlete robot with like zero fuck-ups ever. Which is totally impossible." He looks exasperated. "I'm a fucking human."

"I hate that look on your face and I wish you never had to have it." I gaze up into his eyes. I'm afraid to touch his cheek, but I do it anyway.

His face immediately softens to my touch as he gives me a genuine smile. The Kian I know returns with his jovial eyes.

I take a licorice when he offers the open bag to me. "I hate being shy. I hate when I feel worthless and low. I hate people who are mean to animals and children and weak people, and old people. Anyone vulnerable. It makes me want to cry. I hate that people are hungry and can't get enough food in this world." I chew a bite of licorice as I consider my next confession. "I hate the smell of cooked cauliflower and going to the doctor." I smirk. "And the dentist." Then I eat the rest of my licorice stick.

Kian chucks the bag to Lucas again. A few licorice pieces come halfway out as Lucas catches it. He pulls them out with a smile and an appreciative nod. "I hate running out of licorice because you dumbfuckers took too many bonuses, so we don't have enough for another round of this." He smirks as he waves the licorice bag around, then his face gets serious. "I hate racism and people who pretend to not be racist, but they really are. I hate school, too, but it gives me football, so I guess it doesn't fully count." He takes a bite of licorice and chews as he thinks. "I hate dicks who hurt women. I hate abusers. I hate Brussel sprouts and broccoli and most green foods." He smirks. "And I hate it when Lily gets mad at me."

"Good one!" Lily nods. "I'd like that one on the top of your hate list, please, not at the end." She smirks. She holds up the licorice bag that has only like three left in it. "Good game everyone. I feel like I know everyone more now." She grins, seeming proud of herself for suggesting this game. "Maybe we should make some lunch?" Lily cocks her head to the side.

"Yes, I'm starving," Lucas says as he's finishing up his last licorice.

"Right, starving." Lily shakes her head at him.

"What? I am. I've only had a tiny bit of licorice since breakfast." He raises his hands.

"Yep, me too," Kian says.

"I could eat." Liam rubs Melissa's back.

"I'll make it this time," Melissa offers.

I hop up. "I'll help," I say.

Chapter Nineteen

We head over to the kitchen, and I give Melissa a side hug.

"This is fun, huh?" she asks with a grin. "Being at this cabin with all of us."

"It really is. It's been like perfect for us being here all together. Never in a million years would I have guessed I'd end up with Kian and you'd end up with Liam from being stuck in a snowstorm." I shake my head. "It's seriously unbelievable."

She nods. "Yeah, major, of like freaking epic proportions."

We grin at each other.

"It's so good, though. Delicious." I put my hand on my chest and sigh. "I'm so damn happy. I just can't believe it's happening."

"What's delicious? Lunch?" Kian comes into the kitchen.

I turn around. Oh no! Did he hear me?

"She said you're delicious, Kian." Mandy is sitting on the bar stool at the tall kitchen island.

He barks a laugh and beams a smile at me.

"Mandy!" I scream. My face goes bright red.

Melissa scoffs. "What? It's true."

Kian grins even bigger. "Seriously? You think I'm delicious?"

I cover my face with my hands, peek at him through my open fingers. "I oughta smack you, Mandy. Geez!" I complain. "Really? Friend?"

"What? He already knows you like him. So, what if he knows you think he's delicious, too." She crosses her arms across her chest as she smirks.

"What's delicious? I'm famished," Lucas says.

"Oh, good gawd," I say as I whip around and march into the pantry. "Does everyone have to know this?" I might just die right here.

Mandy is in full tease mode. "Anything delicious in there, Ash? Maybe Kian can go stand in there."

There's laughter.

I stomp my foot. "Mandy you better shut up right now."

"I'm here," Kian says with a smile as he takes a step into the pantry, the very small pantry, that would barely fit the two of us if we were to shut the door. "I like being called delicious." He's still grinning and I'm still blushing.

I turn around and our fronts touch. I gaze up into his eyes and they are full of spectacular teasing, which both thrills me and cheeses me off. I want to swat his chest, but I don't.

"Anything delicious in here to eat?" he asks me with an eyebrow raised.

"Yes," I say with flirty eyes as my heart races. "Lots of things." What is Mandy doing to me? I'll just have to kill her. Imagine how she'd feel if I embarrassed her like this?

"Like you?"

I smirk up at him, give him a half smile, put my hands on my hips. I suppress the urge to tap my toe.

He reaches over my head for something, but his eyes never leave mine. "How about spaghetti?" He brings the box into my line of sight as he loses the battle to suppress his smirk.

"Perfect," I say almost breathless. My heart is trucking like five thousand miles a minute being this close to him, with us touching along our fronts. My chest is fully touching him, like my boobs are pressed to him, and I couldn't move even if I wanted to because he's totally blocking the door. Without taking his eyes off mine, he grabs for something to my right. He presents a large jar of red sauce into my peripheral vision.

"Do you think spaghetti is delicious?" He grins this sexy grin, it just begs to be kissed. "We could all eat that."

"Yes, very." *Heart...slow down*, I command. I want to kiss him so bad I can taste it, but everyone knows we're crammed in here and they're waiting for us, listening to our every word. "We should make it," I say. I flinch. Geez, that didn't come out quite right. I silently laugh as my eyes go big and I fail to suppress my grin. A tiny grunt slips out of me so roll my eyes. "That...didn't come out the way I..."

Kian chuckles and takes a step back. He tries not to grin too hard at me as I blush fifty shades of red. *Awk*!

He gives me a little more room so I take it and plow past him out of the pantry. I need out of this tiny space with him. I go about business, digging in the cupboard for a pot. I feel his eyes on my ass as I'm bending down, peering into the cabinets for too long because I can't seem to find the big pot. Am I always going to blush when he gives me attention? Damn, I certainly hope not. Get over it, Ashley!

"Oh, spaghetti, great meal idea for a big group. I know we have meatballs and garlic bread at my cabin in the freezer. Liam and I could go get them." Melissa's face lights up. "Oh Liam, want run next door with me?"

"You gonna be back in the next half hour?" I tease her.

"Yes, of course, we will! We will just go grab it and come right back." She nods, playing innocent.

"Right, I'm timing you." I glance at the clock.

"Oh, stop," she pleads.

Mandy is looking attentive, sitting with her chin resting on her hands, her elbows on the counter. She bats her dark eyes at me, a completely guilt-free look on her face. "They might find something delicious, too, and stay there."

"Payback can be a real bitch, ya know that, right Mandy?" I glare at her.

"Bring it, baby," she smirks. "I can burn you harder than you burn me any and every day." She giggles. "You're just so fun to tease, Ash."

She's not wrong about being better at payback than me, but damnit, I will get her back.

Kian beams at me amused as he opens the pasta box. Clearly, he agrees with Mandy as his eyes twinkle at me. Oh, gosh, I just want to grab him; my fingers just ache to do it. I yearn to touch his thick biceps. His shoulders look amazing today in his tight dark blue tight t-shirt, but I know I can't just go feel him up in the kitchen. I swallow my urge to maul him and try to breathe normally.

"What?" I demand.

"Oh...I'm outta here, you two are making eyes at each other something fierce. I'm gone before you two flat out make out on the counter." She smacks the countertop with her palms, making me jump. "And I thought you two kissing would make it better, but you two are worse now than before." Mandy slips off the chair and glances at me. She grins, raises her eyebrows in a dare. She covers her mouth with her hand in mock *my bad*.

I'm fuming. My fists are clenched, my muscles are tight, tensing harder by the second, snarling into knots like right before a math test. My cheeks are so red. "You are toast, Mandy. Dead toast."

"Toast was never alive." She snickers as she crosses the room heading towards the door, calling out to Lilly, "Lily, want to go have a smoke?"

"Yeah, sure, just a minute. I've got to pee."

"I didn't know toast could be dead," Kian says with teasing eyes.

Oh, everyone is making me so mad! I ignore him and turn away to let my cheeks cool down. I open the jar of sauce and dump the whole thing into the large black pot, then add two more, topping it off with the lid. The front door slams shut as Liam, Melissa, Mandy, and Lily go outside. When I turn around, Kian is leaning against the counter, arms folded across his massive chest. Geez is he hot, and...we're alone. He is beyond drool-worthy. He rakes a hand through this hair, then places his hands on the counter on either side of him. He tips his head playfully while grinning.

"You hear that? We're finally alone. Need any climbing practice?" He smirks and tries not to laugh but fails and does.

"Aw, shit!" I say. I bite my lip, raise my eyebrows. "Maybe." Did I really just say that?

He takes a step towards me and scoops me up, his hands go under my thighs, and I wrap my legs around him, straddling his middle. He's so swift it takes my breath away. I feel so woozy. I might faint. But I don't get the chance. Our mouths smash into each other and I moan way louder than I mean to as we kiss deeply. He slides his tongue along mine, and he makes a yummy sound. My arousal is churning up fast into a gnarly ball of fire.

He pulls back and murmurs into my ear, "I think you're the delicious one here. Nothing better in this whole kitchen." He sets me on the counter. I hope I'm not sitting on the jelly splat I saw earlier, but who the frick cares, anyway? Kian's *kissing* me.

His mouth lines up with mine again in a rush, and I smile. He smiles, too, and we both chuckle as our lips touch.

"Mmmm..." he moans, then deepens our kiss. "Your laugh and your kiss. Now that's what I like."

I pull back. Stare deep into his eyes.

"Okay, we're both delicious," I whisper. "And we need to stop just saying it."

"Agreed."

His mouth is on mine again so fast I gasp. I rub my hands over his broad muscular shoulders, enjoying finally touching him, running my hands down his thick biceps. I can't believe I get to finally touch him. His hands slide up my back and into my hair as his mouth moves to my neck. I lean my head back and moan.

"Oh, my," I say like a sigh. He kisses down my neck to my collarbone and I know I will explode into a ravenously hungry beast in like three seconds if I don't pull myself away, but I can't seem to get up enough willpower to do it, so I stay and savor him instead, loving every second of his hot wet mouth on me. He slides me off the counter and I wrap my legs around his middle again, as if claiming him. His hands go to my butt to hold me in place. Gosh, his hands feel amazing there. He lets out this hot primal groan that grabs me hard, does things to me I can't even explain, but that I love.

The front door bursts open and I try to struggle to the ground. He lowers me quickly so I can stand. We are both panting, our expressions, and our heavy breathing, giving away what we've been doing.

The kitchen is visible from the door, so I'm pretty sure Melissa and Liam saw us. Liam releases a low whistle.

"We're back," Melissa announces, clearly trying not to embarrass us.

I give Kian a smile, and bite my lip to keep me from laughing. My eyes don't leave his as I say, "Didn't think you two would be so fast. You find it all, Melissa?"

I tear my eyes from Kian.

"Yes, and some frozen cookie dough, too." She makes her way across the living room with it all loaded in her arms.

Kissing Kian was so hot, I need to go outside for a second, or get into a cold shower. I'll go to the brutally cold garage; that won't be as obvious. I need some of this heat stripped off me, so I don't fly into a frenzy and attack Kian again. "I'll get some pop from the garage fridge." I need a task.

"I'll help," Kian says.

Yeah, that's not going to cool me off. Not one damn bit. I whip around and head towards the garage, he follows me fast like a flash. He's so swift. My heart pounds because I know what will happen once we're in that garage alone together, and I'm going to totally lose it.

Liam is clearly in the know because his smirk is pretty strong as we rush past.

Once we're in the garage, without shoes on or jackets, we pad across the frigid concrete to the other side near the car. Kian scoops me up, as easy as he snatches a football off the ground and lays me across the car hood. His body is on me in a heartbeat. His hungry mouth finds mine and we kiss like we might die if we don't. The garage is so cold it feels like we're kissing in a freezer, and the car hood is so frigid, I feel like I'm lying on a frozen lake. I shiver which gets him to lean into me more as he wraps his arms around me and lifts my back into an arch as we kiss.

Kissing him, I can barely breathe, but, yet I want it...and damn, he really is so very yummy. He rolls off me, lays next to me on his back closer to the windshield, and I move to hop on him, straddling his pelvis. I gasp as I sit on him, and he grins. Oh. My. God.

"Yeah, I have no secrets," he says breathless.

I crash down onto him, allowing our mouths to meet again. It's not slow or gentle, it's wild, out of control as we carve our tongues into each other's mouths. I feel like someone other than myself, but I like her, and I want more of her. I'm hungry for it. But, if this doesn't stop soon, I'm afraid we'll go too far, but, still, I can't seem stop myself, it's so utterly amazing. I'm rocking myself on him and I need it.

The garage door starts to open, saving us from ourselves, and a blast of cold biting wind chases Mandy and Lily into the garage.

"Wow," Mandy says when she sees me on top of Kian. "That's hot."

I hop off Kian as if I got burned, and he scrambles to sit up. They came in just in time. I needed that arctic blast to get me to stop. Holy hell, that was impossible to end, I don't think I could have done it.

I meet Kian's knowing gaze. When we kiss, it lights me on fire and makes me even hungrier for him than I was before we started. I run my hand over my forehead and into my hair. I'm at a loss for words.

I swallow my desire and slide off the car, leaving Kian, which goes against everything I want to do. I head over to the fridge and grab several cans of soda pop, plop them in Mandy's open arms, then grab some more, tucking them into the crook of my left arm. They're so cold against my side. But I needed that cold like I need air. I'm super grateful for the task to distract myself from my urge to race right back over to Kian.

"I'll get the door," Lily says, with a little knowing smile on her face.

I nod, giving her the same smile back. "Thanks." I turn back to glance at Kian. He's still on the car, his right knee is bent, and his elbow is propped on his knee, his forehead pressed to his palm.

Oh, dang. "You okay, Kian?" I ask cautiously.

He looks up at me with a sexy grin that makes me want to chuck the pop at the ground and charge him, but I don't because that would be weird with Mandy and Lily watching. He nods. "Yeah, I just need a minute. I'll be right in." His voice sounds strained like he's lifting a giant barbell.

"Shit, Ash, what did you do to that poor boy?" Mandy asks, mocking me with a knowing grin as she enters the cabin.

"Don't you even start, Mandy. Don't even," I warn as I follow her through the doorway. "You're on my shit-list right now, missy."

When the door shuts, she spins around. "I love this for you, Ash. Plus, it makes you even more teaseable."

Ugh! I want to bitch-slap her right fricking now. "So glad I can entertain you," I say sarcastically. "You live to embarrass me, don't you?"

She snickers. "Maybe." She sighs. "I love you, ya know."

I roll my eyes at her, shaking my head. "Yeah, yeah. Love you, too."

Chapter Twenty

Melissa is piling the garlic bread slices into a large serving bowl. Her face is so relaxed. It's doing her some good to be away from her parents for a few days. Again, I'm blessing the repair guy being too busy to come right away. It's been a gift for us all. Melissa's eyes are bright as she says, "I still can't believe we have all these days off of school for cold temps. It's crazy. My mom said this has never happened before in the state of Minnesota where school was closed for four days off in a row due to the cold." Melissa smiles. "Such great timing for all of us to be able to do this, though. And we're lucky my parents need us to stay up here to let the repairman in."

"Yeah, it was like the perfect storm...us here for the weekend, me forgetting my phone, us running out of gas—way to be irresponsible for once, Liss. Damn good timing," I giggle at her as she smiles at me. I love reminiscing about the cabin while we're still in it. "Then your cabin's heat going out, these guys all coming up here. It all aligned, like cosmic fate." I scoop out a noodle from the pot and drop it into the colander to cool.

Kian comes into the kitchen. He looks fine now, calm, normal. Good, he has recovered. I totally agree, that was a tough one to cool down from for me, too. I hold the noodle to his lips. "Taste and see if it's done."

He slurps it into his mouth with a grin and chews.

I smirk as he makes a silly face.

"I like you feeding me."

"Seem done to you?" I ask, loving that he said that.

"Yep. Perfect." He and I exchange glances. His eyes tell me what we will do later. I need to control myself. This is going to be really hard. I don't really want to go far with him, but, yet I do. I'm not going to, though, but it's going to be like running a marathon without any training trying to keep myself from not doing it. Just breathe...just breathe slow. Move slow. Be a turtle, Ash. Be. A. Sloth.

Melissa grabs the plates and lays them out on the table. We're doing buffet style. She's arranging things in prep as I grab the big pot of noodles and drain it. Once I've dumped them in the colander and set the pot down on the counter, I feel Kian come up behind me. His hand slides up my right hip which sends chills through my whole pelvis. Geez, he's a horny fiend! And a match for me.

I jerk my body as he squeezes me, and say way too loudly, "Oh, dear God!"

He rips his hand off me. "Oops, sorry," he whispers. "Didn't mean to make you yell."

"What? What's wrong?" Melissa whips around with alarm on her face.

"Nothing. Umm...nothing at all." I stifle a chuckle as I widen my eyes at Kian. I whisper, "Stop or I'll be forced to pounce on you."

He opens his arms, inviting me; his eyes tell me, "have at it". I shake my head as I smirk at him. *Oiya*, I never thought it could hurt so bad to get hot and bothered, but it's wrecking me something fierce being this close to Kian, him touching me, but not acting on it.

"I'm still waiting for you to climb me," he teases in a soft husky whisper at my ear.

I smack his arm, trying to calm the chills he just gave me. Comments like that are not helping, either. I make shooing motions with my hands. "You need to get out of here before I lose it."

He grins at me and turns, goes over to grab a plate. "Please, please, please lose it," he begs with a tease flickering in his eyes.

I sigh as I try to cool myself down. "Hey all, let's eat," I announce, needing a distraction. I pour the noodles back into the pot and replace the lid to keep them hot. I carry it to the table and place it on a pad, and place a tongs next to the pot for serving.

"Smells amazing," Liam says.

Everyone loads their plates with spaghetti, meatballs, garlic bread, and even Melissa takes a good helping, which is impressive considering her massive aversion to all things carb.

"So, what will we do for our last evening here?" Lily asks. Her hair is in a thick side braid that runs down the front of her, she looks beautiful as usual. She touches her braid as she talks. "We have some games left to play." She smiles at me.

She really is such a sweet person. I cringe remembering how I used to judge her relentlessly and constantly label her as a mean stuck up bitch. I smile back. She's not a mean bitch at all, quite the opposite in fact, which continues to amaze me. "Yep, I'm in. It'll be fun. We've gotta reach our goal and play them all before we have to leave tomorrow. I highly doubt the superintendent will cancel school Friday, too."

"I know, but I so wish he would," Lily says with a sigh. "I'm so ready for college."

"Me, too." I tilt my head to the side. "No doubt about it."

After lunch we play three games before the boys are out, they've had it with games. Lucas heads back for a nap as does Liam. Kian leans back on the couch and watches as all four of us girls play a kids' game we all loved as young kids. I'm sitting on the floor, leaning against his shins, his heels resting against the sides of my butt cheeks. I still can't believe how lucky I am that he and I are becoming something. I want to scream out with joy, but I don't, of course.

I draw the ice cream cone card. "Yes. I used to love it when I got this card as a kid."

Kian leans forward and pokes my sides making me squeal and squirm. "I think that needs to be our next date," he whispers in my ear.

I feel him sniff my hair when he's close. Good thing I washed my hair today. The girls see my facial expression and widening eyes, and they laugh.

"What?" I say with a cross look. Mandy's so pissing me off still.

"Your face is priceless," Mandy says.

"Are you going to stop teasing me or do I have to wallop you?" I send her mean daggers with my eyes.

"Wow, so harsh, Ashie," Kian squeezes his shins against my back. How does even a shin squeeze from him turn me on? Gosh, I'm a freak.

"Well, she's teasing me constantly. She deserves to be bitch-slapped," I say with a huff. I'm half tempted to actually do it, no joke.

"I'd like to see you try, my sweet baby cakes. You wouldn't get very far, I'll tell you that. You know I've got wicked fast moves from basketball." She folds her left hand over her right flexed bicep. "And these." She does work out and she lifts weights enough to have the muscles. I'd want her on my team if I were ever in a group fight. She can throw a punch, I've seen her do it. I've never thrown a punch in my life.

"Yeah, I know." I sigh. "You'd certainly kick my ass."

"Damn straight I would." She's cocky, but accurate.

"I could kick all four of your asses. Like at once," Kian jokes. "But I don't beat girl's asses. So y'all have nothing to worry about. Your asses are safe." His voice is soaked with the smirk I'm sure is on his face, but I'm not looking because I might blush if I do. He said "ass" too many times for me not to, and his heels are still on the sides of mine.

We all laugh.

"Yeah, you're pretty buff, you'd pretty much slay us." Mandy shakes her head. "But I'd go down swinging, just so you know."

"We could always just kick you hard in the nuts to get you to stop." Melissa beams like she's just said the most brilliant thing ever and we all crack up. This is so not a regular Melissa comment. "What? It's true, right?" She raises her hands palms up.

I'm still laughing. "Yes, it's true, Melissa. But I've never heard you say that before. It's rather hilarious coming out of your mouth."

"Yeah, I've got to stop being so stuffy or I'll end up just like my mom." She wrinkles her nose with disgust, then picks a card off the top of the pile and moves her pawn to a red square. "That's something I definitely don't want."

"No, definitely not." I agree. Her mom is the ultimate do-gooder nerd, annoyingly so.

After the game, Kian grabs my hand and drags me to his room. My heart is beating so hard. How am I not going to jump his bones if we are alone together in his room?

"I just want to talk," he declares as he sits on his bed and motions for me to sit too. "I mean...of course I want to do more, but I'm still so angry about what happened to you. This is bothering me so much. Will you please tell me their names? Please?"

At the mention of this, my heart falls. I had been successfully avoiding thinking about this and now he's bringing it all up again. I had been getting excited to lay on his bed and kiss him, but now my heart hurts. Tears spring to my eyes.

"Aw, Ashie, I'm so sorry." He moves over and pulls me into his lap, cuddling me. "I didn't mean to upset you. I'm such a jerk." He rubs my back as I can't seem to stop crying. "I shouldn't have brought this up now."

I gasp. "You know, it was so horrible because they talked about it on purpose, right in front of me at school." I gasp back a sob but fail and it soars out way too loud.

"Ugh," he groans with disgust. "Are you serious?"

I can only nod.

"I want to kill them," Kian snarls. "Please tell me their names. I can make them pay."

I shake my head. I don't try to stop my tears, I just let them flow. I haven't really cried enough about this because I've been shoving it so far down into me, so the tears come fast and furious, and way too damn much. My body shakes with sobs, my nose fills with snot so I can't breathe through it. I do a disgusting sniff. He cradles me, rocks with me, and it feels so amazing.

He coos softly in my ear, "It's going to be okay. I'm here."

I gasp and sob again. The memories of that night flood me and I almost rip myself from Kian because he's a boy, too, and what if he does that to me sometime? I slow and right my thoughts, so I don't start to panic. He's not doing that to me, and he could right now with us alone, but he's not. He's being kind to me. His touch is soft and gentle, not mean, forceful, or invading. He rocks me back and forth slowly, kisses the top of my head so tenderly. My tears are becoming from relief rather than sadness. I feel so safe in his arms. My tears begin to slow down.

"I'm so sorry," he whispers. "I'm a jerk. I shouldn't have brought this up when we were having such a good time. I'm just so furious about it." I feel his muscles tense against me. "This is the only way I know how to help."

"It's okay, Kian. And what you're doing, holding me, giving me the time and space to cry, is helping. I think it was good for me to cry about it. I mean, I've been stopping myself from crying about so much and I think I needed to let myself feel it, so it doesn't eat me up inside." I sniff. "What I'm trying to say is, I think crying about it is helping me. You're helping me."

"Maybe you could talk to a counselor at school about it, too," he suggests.

"No. I can't. Then other adults would find out about it, and I don't want that. It's too embarrassing."

"It's not your fault, it's all on them."

"I know. But it's still super embarrassing."

"I wish you'd go to the police. Or let me deal with them at the very least." His eyes blaze in a fury again.

"Kian, that's exactly why I won't tell you their names. I don't want you to get in trouble for bashing their skulls in. And from the sounds of it, your dad would go ballistic on you if you did, or you'd get thrown off the team for assault and your dad would be majorly pissed at you. I don't want that. I just want to cry about it and then move on." I smile at him. "Okay?"

"I don't think that's the right choice and I don't think it's good for you, either." He strokes my hair in silence, and we stay that way for about five minutes. He plays with my curls, and it feels so amazing. I love it when someone plays with my hair. "Want something to drink?" he asks.

"Yeah, a bottle of water would be great. My throat is scratchy from crying." I slide off his lap and curl into a fetal position on his bed. He places a tissue box next to me and I grab one and blow my nose. My eyes feel so puffy and delicate like raised dinner rolls. Unfortunately, everyone will know I cried.

He leaves the room and my sobs return hard core as I'm suddenly afraid to be alone. The door opens, but I don't look because I'm sure it's Kian returning with my bottle of water.

"Ashie? What the fuck did he do to you?" It's Mandy.

When I open my eyes, she's madder than a herd of bees whose nest has just been smashed by a baseball bat. Her eyes are wild. Before I can react, Kian comes in the room and Mandy pounces on him. She starts wailing her fists on him something fierce, reaching up to scratch his face. She's screaming at him, "You fucker! You fucking bastard! What did you do to her? I'm gonna kill you!" Her right fist smashes into Kian's jaw. He barely moves as she keeps pummeling him with her fist like she's a machine.

He just stands there looking stunned, and takes it, a bottle of water still in each hand.

"Mandy!" I scream. "He didn't do anything to me. He was comforting me." It's like she can't hear me as she's flailing her arms at him totally out of control. I hop off the bed and rush at her.

There is a giant ruckus as Lily and Melissa come blasting into the room. They're yelling at Mandy to stop, but she keeps flailing her arms wildly like fan blades set on high mode. I'm near her and I'm screaming her name but she's in too much of a frenzy to acknowledge me. I scream as loud as I can, "Please, stop Mandy! He wasn't hurting me." I let out a giant sob that ripples through me like a tornado. "You're making this worse!"

Both Lucas and Liam burst into the room and lunge at Mandy, grab her arms, yank her off Kian and they throw her onto the bed. Kian just stands there looking dumbstruck, his jaw looks red and he has scratches down one cheek and his neck.

I'm crying again, cradling my head in my hands, rocking myself back and forth, trying to erase these images of Mandy attacking Kian from my head. I've turned my friends into enemies having an all-out brawl and it's all my fault. I sink to the floor, curl up and pull a soft blanket over my head as I sob.

"Shit! Mandy! What the hell is this?" Lucas asks.

"Man, you okay Kian?" Liam asks. Then, he sternly says, "Don't move, Mandy. Stay there."

I feel someone hug me through the blanket. "It's okay, Ash. It's over now." It's Melissa. She rubs my back through the thick blanket as I cry. "It's alright, Ash," she says to me in a soft sing-song voice. "Shh...it's okay."

"Look at her!" Mandy screams. "He hurt her! She's so upset. Did you see her face? Aw, dammit! I wasn't here to stop it, I couldn't keep her safe." Mandy sounds hysterical. Is she drunk?

I hear Lily's voice say in a calm tone, "Breathe, Mandy. Slow down. She said he wasn't hurting her."

"Aw, shit! Fuck!" Mandy snarls. "Shit..." Then, she spits, "No."

I don't move a muscle.

Another person's hand is on me. "Ash? Is it true? He didn't hurt you?" It's Mandy.

I poke my head out of the blanket. "Yes, it's true, Mandy. He didn't hurt me at all. He was holding me as I cried." I swallow. I can't understand how this happened. "I was screaming at you to stop and you were like a crazy person."

"Oh. I'm so sorry. I messed up big time." She sits on the ground next to me in a hard plop. I follow her gaze as she turns it up to Kian. He's rubbing his jaw, eyes still looking stunned. "Aw, Kian. Damn, I'm so sorry. I've really fucked up here. I saw her like this, and I knew you took her back here. I just wanted to check on her when I saw you come out and she didn't, and then I found her with her eyes all red, she looked so upset, and I assumed you attacked her. I'm so very sorry. I totally suck." She slumps her shoulders. "You can punch me back if you want. I guess I deserve it."

"I don't hit girls," Kian says. "And, actually, I'm really glad you checked on her. You're such a good friend. She needs someone like you watching out for her. I could see how you thought what you did." He rubs his jaw. "You do throw a mean punch though," he says with a grin. How he can manage to smile after that attack is beyond me.

"Ah, man. I'm so sorry," Mandy says again looking so guilty. "I feel like a total douchebag. I'm sorry I didn't trust you. It's just, what she went through, ya know, I don't want that for her again, like ever." Her eyes are so sad, her face sagging, mouth edges turned down. "I'm overprotective of my bestie, I guess."

"Mandy, I really get it. Don't worry," Kian says.

"Open your damn ears next time, will ya?" I flail the words angrily at her. "I tried to get you to hear me, but you were just wild. Why were you so out of control?"

She covers her eyes with her palms. "I'm such a fuckhead." She genuinely looks miserable. "I saw red. I just...you know, I missed out helping last time, and I didn't want that to happen again."

I touch her arm. "Thanks for looking out for me, though, you're a friend. I know you meant well. And last time, you did help me. You got me away before it went too far." I sigh. "But you roughed up Kian's beautiful face, so you suck." I give her a grin so she knows I'm not totally pissed at her.

"But I came too late last time. Stuff happened while I was off having a good time. And I know, I'm so sorry, I wasn't there for you." She hangs her head. "You're right, I was a maniac. Please forgive me."

I nod. "Of course. You were just protecting me, and I appreciate that."

Next, she glances at Kian, then grimaces. "You forgive me?"

"You're already forgiven." Kian gives her a compassionate look. "I'd have done the same thing if I suspected someone hurt her." He smirks. "Hell, I actually admire you for it. Coming after someone built like me so fearlessly to protect your friend. That's admirable."

Mandy grins. "No, with those pipes of yours, you would have done much more damage than I ever could."

He smirks. Nods. "True. That's very true."

"Is everyone okay now?" Lily asks in a little meek voice.

"I'm good, but I look like a freak now." I touch my puffy eyes that feel red and swollen as a ripe garden tomato.

"Don't worry about that, Ash. We're all friends here." Lily gives me her gentle eyes and a small smile.

I smile back. She's right. We are.

Chapter Twenty-one

We're all sitting around the living room sipping on beverages. I'm snuggled into Kian's lap on a single person recliner. Liam and Melissa are cozied up on the couch. Mandy is stretched out on the floor, leaning on a large blue pillow, her shiny dark hair flowing down her toned shoulders, visible only because of her tank top, her sweatshirt balled up by her side. Lucas and Lily are in their usual chair with Lily sprawled across Lucas's lap. Music is playing and we're talking about nothing and everything all at the same time. It's simply perfect.

I'm super satisfied with where things are with Kian right now. I'm totally convinced he's a good guy, a guy I'd want to be my boyfriend, if he'd have me that way. I'm not fully convinced yet that he does, though. This could just be a cabin thing, and it all could go back the way it was once we get home. My heart goes pitter-patter when I glance at him, and his eyes brighten when he smiles at me. He traces my cheek and jawline with his index finger, ending in a graze along my lips—I nuzzle into the sensual touch of his finger. After everything that's happened, I might be daring to hope for some sort of future with Kian.

I'm so super thankful he doesn't hate Mandy after she pummeled him. I couldn't handle my potential boyfriend hating one of my best friends. I curl my finger at him in a repeated motion to get him to lean his ear down closer to me. I whisper, "Thanks for not hating Mandy."

He cocks his head at me. "I don't hate her. She clearly loves you something fierce. Like I said before, I admire her."

"Yeah, she always has stood up for me. Mandy doesn't love lightly." I smirk.

I glance at my friend on the floor. She's so lovely and I can't wait for her to find the right person. I can't wait for her to fall in love with someone who falls right back in love with her, too. As she's talking with Lily about music, her eyes light up and her expression changes rapidly as she speaks with great animation about some song. Their friendship is growing, and I see that familiar fierceness she has for me growing for Lily, too. I mean, they did kiss, that's totally true, but I think their friendship is stronger than that, sort of like her friendship is with me. And Melissa, too.

I whisper to Kian, "She's a good person, she just loves so deep when she does. She thinks of herself as my protector."

"That's not a bad thing," Kian says back in a low voice. "She just needs to let me help protect you, too, because I can't not do it. I want to keep you safe from all harm." He grins. "You're stuck with me, now."

His words give me tingling chills. "I want nothing more than to be stuck with you, Kian."

"I can get you stuck in all kinds of good places," he grins a suggestive grin. "I promise."

I give a short laugh and feel a swirl of desire dance inside my pelvis. "You are naughty, aren't you?" I wonder how much of a bad boy Kian really is under all his goodness.

"You have no idea," he teases.

Maybe not, but I want to know.

I murmur in a hushed tone, "Hmm...I can't wait to find out." I touch his cheek and gently run my finger to his red jaw. "Does it hurt?"

"Yes. I was serious, she throws a mean punch. I'm definitely impressed." He nods towards Mandy.

"Yeah, she lifts weights. She's slim, but tough as steel. She's got herself some hefty muscles."

"Who does?" Mandy asks. *Ack*, dang it, she heard me.

"You do." I glance at her. "I told him you're tough, for a girl."

"For a girl?" She scoffs. "I'm just tough, period. Don't throw 'for a girl' into that. That's crap."

"I just mean you are tougher than me, Melissa, and Lily, 'cause we aren't really what I'd call tough girls." I smile. "I didn't mean it negatively. Plus, you have a fierce drive which makes you a serious force."

"Right. I get it." She nods, looking satisfied with my answer.

"You've got my back, and I appreciate it, Mandy. Remember the time last year when Alex Jenkins grabbed my ass and started grinding into it at that party? That's the last time I saw you go ballistic on a guy for me. He wouldn't let me go and Mandy saw and ripped him off me. Beat the crap out of him."

"I gave him a black eye." She grins rubbing her fist. "Fucker deserved it."

"That was you who gave him that black eye?" Liam looks at her incredulously. "I remember when he came to school with that shiner." He laughs. "He made up some story about getting into a fight with a guy from another school over a girl."

"Nope, it was from me." She flexes her bicep. "I'm a badass when I need to be."

Liam laughs. "I'm going to throw it in his face that he got knocked out by a girl. That's hilarious. The guy is really a dick." He looks at Mandy. "No offense. You are tough."

"Thanks. And yup. I know he is." Mandy nods her head. "He kept bugging Ash after the party, too, so I had to threaten him to blacken his other eye. All I had to do was threaten him and draw up ready for a punch and he left her alone after that." She snorts. "Guy couldn't take a damn hint to save his life."

"Yeah, he was gross. He kept coming up to me at school and he would put his hands on me. We weren't even dating, and he was trying to claim me, grabbing my ass, coming up from behind me and draping his arm over my shoulder in the hallway at school. I kept telling him to leave me alone, but he wouldn't. Guy was a total jerk." I sigh. Shake my head. "He wouldn't take no for an answer until Mandy threatened to pummel him again."

"What an asshat," Kian says, looking very cross.

"Yeah, I went to elementary school with him," Lily says. "He was a jerk kid even back then."

Melissa and Liam are silent. I glance at them. Ah, it's because they're making out, which is so unlike my friend; it's just so shocking to see. I look at Mandy and nod in the direction of our friend majorly sucking face with Liam. Mandy nods with a smirk.

She pumps her fist. "Yes! I know, right? So weird to see her like this." Mandy shakes her head. In a louder voice she asks, "Hey Liss, coming up for some air soon?"

"Wh-what?" she asks all dazed and confused. "Um, yes." She smiles sheepishly. "Give me a drink and I guess I'm suddenly okay with PDA." She blushes, glancing at Liam who grins back.

"Works for me," Liam says as he wraps his arm around Melissa and gives her a squeeze.

She giggles and snuggles into him, laying her hand on his chest, tucking her head under his chin.

"Ah, you are the best, Liss," Liam says into her ear, but loud enough for us all to hear.

"Alright, let's spice up the night. Who's in for a drinking game?" Kian asks.

"I'm in," Lucas calls out. "Pick your poison."

"King's Cup, Avalanche, Up & Down the River?" Kian asks with a hand in the air.

"Let's play Avalanche. That's easy for those who haven't played it before." Lucas stands after Lily gets off his lap.

"Works for me," Liam says.

"I don't know how to play," I say.

"Me neither," says Melissa as she stands and stretches her arms straight up in the air. Liam tickles her armpits when she does. "Hey!" He gives her a devilish grin.

Mandy pipes up, "You know how to play, Ash. It's that game we played at Erica's party where someone yells 'floor' and everyone has to fall to the floor and the last one down has to drink their full cup."

"Oh yeah, I remember that one. I got tanked that night because of it. I was too slow and always distracted so I kept being the last one down." I smirk. "I sucked at it."

Kian raises his eyebrows with a mischievous grin, actually it's almost scandalous in nature, which sends ginormous shivers rippling through me. "Let's get down to it, then," he says. "We can grab dice out of one of those games on the table."

It's no surprise, I do terrible in the game. I'm watching Kian intently. It's going to be a tough night for me trying to keep myself off Kian. Right now, I just want to tackle him to the ground and slam my mouth onto his and go at it. He keeps giving me these passion-filled glances that are firing me up from across the table. We're all standing so we can drop to the floor when it's time. I'm about ready to sit down and stay there; this standing is getting too hard for me. I'm feeling a little wimpy.

I raise my left hand. "I need to be done. I'm waving the white flag." I make my way to the couch and sit beside Melissa. She quit twenty minutes ago.

"Whatcha drinking?" I ask her.

"Pop. I just can't play games like that." She puts her palm on her forehead and lets out a big sigh.

"Yeah, I can for a little while, but I can't for long. Honestly, all I want is to kiss Kian."

"I know, right? I'm missing Liam right now, too, but I want him to have fun playing the game. I keep begging him to sing. He brought his guitar. I'd love to hear him sing." She glances at him and sways like she's swooning to his singing voice.

"Yeah, that would be cool if he did. I agree. He's got an amazing voice."

"Liss, can I talk to you about something?" She nods. "I'm scared that Kian will stifle his desire for me now that he knows what I went through. I don't know how to tell him I don't want him to hold back." I look at her without hiding my fear.

"Just tell him that if he seems to be holding back." She gives me a small smile. "Though, maybe it's good if he does take it slow, so you don't get overwhelmed while you're still healing."

I shrug. "True. I'll have to see how it goes. I don't want him to treat me like I will break though." I scoff. "I'm not going to break." I give her a big grin.

"Uh, no, you won't. You've been waiting for him for a long ass time." She giggles.

I glance back at him, and he notices my direct gaze. I raise my eyebrows at him then return my eyes to Melissa. "Goodness, that boy riles me up. I'm afraid I might go all beast mode on him later."'

Melissa laughs. "I'm pretty sure he wouldn't mind that."

"Uh, no, I'm thinking not."

"Melissa, that boy makes me horny."

"I get it," she blushes, then grins. "Same for me with Liam." She eyes up Liam and sighs. "How did this happen? I feel like the luckiest girl in the world right now." She shakes her head. "How did I land Liam in my life like this?"

"I know, I feel it the same," I say.

Kian yells, "Floor!"

Lily moans. "Oh no, it's me again. You guys are killing me."

"You can quit and go sit with Ash and Melissa," Mandy suggests, giving her an out.

"I might need to, or I might be done for the night and have to go to bed." Lily shrugs.

"Bed?" Lucas asks with interest.

"Not that kind of bed," she says with a laugh. "It'd be a passed-out kind of bedtime."

"Okay, time to quit now," Lucas says and Kian laughs.

"And we're down to four," Liam snickers. "Who will be the champion?"

Lily meanders over to us and plops down in the bean bag that Lucas dragged out to the living room from his bedroom earlier.

"What's happening over here, girls?" She looks rather sleepy.

"We're talking about boys." I grab a handful of potato chips from the bowl on the table.

"Ooh. My favorite topic." She sets her cup on the coffee table and falls back onto the bean bag, throwing her arms up over her head.

"You and Lucas going to prom this year?" Melissa asks with a hopeful look.

"Yes, I've been dress shopping. Can't find the perfect dress yet, but I'm on the hunt."

My heart does a leap. Oh, how I would love to go to prom with Kian! I wonder if he will ask me. I really didn't think anyone would ask me this year, but now I'm hoping Kian will. The thought gives me butterflies in my stomach.

"How fun. You'll have a blast." I grin at her.

"Maybe we could all go together. Wouldn't that be so much fun?" She rubs her temples with her index fingers as she yawns.

Wow. I would have thought she'd want to go with her other friends or other cheerleaders and their boyfriends. So, I say it. "I would have thought you already had plans with friends to go with."

"No. I don't want to go with those fake girls. They really hate me, anyways. They will just be downers if I go with them." She rubs her eyes then pops them open, giving us a smile. "I like you guys way better."

Melissa glances from me to Lily, as if she reads my mind. "We like you too, Lily. I'm so happy we've gotten to know each other these past few days," she says.

It gives me warm fuzzies as they both look so happy, and so relaxed.

"Me too. It's been so real getting to know you all." Lily hops up. "I need cheese. You two need a snack?"

"Yes, definitely." I follow Lily to the kitchen. "Something cheesy sounds perfect right now. Maybe some crackers, too."

Lily nods. "Yeah. I think we have some cheese left and there are tons of crackers in the pantry."

We've got big plans.

"We could make up a platter and add some of the sandwich meat, too. I think all of them should eat something while playing that game, plus they are always hungry, anyway." I start pulling out meat and cheese as Lily looks in the pantry for crackers.

We build a nice platter, garnish it with fruit and pickles, and then carry it to the table where they are still playing the game.

"Snack break," Lily announces before grabbing a slice of cheese, piece of ham, and a cracker.

"Come on, Liss. Have a snack with us." I swing my arm her way and curl it back, beckoning her to join us.

She shakes her head. "I'm good."

I give her the *you-need-to-freaking-eat look* and she reluctantly comes over but takes only one piece of cheese to nibble.

"That's weak, Liss." I roll my eyes at her.

Liam grabs a piece of turkey, a slice of cheese, and a cracker, stacks them up and presents it to Melissa's mouth. She gives him a tiny grin and lets him slip it into her mouth. Liam smiles, clearly, he thinks it's hot to feed her. Good. Maybe he will be very good for her and make sure she eats decently. That's the kind of boy she needs, a caretaker.

"What am I? Chopped liver? I stink all of a sudden? Why are you way over there, Ashie?" Kian's eyes are so bright and sparkling. He sticks out his bottom lip in a pout and points next to him. "Please?"

"Chopped liver?" Liam asks in mock shock.

"My mom says that," Liss states in an amused tone.

I want to suck Kian's protruding lip right into my mouth. I scurry over to him; his arm goes right around my waist and he plants a soft kiss on my lips. I can't resist, I part my lips and suck that luscious lower lip of his right into my mouth, which makes him sigh.

I release his lip from between my two and hold his gaze. Aw, shit, this is going to be a hot night.

"Hungry?" he asks with clear desire in his eyes.

"Yeah."

He grabs a slice of cheese and a cracker and hands it to me. "Want meat, too?"

Meat. I gasp, flaring my eyes wide. Being near Kian makes my brain go there, so I blush and then I realize he didn't mean it that way, he meant real meat, like ham or turkey with the cheese slice and a cracker. But it's too late, he catches my drift and instantly he's laughing his ass off at me.

I groan. "Oh, what's wrong with me? I can't keep a clean thought in my head worth crap around you."

He's grinning at me as he pops a cheese slice into his mouth. "That's the best sentence I've ever heard in my life."

"I need to scrub my brain clean." I cover my flushed cheeks with my hands.

"Don't you dare. Please don't," Kian says as he's chuckling. "I love your brain just the way it is." He rubs my shoulder.

"Yeah, Kian, watch out for her brain," Mandy says. "Don't let her shyness fool you. She's got some doozies in that brain of hers. I know, trust me." She points at me with a saucy look.

"Mandy, you're so impossible. Shut up already!" I send her a nasty eye glare. "You're not one to talk with your naughty potty brain."

"I'm not the one claiming to have many pure thoughts in my pretty little head." She cackles with lit up eyes.

"Guess I'm not far behind you, am I?" I ask with a sigh.

Kian chews with a gorgeous, big irresistible grin. He's highly amused by our banter. "Keep going, I'm learning so much."

I glare at him flirtatiously.

"This was yummy, thanks ladies," Lucas beams a *thank you* grin.

"Yes, thanks, hit the spot," Liam says.

We finish up our snack and they go back to playing their game. The snack helped me considerably, but I can feel a stirring in my gut that wants me to launch myself at Kian the next moment I get him alone. I'm not so sure I will be able to control myself.

Chapter Twenty-two

Melissa is successful in her quest to get Liam to sing and play guitar for us after they finish their game. We are all lounging about the living room as Liam sings us a song. Melissa watches him all doe-eyed like a lovesick fan at his show. Liam's good, really good, practically a professional musician already at eighteen. I think this boy is going places.

"You fucking rock, man," Lucas says, shaking his head once Liam is done. "You still thinking about going into music in college?"

Liam nods. "If I can get my dad to fucking agree to it and help me pay for it. You know my dad, he's all about himself and I get anything leftover, if I'm lucky." He shakes his head. "Or I'll just keep doing the band if we get enough paying gigs. Who knows, time will tell, but I definitely want to do something music related."

Melissa is glued to his leg like his number one fan. She's looking at him like he's a mega star and she wants to jump his bones. I want to whisper into her ear that he's hers now, clearly.

Kian has gone to his room with the claim that he needs to change because he spilled on his shirt. I want to go check on him so badly. He's not returning so I head towards the bathroom. Well, I don't really need to go, I just want to try and peek in his room, be a little naughty because my hormones are driving me there. As I get nearer the bathroom, I hear a sound.

"Pssst…" Kian's door is cracked open, and I see his eye and half of his smile through the crack in the door.

My heart pounds in my chest as I walk along, it's crashing inside and pumping about like the flames of a bonfire licking the air. I bypass the bathroom and walk towards his room. He opens the door wide, and I quickly slip inside. He shuts the door behind me and envelopes me into his arms. His mouth is on mine and his kiss is so wet and powerful, aggressive that it overwhelms me, and I go weak in his arms, almost fall, but I don't because he's holding me up. He backs us both up towards the bed as we keep kissing. His tongue slides against mine and I moan, which makes him groan as he kisses me hard.

He gently lowers me to the bed as my body trembles.

He stops kissing me, I'm guessing because I'm trembling. He sits on the bed. "You okay? You're shaking." His eyes are full of concern.

"Yes. Please, don't stop. I don't want you to stop or treat me like I'm fragile, because I'm not." I give him a sexy grin and push his shoulders back onto the bed with my hands.

"Wow," he says as I climb on him to straddle him.

He groans as I settle myself to sit upon his firm desire and I attack his mouth with mine. I travel with my kisses along his jawline, the one Mandy didn't punch. For my next move, I kiss up to his ear and clasp his earlobe between my lips and take it into my mouth to suck, caressing it with my tongue, my lips. I gently bite his lobe.

"Oh, God," he groans in response. His hands are on my outer thighs traveling up towards my butt and he wraps his large hands around my hips, and I can't help it, I start to move, and he lets out this super loud moan, which does things to me. I keep grinding, and I'm in big trouble. I'm not going to be able to stop and the way his hands are traveling me, I'm afraid he won't be able to stop either. We're both breathing heavy as our mouths join again, our tongues find each other. I feel him smile against my mouth.

"You're so sexy," he murmurs as his mouth kisses my neck. "You're driving me just wild." He hops up and flips me on my back and presses his body to mine, his eyes ablaze with passion. I part my legs and he leans against me.

I sigh with the pleasure of our bodies touching. He feels amazing everywhere. I tingle as he kisses me near my throat.

I moan. "Kian, that's so good."

His hand cups me, but then he rips his hand off. "Oh, sorry, I lost control." He hovers above me. "I want you so bad it hurts, but we need to slow way down." He starts to lift himself off me.

"Wait. Why? I don't want to stop. Please?" I beg.

He chuckles. "Aw, don't do that to me, I can't resist you anyway, but when you say that, I'm a total goner."

I smile a sexy smile and stick it to him. "Good. In that case, pretty please with Kian on top?"

He cracks up. "Damn, you're no help in stopping at all."

His heavy breathing is turning me on more.

He settles back down on me. His mouth finds mine again and his kiss overwhelms me with how passionate it is. His mouth travels down my neck where he nuzzles me, kissing me just under the hem of the neckline of my shirt over my upper chest.

"More," I murmur which inflames him into a frenzy of movement.

I have, like, zero self-control as my hands travel across his shoulders, down his back and down to his butt which causes him to grind against me and we both groan.

"Shit, I just can't stop," he murmurs.

"Don't then," I say it like a sigh.

He does stop, scaling back the steam, yet he looks so hot and bothered. "We can't. It's way too soon." He sighs. "I don't want you to think that's all I want from you."

"I don't think that," I assure in a cooing tone.

He lifts himself off me enough to gaze into my eyes. "You make me crazy, you know that?"

I pout and say, "Hmpf. I want more." I frown.

"You're damn cute when you're mad and horny." He sucks on my lip and sticks his tongue in my mouth. His body presses into mine hard.

"Oh, yes," I murmur.

We grind our bodies together as we kiss for several minutes, getting hotter by the second.

He breaks our kiss and hops up off me, throws both his hands into his hair, which is mega-hot. "Fuck. I cannot stop myself. We need to go back out there or we're going to do more."

How is he better at stopping and I'm the one wanting more? I sit up and let my arms flop between my bent legs. I'm fully aware I have major cleavage right now as my top buttons came undone as we had rustled together. His eyes go right there, and I like it. I give him a sexy grin.

He shakes his head. "Damn. I'm powerless against you, which is why I need to go throw myself outside for minute." He runs out of the room which makes me giggle. "No laughing at me," he calls from the hallway. "This is not easy for me!"

Poor guy. I know it'll be harder for him to come down from this makeout session than it will be for me. It's less visible for me. I giggle. I sigh and slowly enter the hallway. As I walk towards the living room everyone is laughing while they're looking out the front window. My cheeks go red even though no one is looking at me because their eyes are all glued to something out in the yard.

"Hilarious," Mandy says as she cracks up.

"That's the funniest flipping thing I've ever seen Kian do," Liam is cracking up.

"Poor guy," Lily says, but she's got a little smile.

"Poor guy? What did he do?" I walk towards them. As I approach, I see Kian has face planted himself and is lying with his front side fully smothered in the snow. "Oh my gosh!" My hand goes to cover my mouth. "Holy shit! That's got to hurt. It's so cold."

Mandy's laughing so hard she's doubled over.

Lily giggles as she tells me, "Ash, he was so hilarious. He came running into the living room in a big rush with his hands in front of his crotch, chanting under his breath, 'I need the cold. I need the cold.', and then he ran out the front door and dove face first into the snow, and he hasn't moved a muscle."

Lucas is consumed with uncontrolled laughter, too, so he barely gets the words out, "He—he—he, like, just launched himself...right into the snow. Funniest thing I've ever seen."

"He'd better come in, he's going to get frostbitten," Lily says with a worried tone. "It can happen within minutes in this weather. We don't need this again."

"Oh, wait. I've gotta bust his balls first." Liam runs to the door and whips it open. "Kian, don't get frostbite, your dick might fall off!" He cracks up.

Lucas runs to the door, too. "You're making them even bluer, jackass!" I lurch at that one as he pauses for a giant laugh. Then, says, "It doesn't take long to get frostbite in this weather, fucker. It might turn black and fall off, dude." He laughs. "And not black like me, black like dead cock."

Lucas and Liam crack up together like little boys in on a prank and slam their clenched fists together in a fist bump.

Kian lifts his face and yells, "Shut up, fuckers!" He's using a joking voice. He immediately rolls over to his side, though and rests his head on his bent arm. He has this big shitty grin on his face. He waves at us girls in the window and we all wave back. He's a ham.

"Make him come in, please, Lucas," Lily pleads.

"I'll get him," I say.

"He really could get frostbite quickly in this extreme below-zero wind chill." Melissa nods. "Lily's right."

"Oh, that was so funny, you should have seen his face, Ash, as he hurled himself into the snow. He was all googly-eyed like a cartoon character." Mandy cracks up. "It was like watching an animated kids show as he flailed arms in the air and landed in the snow with a heavy plop." She gasps trying to catch her breath. "He didn't even flinch or anything when he landed in the snow." She snorts. "It was so hilarious!"

"Wow. Just wow," I say as I shake my head. "He's so crazy." I make a move towards the door to go retrieve him. I want to say I wasn't the one voting for blue balls.

By the time I get to the door, Kian has lifted himself out of the snow and is tromping through it, knee deep, towards the driveway. His whole front is caked with snow, some of the pure white crystals stick to his face and he has clumps of it in his hair. He shakes like a wet dog and flings the snow off himself. He makes his way to the front door in a mad rush with a wild yell like a war cry.

He bursts through the front door, a grin across his face. His facial skin is flat out bright red. "Ah, that's much better. Best part, the cold barely even hurt." His cheeks are all round and rosy like a little boy who has spent an afternoon sledding. He's just utterly beautiful.

We all crack up at the sight of him, but there's no covering this up. Everyone knows what happened between us, it's all over their faces. I'm so freaking embarrassed. I'm not sure which is worse, everyone knowing we didn't do it or having everyone assume we did. He basically slammed his boner into a snowbank after he ran away from me...though, I have to admit, that is pretty funny. I bite my lip and then uncurl my frown into a smile as he holds my gaze.

"Ashie, you need a cooldown, too?" He starts to chase me, all awkward like a zombie at first, then he rushes me.

I squeal. "Crap! No, Kian, I don't need a cool down. No!"

"Oh, the hell you don't! I was with you. I know. Come on, now," he scoffs while nodding as he rushes at me. "Come here. I've got some nice cold snow I can share with you. Make you all better. Kian'll fix you right up, baby." He shakes his head vigorously like a mad dog, his hair wetted together in chunks. His grin is one of a rascal. He catches me in like three seconds flat. He presses his wet body to me.

I groan and squeal super loud. He's freezing cold and some snow falls off him down onto the bare skin of my chest, snakes its way down beneath my shirt as it melts fast against my hot skin. I scream as it dribbles down onto my stomach. He shakes the melting snow out of his hair and the freezing cold drips land on my face as a spray.

"Too cold!" I scream as I pummel his chest with both fists. He releases me.

"Just sharing, thought you needed the cold too after all that." He smirks.

"You're a devil." I want to smack him and kiss him, both at once.

He winks at me and goes to the kitchen and starts rummaging in the fridge for food. That boy is a total beast! All the boys follow him like hungry drones.

I watch them in the kitchen as I follow the girls to the living room.

"Kian, that was the funniest damn thing I've ever seen in my life." Liam claps him on the back as he heckles. "Priceless, man, just priceless. Thanks for the entertainment."

"Worked though, didn't it?" Lucas asks, nodding.

"Hell yes, it did. I needed that." Kian throws his head back and lets out a howl. "This boy needs a hefty snack."

"Oh, my." I shake my head. I'm falling for this boy, and hard.

"You okay after all that?" Mandy asks me through her laughter. "That boy of yours is a wild one."

"Yep, before, in the room, that was...just...indescribably hot. Unbelievable. Seriously, wow." I cover my mouth, totally failing at hiding my grin. "Let's just say, he has better self-control than I do."

Mandy blows a mouthful of air out of her mouth in a cackle. "Wow, do tell. That's impressive, Ash."

"I know, right? Yeah. I think I need to sleep in the cold shower tonight. And handcuff me to the bedpost so I don't go to his room, will ya?" Laughing at myself, I try to wipe the rest of the melting snow off my front. "Now I'm just sopping wet. Really? I've changed clothes more than anyone else in this cabin." I shake the tiny wet snow chunks off me with my hands.

"Did you girls just say something about handcuffs?" Liam cracks up. "Who said that? I want to know."

"I know, right?" Kian says cracking up. "Sign me up!"

Lucas shakes his head at them with an amused look. "Y'all would like that shit, wouldn't you?"

"Just saying..." Kian shoves a meatball in his mouth and says while chewing, "Yum, this is an awesome meatball."

"Yeah, they're a little over the top, huh? Ash, just go get a sweatshirt on to cover it up," Melissa suggests.

I nod and take her suggestion. I go find a thick shirt to cover up my wet one, but that's annoying so I change my shirt anyway. I wave at Kian as I walk past the kitchen. His eyes follow me, a grin on his face as he shoves a leftover piece of garlic bread into his mouth.

"Let's play a game," I hear Lily say as I enter the room.

Chapter Twenty-three

L ily is setting up a game.

"The boys are going to play a card game and we're going to play this, that okay, Ashley?" Lily hands me my hand of cards.

"Yep. I love this game." I take the cards from her and glance over at Kian with his buddies. They are joking and laughing, having so much fun.

"Yeah, they're gonna crash hard here at some point and just pass out." Lily rolls her eyes. "I can just see that's where it's going."

"Okay, let's start." Mandy sits on the edge of her seat.

We play for about an hour. Melissa is winning. The boys are loud as they laugh and egg each other on.

At 9 o'clock we hear a knock at the door.

We look at each other, wondering who could possibly be at the door in this weather? I shrug, hop up and run over to the door. Maybe someone had car trouble and needs help?

"It's okay, Ash. You can let them in, we were possibly expecting them," Lucas calls.

I open the door and gasp loudly, shrinking back as terror fills me. Standing there in the blustering wind are Joey, Jack, Alexa, and Gabriela from school.

Everyone is silent, staring at me, for what feels like forever. They look confused and I am gripped with horror, unable to move as all the bad memories flood my brain.

Jack goes, "What the hell are you doing here, Ashley?" He smirks at me and stares at my chest longingly. "This will be quite the party now, heh?" He cocks his head at me, his eyes mocking me.

Joey grins at me and it's such a sick look, I want to vomit. "What a pleasant surprise...would love to hang out with *you* again." His eyes are feeling me up and it's like he's stabbing me with his gaze, piercing through my clothes to see my nakedness, eye-fucking me when I can't hide from his eyes.

I feel my face drain of all color and I step backwards as if they are a raging flame and I'm paper. I'm silently screaming inside myself along the entire surface of my skin. Memories from that night flash into my head stabbing me with repeatedly as a yell bubbles up from deep in my gut, reloading my terror as I recall these two boys' parts in my attempted rape. Their hands on me where they shouldn't be.

"Well, let us in. It's freezing out here," Gabriela says in annoyance with a flick of her red hair.

I step back. I will not cry. I won't. I'm frozen, petrified, like I'm dead. Kian comes over.

"Hey, what the hell took you guys so long?" He glances at me. "Ash, what the fuck is up? You look..."

I don't move a single muscle. Mandy flashes to my side and touches me. I grimace. I don't want anyone to touch me right now.

Kian's face goes into this horrid twist as he must guess why I'm acting this way towards these boys. He goes, "Them? It's them, isn't it, Ash?" He glances towards Mandy and me. In a flash, he explodes like a tornado and grabs Joey by the shirt and screams, "Joey! Was it you who tried to rape Ashley? Huh, was it? I can tell by your eyes, ya fucker!" His biceps are rock hard, flexed like mounds against his shirt. "It was, wasn't it!" He looks like a superhero gone evil.

Kian looks back at me, his eyes are full of hate, flaring without restraint like a madman. He turns that charged gaze to Joey next, raises a fist and smashes it into his jaw. Joey cries out as he falters backwards from the punch. Alexa and Gabriela shriek and scatter. Joey bends over moaning, holding his jaw. "Or was it you, Jack? I always knew you were a shit fuck piece of shit like that." Faster than lightning he smashes his fist into Jack's cheek. Jack's head slams into the door behind him. The girls scream again, taking more step backs.

After Jack's head reverts back to upright, he hollers, "Kian! What the fuck?" He cups his cheek with a hurt angry look in his eyes.

Chaos erupts. I can't focus on anything; it's all a blur and I feel distant yet present. Everyone's words flail about my head like gnats I have no energy to swat away. Everyone is yelling, so many girl screams wail out, but I can't scream because my screams have no voice.

My vision is blurred in the frenzy, but Liam and Lucas seem to be restraining Kian. My vision refocuses. Liam and Lucas each hold one of Kian's arms as he tries to lunge back at Jack and Joey, and he's so strong, so enraged that they're struggling to control him.

"Get out of here," Lucas yells at Joey and Jack.

"You're a strong fucker, Kian," Liam complains with a grunt. "You have to stop," he commands.

Mandy ushers me to the living room. I obey her lead. I've fallen into zombie mode. I can't even make tears I'm so shocked at seeing their faces here at this cabin where I've felt safe and had so much fun. I take in a deep gasp that sounds oddly like a death rattle.

"It was them, wasn't it, Mandy?" Lily asks in a voice full of unmistakable dread.

I'm not looking at Mandy, but she must have nodded because both Melissa and Lily react.

Melissa says in a small voice, "Oh dear, no. No. No."

Lily gasps. "Oh no. This is awful. This is so bad. Ah, Ash, I'm so very sorry." She's gushing, almost doing a whimpering purr as she speaks. She gently pets my arm.

The guys are all yelling. Lucas is telling Jack and Joey to leave again, to just go back home. I cringe as they protest and deny they did that to me, but one of the girls calls from outside, "Let's just go, Joey."

Kian is snarling, grunting like an angry lion. "Let me smash their faces in, fucking bastards!"

"Kian," Liam shouts. "Kian! You've got to calm down. Kian!"

"I'm gonna fucking kill them!" Kian growls like a bear. "Let me fucking go!"

Someone slams the front door shut.

"Dude, you've got to stop! Kian! Stop!" There's a pause before Lucas says in calmer voice. "Bro, if we let go of you right now, I'm afraid you really will kill them." He groans. "Stop fighting us, Kian. You ain't fucking going after them. Not happening, bro."

"You'd do the same thing, Lucas, and in fact you did it for Lily. Let me go! You should get this."

"I do get it. I do, Kian, but you can't." Lucas, is calm and direct, the voice of reason again.

"Right, Kian. You're damn lethal right now," Liam says with absolution. "No fucking way, Kian, I'm not letting you throw your life away on assault charges, or something, worse."

I'm rocking myself back and forth on the soft couch cushion and then I feel this avalanche fall inside of me. My shock gives way to the dam of my zombie mode and tears fall from my eyes like a faucet on full blast. "Oh my...oh my...they..." I whisper in a raspy chant, then a loud wail escapes my mouth and I cover my face. I want to scream! How could they deny doing that to me? It's ripping me to shreds inside. I slip off the couch, crumple to the ground. Mandy grasps at my arm as I sink to the floor. I fall into a full meltdown, sobbing heavily.

"Where is she?" Kian bellows. "Ashie? Are you okay?" I hear something crash. "Let me go you fuckers. I need to get to her." Another crash.

He's at my side in like what feels like two seconds. He's pulling me onto his lap and cradling me, rocking me, shushing me, cooing in my ear a slew of many repetitions of "It's okay. I'm here. You're safe."

He smells like garlic and red sauced meatballs and Kian. Lovely Kian. Only Kian. I want to carve myself a spot on his chest and stay there forever. He strokes my hair and I hear people talking, but I have no idea what they're saying. I can't focus, their words are like a foreign language to me. I'm terrified now that Kian knows my attackers' identities, and he'll go beat them up and then his life will fall completely apart because of me. It will be all my fault. I'm crying because I don't want to ruin Kian's life. I'm crying for their denial of what they did to me, and almost did. My sobs are tearing me apart while Kian is holding me together in his strong arms.

"I can't believe this," I hear Lily say. "I would never have guessed they would do that to a girl. This makes me want to throw up."

I start to tremble, and Kian snuggles me closer, kisses my forehead, then the top of my head. "They're gone. They will never do that to you again...I'm going to beat their asses to bloody pulps."

I shake my head vehemently. My voice fills me again so I can speak. "No! Kian, you can't! Please, promise me you won't do that. I don't want you to get kicked off your team. Please, I don't want you to get an assault charge. Please! Kian! Don't!" I look up into his eyes and plead with him not to do it.

He lets out a huge breath as his body twitches.

He looks at me. Rage leaves his eyes as I touch his cheek.

"Please, promise me you won't do it." I'm rubbing his cheek gently. "Please..."

He sighs. "Will you go to the police and report them, then?"

I stare at him right into his eyes. I blink and swallow. Shake my head.

His eyes rage up again, but he says nothing. He gently pushes my cheek to his chest and completely envelopes me in the cocoon of him. The room goes silent, and I wish someone would talk or laugh or crack a joke. Anything. But it's nothing. It's just this horrid awful silence, and silence is what I've been living in so this quietness rakes my heart up into a roughed up bloody lump as it thumps inside my chest. Tears fall off my lids, free fall down my cheeks and plunge off my jawline to die a sure death of nowhere important.

Chapter Twenty-four

Kian stands with me in his arms and carries me back towards the bedroom. I let him carry me without any fight. He pushes his bedroom door open and carries me to the bed. He lays me down gently and lays beside me. He pulls me to him. I'm so limp, he easily molds me as he guides my head to his chest. I settle against his shoulder as he cradles me.

We're silent for a very long time. The rhythm of his breathing as his chest goes up and down is hypnotic. I must have fallen asleep for a while because when I stir, he stirs as if waking from sleep.

He clears his throat. "You okay?" he asks.

I nod. I feel drained of all energy.

"You fell asleep. I guess I did, too." He tucks a strand of my curls behind my ear and runs his hand across my cheek so gently I almost cry.

"Did everyone go to bed?" I ask.

"Yes, about 11:30, midnight."

I sigh. I can't think of a single thing to say to him. My head is swirling with the chaos of the night. "What time is it?"

He arches to see the clock. "It's about one."

"Do you have water in here?" I ask him.

"Yes, Melissa brought us some water bottles before she went to bed." He hands me one and I see his fist looks swollen and there are a few streaks of blood across it.

I take the water bottle. "Thank you." I sit up and take a long drink, the water is so luxurious against my throat. Then I say, "Is your hand okay? It looks like it hurts."

"Yeah, it does hurt, but don't worry about that. They deserved it, and much, much more." His eyes are heading full bore into angry mode again.

I give him my worried eyes. "You won't go after them again, will you?" I shake my head. "Please, I'm begging you not to. Let this be enough. Okay?"

He throttles back his anger. "Will you consider going to the police?" His eyes are so worried.

"I'll think about it." But I won't do it. I don't want my mom and dad to know. I don't want everyone at school to know either, but it might be too late for that now. Gabriela is a huge rumor mill provoker, and I bet she's already spread it all across social media by now and everyone knows.

"Will you tell me the third guy's name? He deserves at least one pop." Kian's eyes flare with aggression.

I don't want to tell him. Henry was the worst one with how relentless he was with my pants, and the look in his eyes had terrified me. I take another drink of water. I don't think I should tell him, but he really wants to know. He keeps asking and I'm afraid he won't stop. "Are you going to hit him? He will be expecting it now that you hit Jack and Joey. They will warn him."

"Maybe. Or I'll get some other revenge on him, but something is happening to the fucker, that's for damn sure."

I cap my water and snuggle back into him.

His hand goes to stroking my hair. "So, who was it?"

I sigh. I'm going to regret this. "Henry."

"What? Are you serious? He's a guy I hang out with all the time. That freaking low-ass fucker." Kian starts to rise and clenches his fists. I can hear him clench his teeth as he seethes, "He's dead."

"Kian, not dead. Please..." I plead with him with my eyes. "Don't."

"He deserves the worst. Rapists are the worst pieces of shit. What gives them the right?" He's being way too loud. "Guys like that make girls have to be constantly afraid and that's just not okay."

"Shh...you'll wake everyone up," I whisper.

"This makes me so mad I could literally punch my fist through a wall right now." His body is quivering, jerking.

I run my hand over his chest to try and calm him down. It works and he sighs.

"I'm sorry, I'm getting riled up again. It just hurts me to know they did that to you." He snorts. "And those asses denied it?"

I sigh. "Kian, I'm so horrified it happened to me, but I'm also grateful they couldn't finish. Imagine how I would be then, if they had gotten their...in me? I would be even complete worse garbage right now."

"Attempted is bad, Ash. They deserve a beat down for that. Jail." He sucks in a long breath. "Shit, if they had gone all the way...I'd be killing them for sure...no one could stop me."

Well, that right there scares me. "But that didn't happen. It didn't. Let's focus on that. Okay?" I'm not going to mention it was within like a minute or two of happening before Mandy walked out and saved me; that won't help him calm down. I shudder.

He pulls me closer.

"Can we talk about other things now?" I ask as I glance up at him.

He meets my gaze. "Yes. That would be a good idea."

"I wish we didn't have to go home tomorrow. I've loved hanging out here with you and with everyone. It's been like a big long giant party."

"Yes, I've had a blast, too. And I've loved getting to know you better." He kisses me on the top of my head. His lips give me a warm tingle. "I was so thrilled when I heard you were coming over that first day. Didn't you think it was odd that I opened the door for you? I was waiting for you."

I drop my jaw. "I had no idea. Like zero clue. I guess I'm a little clueless, huh?"

"Yeah, kinda." He rubs my arm. "This cold weather has been a gift because we got to spend so much time together to get to know each other."

"Yeah, it's been awesome. I'm bummed we'll never get to do this ever again, so that sucks." Relief fills me as he seems to have fully calmed down.

"But now we get to go on our date. Where should we go? We could go to a movie and out to dinner. Pizza? Pasta? Burgers? You pick." I hear the grin in his voice. "I can't wait to take you out."

"Ha! We're together now and have been for days. I think we've already had the equivalent of multiple dates with all the time we've spent together."

"You're right." He pauses. "Does that mean I've earned the right to ask you to be my girlfriend?'"

My stomach flutters and I smile. "You mean, like, make it official?"

"Yeah," he says it soothingly, like he's in a hot shower.

I'm all warm inside just thinking about being his official girlfriend. I hop up on my elbows and gaze at his beautiful shining eyes. I press my lips to his in a peck kiss, then I grin.

"So...that's a yes, right?" He raises an eyebrow.

I nod. "I'd love to be your girlfriend." Oh my gosh...melt me to a puddle right damn now! I lean back down and take his bottom lip between my two lips. "Does this mean I get to kiss you whenever I want?"

"Yes, yes, yes, oh yes." He pulls into a deep passionate kiss that leaves me breathless, and very randy.

He pulls back. "We need to slow down, though." He clears his throat. "If we stay on this bed together tonight, let's make some rules."

"Rules? I hate rules. I'm a rebel at heart." I crawl on top of him and lay flat so we are touching all along our bodies.

He coughs and gently rolls me off. "That is Rule Number One, you may not lay on me because that does things to me."

"What's your point?" Duh. Clearly it does. I sit up and smile seductively, hoping to entice him. "Oh, you're no fun at all." I pout when he doesn't cave, crossing my arms across my chest. I finally get this boy after months and months of wanting and I still can't have him? This is so unfair and wrong.

"And no touching below the upper chest level." He scoffs. "Wait, no, *my* chest you can touch." He grins mischievously. "I can't touch yours."

I blush and hide my face away from him by diving down and snuggling into his shoulder. "Oooh..." I growl. "I hate these rules."

"And we can kiss, but no body touching." He tries to look at my face, but I tip it down further against his chest so he can't see me. "We kiss with a blanket between us."

"You've just turned into zero fun." I poke his side with my finger which causes him to wiggle.

"Ash..." he scolds.

How is he the one of reason here? I stifle a laugh.

He cracks up. "I can't even believe this is me making up these rules." I sneak a look at his face and his eyes are lit up with teasing me. "But, how else are we gonna behave here together?"

"And why do we have to behave?" I put my free hand on my hip, my elbow pointing at the ceiling. "I'd much rather be naughty."

"And that right there is something I love about you, but we just started dating and I really don't want to go there with all that's gone on this week. It's just too soon, especially with the trauma you just recently went through."

"I thought we were done talking about that," I huff. Though I'm reeling with delight from him using the word "love" in his sentence, even though I know he didn't mean it in that four-letter-word way. But I liked hearing it come out of his lips in relation to me regardless.

If I'm being honest with myself, I'm having such mixed feelings. The duality of my own sexuality alarms me. On the one hand, I'm a bit terrified of what boys could do. I had no power to stop what they were doing to me that dreadful day. I felt so helpless. Yet I want Kian. What if Kian does something to me that I don't like? Am I going to have the guts to tell him or am I just going to take it? I shudder. I'm just so confused because I really, really want him. I really want to be with him, but I'm scared, too. But, then, mostly my hormones are taking over here, and I just want to jump on him, rock his world, and mine.

But there's this little mean gnome of doubt that sits in the back of my mind. He whispers horrid words to me. Words that instill fear in me and darken the brightness of my desire, and that's just not fair to Kian. Nor to me either, for that matter.

Ugh! Damn, those fucking shitheads! Why did they have to do that to me? I stifle the start of tears. I feel so fucked up right now. So, utterly confused.

Kian breaks our silence. "We are done talking about it. I promise. Let's talk about something else now that we have the rules established." He glances at me and concern clouds across his eyes. "What's that look about?"

"Nothing." I press my lips together as he watches me, but I drop my gaze away from his. I refuse to show him my eyes, they will tell him too much. I repeat Lily's sentences in my head. *I decide when. I decide how. I can change my mind.* She's right, it does help me. I repeat them again in my head. Feeling better, I speak up. "Okay, brilliant one, what should we talk about then?" I pop up my eyes to meet his now that I have controlled my fear a bit, and I bat my eyelashes at him.

He buys it, grinning. "Okay. Tell me your favorite meal."

"Pizza. You?"

"Burgers."

"Besides dance, what else do you like to do?" He gives me a little squeeze. It feels so wonderful.

"Ski and snowboard."

"Sweet! You like to do that? I love to ski. I've never snowboarded, though. We should go. You can teach me to snowboard, too. That'd be an awesome date."

"I'm in." I smile at him. I love him so much already. Wow, do I? I need to cool my emotions.

"You ice skate?" he asks with hopeful eyes.

"Yes, I can skate."

"Music to the ears of this hockey player." He pauses. "How about summer?"

"Swim, water ski, go to the beach," I say.

"Sweet, I love those, too. You fish?"

"Nope."

"Damn, I knew you were too good to be true." I glance at him as he smirks.

I swat his chest. "We don't have to do *everything* together."

"Hmmm...I guess not. Maybe you can come along and read a book."

"True. I do like to lay in the sun, though, and go boating."

"Bikini or one piece?" he sucks his lower lip into his mouth.

"Bikini."

"Yes, thank you, God!" he practically screams it out, falling into his dramatic mode again.

"Shhh! Oh my gosh, Kian, that was so loud, everyone will think you're having an orgasm."

"Good point." He gives me a rascally grin and I want to rub my fingers across those lush lips of his, touch them somehow, someway.

"Can we kiss now?" I ask with a coy look.

"Not sure I can handle it and behave myself, but I'm willing to try." He winces a tiny bit like he's scared.

I grin.

So, we kiss, without our bodies touching, and a blanket between us. My heart begins to thump something fierce, my breathing speeds up and I'm fighting a serious urge to climb on top of him. I'm trying not to take action, but my chest is suddenly on his. I'm a natural born rule breaker. He shifts his position, rolls me to the side so we're both face to face on our sides instead. Our mouths find each other, and our kiss deepens. Oh, even this is too much...I want him.

We kiss for two minutes before he pulls away and having his mouth leave mine is agonizing. "I need a breather, I'm...wow. This is way harder than I thought it would be." He clears his throat. "Want to go get a snack?" He sits up in the bed, faces away from me.

"Sure. I could eat."

"Perfect." He stands up and I follow him out to the kitchen.

He rummages in the fridge and I raid the pantry. I pull out some chocolate cookies and he spots them, and responds with a grab of the milk jug, and a half a block of cheese, so I return to the pantry and snatch some crackers.

He pours us two huge glasses of milk and I grab plates. We load them up with cookies and crackers. I slice some cheese and we each take a pile. We carry our plates to the coffee table and take a seat on the floor opposite each other.

I take a tiny sneak of a glance at him. His face looks eager as he eyes up his plate. How cute. "I think there are some grapes left, too. Want some?" I ask. "I'll get them."

He nods. "Yes, please." His eyes are saucers, seeing Kian with this look really tugs at my heart. I go to the kitchen and wash some grapes and place them in a bowl.

"We need some fruit in our lives." I pop one in my mouth as I set the bowl on the coffee table.

"Yeah, I love grapes." He finishes chewing whatever he's devouring. "So, you girls need some gas tomorrow before we go, right?"

"Yep, we're out. That was our initial problem after coming back for my phone. Part of why we got stranded. That, and of course, the weather."

"Okay. We can easily fix no gas. Maybe Liam and I can run up and get some in a gas can while you all pack up. And isn't the guy coming with the propane refill late morning for Melissa's cabin?"

I nod. "Yep, he's coming at, like, 11:30, I think." I scoff. "Yeah, right. I'll believe that when I see it!" I certainly wouldn't mind him delaying it one more day. "Not sure how long it will take. Melissa said he's going to do a maintenance check on it all, too, to make sure it works. Then we'll be free to drive home. Wish we didn't have to."

"I know, right? Guy must be extra busy right now with the storm." He smirks. "Honestly, I think I could stay here forever with you and our friends, and be very happy." He grins as he pops three pieces of cheese into his mouth at once.

"Same. You would miss your sports, though. Right?"

He nods. "True. I would." He grins. "But I'd have you."

Aww. His words send so much warmth through me, not even the cold brutal polar vortex wielding its power outside could touch it.

We finish up our snack and clean up. We head back to the room and as we pass through the door, he flips the lights off. We crash. The bed feels so good as I settle in. I squish the pillow under my head, but then turn to face him. I want to know what he's doing, what he looks like in bed in this low light. It's positively scrumptious.

He's smiling at me. He was watching me adjust my pillow, and this makes me smile back.

"I guess we should get some sleep, huh?" I say with my eyes half closed.

"Yeah, that food is making me sleepy, too. You can use the bathroom first," he says as he snuggles into the comforter. "That way I won't gross you out if I'm stinky." He smirks at me.

"Are you usually stinky?"

"You have no idea," he jokes.

I slip off to the bathroom, brush my teeth first, wash my face, change into pajamas. Again, I'm contemplating bra or no bra. I take it off; it sucks to sleep in. I open the door. As I leave the bathroom, he starts to enter. I feel awkward and shy as he passes by me, our fronts almost touching, which makes zero sense with how we've been mauling each other.

"Meet you in the bed," he says. "Wow, that sounds...yeah...right." He looks past me, his face just about to have an expression of ecstasy.

"I'll be there." I whip around before I finish my words so he can't see my cheeks flush.

I lay on the bed and sneak under the covers, waiting for him, wanting what I can't have. Am I really going to sleep in this bed with Kian and actually be able to sleep? I don't want to leave it though, no way. This is just too delicious to not do, even if we don't do anything other than sleep. Plus, I don't want to wake up Mandy and Melissa if I were to go into our bedroom now. It's settled. I'll stay.

Kian comes into the room and slips into the bed under the covers, which sets my pulse raging. "I want you to stay with me because I want you to feel safe. Hence, our rules, which apply and I'm going to add no kissing, after we do one more."

"Shit, Kian, you suck!" I lightly slap his chest. I'm so frustrated. I finally get to kiss this boy and he's taking it away?

He reacts by grabbing the back of my neck and pulling me towards him. His minty hot mouth is on mine instantly and I moan against its hotness as our fronts smash together and I'm instantly filled with heated passion I can't stop my hands from flying to rub up and down the sides of his abs. He groans as I travel them down his abs to his lower belly. Good God, that one muscle...

He jerks himself away from me, lays flat like I slapped him. "Hand me that extra pillow, will you?"

I sigh, but I do hand it to him. He shoves it between us, as I giggle. Damn, I was so close to getting him to cave.

"Is that our shield?" I snicker.

"Yes, we clearly need a physical barrier." He pulls my face back to his. "One more kiss and we go to sleep. Deal?"

We share a sweet, short kiss.

"Good night, Ashie."

"Good night, Kian. And thank you for hitting Jack and Joey." I scoff. "That sounds really weird. Hey, wait, how did you know for sure it was them who attacked me?"

"When you were just standing there staring like you were in a coma, I looked at Mandy and she held up two fingers and pointed them at Jack and Joey with a nod, so I knew immediately why you were so upset. I think Mandy was quite satisfied I slugged them both."

"Ah. I see. Yes, that makes more sense now. Yeah, I know she's wanted to hit them since the attack. I've wanted to hurt them, too. But I have, like, no way to do it."

He releases a big scoff. "I'm glad I hit them, but please know that I don't go around hitting people like that." He sighs. "That's not who I am."

"Yes, I know. I believe you." I scan him. His face is slightly lit up by the light from the clock on the bedside table. "I have a confession.

I'm not sure I can sleep with you in this bed with me. It's going to be a challenge, but I want to stay with you."

"I know, same here. And I want you to stay here, too, so I can be close to you. I want you to feel safe, protected." He sighs. "Plus, who knows when we'll ever get to do this again."

I nod. His words warm me better than fire. "Kian?"

"Yes?"

"Can I just tell you that you're amazing?"

"If I can tell you that you're my dream." His sexy husky voice is so pure.

"Hmmm...I like that," I murmur.

"Sleep good."

"Sleep good." I pause and doubt stabs my heart. I fear this won't last, it's just a-stranded-in-cabin effect. I'm instantly terrified to leave this little humble cabin. He might feel differently about me after we leave. "Kian? Can I ask you something?"

"Yes, anything, Ashie."

"Are you going to dump me right when we get to school because you'll be reminded that I'm...like...a nobody at school?"

"Don't you say that. I told you to never say that again. You are not a nobody. You're an amazing somebody. Don't you get it? Ashie, I've been eyeing you up for months, remember? I caught you staring at me and that's when I noticed you. I've been trying to get your attention for months, but you never returned my glances, so I thought maybe you weren't interested in me anymore, so I left you alone. Dreamt of you from afar." He sighs. "I should have realized how shy you are. I'm not shy at all. I should have made a move to talk to you. At least tried, anyhow."

His words cover my heart in warm glitter as if it were basking in the shining summer sun and not in a cabin in a dreadfully bitter anomaly of frigid weather. "Ha! That's really hilarious to me because I've wanted you from afar for months and months and months.

When you looked at me, I felt like you caught me, so I'd look away as fast as I could. I even became afraid to look at you and avoided it, which is probably why you thought I wasn't interested. The last thing I wanted was for you to hate me, or think I was annoying." I touch the smile living on my lips. "So, we're really lucky we got thrown in the cabin together, huh?"

"Damn straight we are. I've got you now and I'm not letting go." He pulls me close, up and over the pillows so our whole fronts touch as he kisses me deeply.

"You're breaking your rules," I murmur as he kisses my neck. I feel his desire grow against me and he jerks back. Damn, why did I open my mouth?

"Uh. Oh, right, my bad." He grins at me, it's dark but a bit of the moonlight sneaks in through the crack in the curtains, enough for me to see his sexy impish grin. He lets out a big breath. "Guess I'm the naughty one now. You're just so irresistible, I can't stop myself." He clears his throat and says, "But, seriously. We'd better get some sleep, so we aren't zombies tomorrow."

"Right," I say with an exaggerated sigh.

He sighs, too. "I get that. Good night."

"Good night." I roll over the pillows and land on my side of them, facing away from him even though every fiber in my body is aching to lay fully alongside him. I'm yearning to have every possible inch of our bodies touching again.

He firms up pillows in between us, finding another to add. "Just in case my asleep-self gets naughty without my awake-self's knowledge," he says in a playful tone.

I giggle. "Just saying, I'm totally wishing for that to happen."

Chapter Twenty-five

The morning comes way too soon. Kian and I are able to sleep, clearly, and when I wake it's ten. It's totally amazing to wake up next to Kian. He looks so freaking hot in the morning sun streaming through the curtains. I wish I could hop on him and kiss him, but that would break our stupid rules. His eyes are like slits. He sees me gazing at him and he grins.

"Good morning, beautiful," he says.

"Good morning, sexy," I gush.

His grin widens even more, making him completely irresistible. He chucks our pillow fence from the bed, pulls me to his side, and gives me a peck on the lips.

"Shh...that one doesn't count against the rules. I won't tell if you won't," he murmurs kissing my chin, then starts traveling down my neck with his kisses.

I smirk, almost moan. "I'll keep that secret. They're our rules, we can break them, you know."

He pulls his lips from my throat, tips his head back. "There is a huge part of me that agrees with you right now." He laughs, clears his throat. "And I need to throw myself from this bed right effing now before that part completely takes over my brain." He whips his body around and sits on the bed facing the other wall. "It's too late."

"You okay?" I try not to laugh. I know damn well what he's hiding.

"I'm good. Just great." He runs his hands through his hair. "Peachy."

Damn, is he cute.

I roll towards him and tickle his sides.

He lets out a loud gasp as he arches away from my touch. "Oh, whew! Don't do that!" He hangs his head. "You're not allowed to touch me, even for a tickle."

"Poor baby," I tease him with a wicked glint in my voice.

"Uh. I can't believe I'm going to say this, but will you please leave?"

"What? I can handle it, Kian. I don't need to leave."

"Shit."

"Okay, okay. I'll leave you alone. I can go shower."

He scoffs. "Not helping, Ash."

"Oops. I'll go do something disgusting, like clean the toilet."

"Okay, see you soon, buh-bye now."

He glances up at me, grinning and shaking his head as I leave his room. I want to run back in and push him down on the bed, but I'm gonna be a good girl and walk away.

Lily is in the kitchen making eggs. "Hi, Ash. How are you feeling today?"

"I'm okay, Lily. Thanks. You?"

"Good, I slept well." Her cheeks are rosy.

"Kian is so sweet." I should explain myself; I'm sure I look sort of goofy right now.

"Yes, he really is. He's a good guy. I've never seen him punch out anyone before, he doesn't go around doing that kind of thing, you know." She shakes her head. "Boy has got quite a swing."

"I know. He was like a damn superhero or something hitting the both of them like that. He was so mad last night, though, he was a bit frightening, I mean, if you didn't know who he really is, that is."

"Yeah, but they deserved it." She comes over and gives me a hug. "I just hope you're doing okay with all of this. I'm worried about you and if you are really letting yourself process all that's happened to you." She steps back. "Call me to talk anytime, okay?"

"I will. And thank you, Lily. It's been so much fun getting to know you."

"I feel the same way. I hope we can all hang out again soon. I seriously had so much fun with you all." Her eyes are so soft, and her smile is so sweet. How could I have ever hated this wonderful, kind-hearted girl?

"I had an absolute blast. The most fun of my entire life." I grin at her. "And, Lily, thank you for those sentences. I've already used them several times and they've really helped me. Did you read them from somewhere?"

She sighs. "No, they came from my brain. I made them up."

"They're perfect."

She smiles at me, rubs my arm, and nods.

Melissa comes out of her room. "Hey you two, sleep good?"

"I did sleep well, and you, Melissa?"

"Wonderful. Like a baby." She smiles at me.

"How about you, Ash? Were you able to sleep?" Melissa pulls her hair into a messy bun.

"I did, but Kian and I stayed up too late. We were talking forever and had a snack."

Lily heads over to tend to the scrambled eggs in the pan. "There's coffee made if you two want some."

"Thanks, sounds wonderful," I say. "You need help? I can do something."

"Yes, you could check the bacon in the oven and the blueberry muffins. Need to cut some fruit up, too. There are some grapes and oranges left."

"Oops, Kian and I ate the grapes last night."

"Ah, well, we can cut up the oranges and I think there may be one apple left."

Melissa offers, "I'll cut the fruit up."

We work on breakfast and talk about school. None of us wants to go back to school tomorrow, but surely, we will have to. The superintendent wouldn't cancel school for a full week, plus, it's supposed to warm up. I think our polar vortex extreme cold temperature spree is over now. Life has to go back to normal. Well, not *normal* as I've gained an amazing new boyfriend and several fantastic new friends.

Lucas ambles out of his bedroom and goes right to Lily to plant a kiss on the back of her neck beside her braid, which makes her squirm and squeal.

"Hello, ladies. How did y'all sleep last night?" He beams with his spectacular grin.

"Wonderful. Never better. It was an exhausting night though. Too eventful for my tastes." I tilt my head to the side.

"Right, well, eventful is fine as long as it's all good." Lucas rubs my arm, gazes into my eyes. "You okay? We were all worried about you." *Aww*. How sweet.

"I'm good, thanks for asking, Lucas. It means a lot to me that you all care so much."

"We're friends now. You're stuck with us," Lily confirms.

I grin. "I wouldn't have it any other way."

Melissa waves to me. She's heading off down the hall to check on Liam. She'll be gone for a few, I'm sure. "I cut the fruit up already," she hollers over her shoulder.

"Thanks," I call her way.

Kian finally comes out of the room which reminds me I forgot to shower. He wraps his arm around my waist.

"Breakfast smells amazing. I'm starving." He grins down at me. "When Liam gets his ass up, and after breakfast, we'll run and get you girls some gas. We need anything else?"

Lily shakes her head. "Nope, we have food leftover, so we won't need anything else. It's a good thing Lucas's mom keeps the fridge and freezer stocked up for weekends of ice fishing, it totally made us staying here this long possible." She laughs. "We sure as heck would not have starved." She dumps all the steaming scrambled eggs into a bowl and covers it with a lid. Next, she checks on the bacon, pulls the pan out of the oven.

I gaze out at the frozen lake through the large windows facing it. Its stillness is calming and unmatched, white and glistening in the sunshine without evidence of wind. I don't miss the howls of the storm. Lucas's family has a large wooden ice fishing house out in front of their cabin; there are several other fish houses peppered across the lake. A person is walking around pulling a sled with gear behind towards one, and a dog is running ahead and back to him over and over again, leaping and jumping. I smile. It must be warmer out. I turn to my task and set plates and silverware on the table. Kian helps, too. We exchange grins.

Once the bacon aroma has wafted over to the other side of the cabin, Mandy saunters out of the bedroom, her hair all askew. She smooths it down and comes to hug me.

"You okay, my sweet baby cakes?" She rubs my arm and pulls me into a full-frontal hug.

"I'm good. You all took good care of me." I step back and flatten her still mussed up hair.

"Bed hair, huh?" she asks with a grin.

"Yes, crazy bed hair. You look like a wild woman." I grin.

"That's because I *am* a wild woman," she smirks. "That smell woke me up. This smells like heaven, Lily. You rock." She walks over and takes a big exaggerated whiff.

Lily is setting more food onto the table as she smiles appreciatively at Mandy. "Should we eat at the table this time like normal people?"

"Yes," I say. "We could do that."

"That will be kind of fun." Lily places a pile of napkins on the table.

"I'll get Liam and Melissa." I walk down the hall and decide I'd better knock hard and just yell through the door. I rap on the door three times. "Breakfast time, kids!"

We all pile around the table and eat a meal like real friends, because that's what we are.

Liam and Kian run into town to get gas after we're done eating. Lucas and the girls and I clean up the cabin and pack. With many of us working on it, we're done in no time and now we have a half-hour before the propane person comes.

I text my mom my expected arrival time. I'm still debating whether I tell my parents about the attack. Everyone has me thinking. I don't want them to get super overprotective of me, though, so that's the other reason I don't want to tell them. They might put me under house arrest. Plus, I'm scared to tell them I was even at a party. Seriously, I'm outright horrified thinking about telling them exactly what happened to me. I don't want to say those words in front of my parents. I honestly don't know if I can do it. Will they blame me? Will they think I'm a slut for being drunk at a party alone with boys? Will they lock me in my room until I'm twenty-five-years old? Ugh. What will they think of me? It makes me want to cry.

They won't understand. They'll think I'm a liar and blame me. I just want to forget about it all, but after hearing what Joey and Jack said to me last night tells me they will do this again to another girl, so I need to take action to stop them from hurting someone else. It might feel good to be an example to others and speak out, but still, I'm petrified to do it. If nothing else, maybe it will scare the crap out of those two jerks and force them to change. If I can prevent another girl from being attacked, from suffering at their hands, I should do it. I feel resolved to it as I put the clean sheets on Kian's bed.

I head out to the living room. All my friends are sitting around as there's nothing left to do but wait for the propane guy and load up the vehicles.

"Lucas, we loading up the ice fishing poles, or should we leave 'em here?" Kian asks.

"Let's leave them here so we come back up to ice fish soon," Lucas suggests.

"Good plan," Kian says. I sit next to him, and he pulls me close with a big grin, which I return. "We didn't exactly get any ice fishing in, did we?"

"Nope," Liam says as he tucks a strand of Melissa's hair behind her ear. "We did something way better."

"That's for sure," Kian says as he gives me a squeeze. "That's for damn sure."

The repair guy arrives, and it prompts us all into action.

The boys head outside to start loading up some things into the vehicle.

I glance at each of my friends, old and new. I decide for a final decision; I'm gonna do it. "I'm thinking about going to the police to tell them about the attempted rape."

All four of their eyes flip to me.

"Well, you have two witnesses. Me and Ruby saw them with their hands on you." Mandy nods vehemently. "We can come with you as witnesses."

"I know. But I didn't want to have to bring you into it, Mandy." It hits me like a thick brick of sludge in my gut as I realize I won't even be able to blame Jack because he just watched, he never even touched me. That seems so wrong. He was there, wanting it, too, but not stopping it. He's a sick bastard, and will he even get in trouble if I report it? Or will he get off free and clear for not touching me? I don't know.

"Don't worry about that. If you want to do this, I'm there for you and I know Ruby will be, too. She was just as livid as I was about it all."

"I just can't decide." My voice, and my resolve, wavers yet again.

"You'll make the right choice," Melissa says with kindness in her eyes.

"Yeah, I think you'll make the right choice if you really take the time to think about it. Spend some time evaluating it." Lily smiles at me.

Melissa pipes up. "Yeah. It's a crime to even attempt to rape someone."

Mandy nods. "Hell yes, it is. I think it's like a misdemeanor or something."

"My parents will make me go to therapy and it will be harder for me to do what I want. But I think about preventing other girls from going through what I went through or possibly something even worse. So, it will be hard to go through, but, in the end, I think it's worth it." I feel tears sting the backs of my eyes, but they die there and don't make it to full existence because I get distracted when Liam and Kian storm into the cabin. They're joking and laughing, falling into the cabin like a circus. Lucas runs into the cabin after them, laughing, too.

"Propane guy has a question, Melissa," Liam calls out.

She hops up and joins him at his side. He grabs her coat and hands it to her. After she is dressed in all her winter gear, she hooks her arm through his and they waltz out the door.

"Ah, young love," Kian says in a crotchety grandma voice. "May the force be with them." He heckles. "It's still brutal out there."

I make my way towards him and fall into his arms for a hug. I grin up at him, thoroughly amused. "You have more voices than anyone I know."

"It's a talent," Kian says, winking.

"It really is, Kian. I can't do that." I really think it is a talent.

"You girls now have gas," he snickers and puts his hand in front of his nose. "Pew!"

"Dork," I say. Fart jokes are apparently funny to teenage boys. Though my dad laughs at them, too, so maybe it's just a male thing.

He plugs his nose as he smirks. "Ashie, you stink."

I lightly slug his bicep as he laughs.

"I guess we should pack up the rest of the stuff in the car, then, huh?" Lily says. "That sucks."

"Yes, it does suck." I grimace. "I don't want to go."

No one makes a move.

Kian perks up. "Hey, maybe Liam can switch spots with you and go in Melissa's car, and you can ride with us, so we get more time to hang out."

I nod perking up for this idea. "Sure, works for me."

Kian looks proud, like he's a genius. "Yes, then we can stop at a gas station near home and switch you two out. The 'rents will never know."

"I like it. You and me in the backseat." Thoughts of kissing him for the next few hours invade my head.

"Just don't make too much noise or you'll make Lily and I jealous." Lucas grins at us from his seat on the couch as he pats Lily's thigh. "Right?"

"Right," Lily says with a smile and a bob of her head.

Melissa and Liam come in the front door. "All done," she says.

"Wow, that was fast," I say.

"Tank had a leak, which he fixed. Now, he can feel the heat working, so it's all good to go."

"You guys think we'll ever get to do this again together?" Mandy asks.

"Well, I'm tempted to ask my parents. They might let us, who knows?"

"Yeah, it'd be like a reunion." Melissa grins. "I'll beg my parents. Maybe if we promise to have all the girls in my cabin and all boys in Lucas's cabin, they might let us?"

"You better learn some magic to get your parents to go along with that one, Liss," I say, shaking my head.

"I know, right? It's wishful thinking." She slumps her shoulders.

"I don't know, we didn't do so bad for ourselves," Lily says. "No one died and we had several crises, but we handled it. We cooked actual meals and cleaned up. I think we did pretty good."

Lucas says, "I think I could get my parents to go for it. They're pretty liberal. They let Lily and I come up here alone. So, I think they'd allow it for all of us. Summer would be more fun, too, because we could be outside, swim, go boating, and do bonfires. Dang, man, that sounds really fun. I'm really gonna ask." He grins.

"I'm afraid my parents wouldn't likely let us up here alone on purpose, but maybe they'd come with us, and the girls could come over during the day but sleep at my cabin. It wouldn't be as fun because we couldn't be together overnight, but we could still hang out. It would be awesome."

"Well, kiddies, we should head out," Liam says. "I've got to meet with my band later today."

I gasp. "Oh, no! Mandy, about that bottle?"

Her eyes go wide. "Shit! I forgot about that. Like, I totally forgot." She groans. "I bet we drank it."

Kian grimaces. "I think that's the one I drained on the second night."

"Fuck," Mandy says, frowning.

"You didn't!" Melissa's hands go into fists along her tiny frame. "You took the one from my cabin? Mandy!"

"My bad. I'm so sorry, I meant for us to only drink half, then put water in it to fill it back up." Mandy shrugs sheepishly.

"My parents are gonna freak!" Melissa's eyes are wide, her lips in a tight firm line.

Lily offers, "Could you tell them you dropped it, and it broke? Like you were getting something else out and bumped it?"

Melissa's face lights up. "That's brilliant, Lily!" She smiles. "The popcorn popper is also in that cupboard."

"Just tell them I did it," Mandy offers. "And if they still don't believe you, throw me under the bus and tell them I drank it, all by myself."

"Thanks, Mandy, but I think they'll buy this. My parents won't believe I drank that, so I think this will work. Good thinking, Lily."

Lucas and Lily stand up.

We all meander outside because we have to. We stand on the driveway to say our goodbyes. I hug each person, all the girls hug all the other girls, and the girls hug the guys. We're ready to go. We load up the cars with the final stuff and the remaining perishable foods. We agree to stop on the way down for a bite to eat.

I'm thrilled. I will get three more hours with Kian and another meal. The car door isn't even shut yet and Kian is pulling me to him. He plants a kiss on my mouth, and I moan.

"Stop it, right now," Lucas shoots us a glare in the rearview mirror, but I can see the grin in the crinkles around his eyes.

"Sorry, I'll be more silent." I give Kian a silent giggle. "That was actually on purpose, just to tease you, Lucas."

Kian grins then pouts. "Aw, I love her sounds, you party pooper, Lucas."

"Hardy-har-har," Lucas mocks.

Lily glances back and smirks at us. "You two are adorable."

I turn my face back to Kian and his mouth finds mine. It's going to be a real nice ride.

THE END

Thank you for purchasing this book!
Please write a review on the site you
purchased this book from. Thank you!

About the Author: Julie Hoag

Julie Hoag is an author, blogger, and podcaster. She writes romance and nonfiction. You can find her first published YA Romance, *Hungry Hearts*, Book 1 (published by Month9Books, Swoon, on multiple bookseller sites and it is available in ebook, paperback, audio CD, and audiobook. https://storyoriginapp.com/universalbooklinks/70dde6a6-7ebc-11ec-840a-bf1a7394423e)

She also is a cookbook author, and blogger at https://www.juliehoagwriter.com/ where she writes about family life topics such as family travel, family life, recipes, cooking for split table families (hybrid recipes for vegetarians and meat eaters in one recipe), tips for life with pets, gift ideas for the family, DIY topics, and more.

Her podcast can be found on podcast apps and YouTube and goes by "Vegetarians & Meat-Lovers: Split Table Recipes". On the podcast she shares recipes, tips, cooking advice, and hosts guests in the food arena, as well as sharing fun anecdotes about her life. She has a short ebook that is also in Kindle Unlimited called *How to Cook for a Split Table of Vegetarians & Meat-Eaters* in addition to her cookbooks. She also has a small self-help book *40 Ways to Honor Your Mom After She Has Passed Away* which originally was a blog post she shared about her own lived experiences with grief. In ebook and paperback https://storyoriginapp.com/universalbooklinks/99fe93ac-c988-11ec-ba89-6bce7826f47a

Sign up for Julie's newsletters here: Subscribe to Newsletter • A Family Lifestyle & Food Blog[1]

Cookbooks on Amazon:

One Dish Two Diets: Recipes for Hybrid Families Composed of Vegetarians and Meat-Eaters is a cookbook that is available in ebook, paperback, hard cover, and audiobook, and on Amazon on Kindle Unlimited. https://storyoriginapp.com/universalbooklinks/36b9ce90-6b57-11ec-837f-8f2460b6a963

American Midwest Cooking: Quiches in ebook and paperback The book is available on Amazon and Kindle Unlimited. https://storyoriginapp.com/universalbooklinks/07baee4a-61dc-11ed-ba27-277909561aeb

---

1.   https://www.juliehoagwriter.com/subscribe-to-newsletter/